SERAPHIM

E. M. Wright

PARLIAMENT HOUSE PRESS

Seraphim

Copyright © 2024 by E. M. Wright

All rights reserved.

Edited by Megan Hultberg and Hayley Frerichs

Cover design by Shayne Leighton

Ebook ISBN: 978-1-956136-45-6

Paperback ISBN: 978-1-956136-63-0

PARLIAMENT HOUSE PRESS

WWW.PARLIAMENTHOUSEPRESS.COM

To Ellie, my first real fan
Never stop writing. It's worth it.

PROLOGUE

The sea was on fire.

The merchant ship floated in scattered pieces across the waves, still burning, like hellish Greek fire. Lord Anthony Erikkson gazed over the wreckage with a heavy heart, his mouth creased. So much destruction. This trip across the sea back to England from India had been a difficult one. They were traveling in the wake of a group of air pirates, each day finding more carnage in their path. The salt air had tasted of acrid smoke for almost a week. He mourned the loss of all those lives, all the beautiful merchant ships destroyed by greed. As he surveyed yet another morning of devastation, Erikkson wondered when the pillaging would end.

Sailors' bare feet pounded across the deck. Above the Cockney accents babbling instructions, Erikkson heard the lookout shout, "Someone in the water!" A sailor, perhaps, or some passenger from the merchant vessel? He made his way to where the men stood at the rail, casting ropes into the water and calling out to the body floating below.

In moments, the sailors had expertly hauled a boy from the water, dressed in sopping wet rags, seawater cascading down his slight figure. He had black, shoulder-length hair and mahogany skin. One eye was swollen shut, blood staining the left half of his face, and his limbs had that gangling quality seen in young adolescents, emphasized by how thin he was. About one ankle, he wore the remnants of a shackle, the chain dragging along the deck. The boy did not cough or splutter, though water dribbled from his blued lips as he crouched on the deck, watching the sailors warily with his one good eye, shockingly bright green against his dark skin.

Erikkson shoved through the crowd, "Please, let me through! I am a doctor!" It was not entirely true. He was a biomechanick. But the medical principles were essentially the same, and he felt inexplicably drawn to this boy.

The boy scrambled backward as Erikkson tried to approach, holding up his hands in a gesture of peace. "It is all right. We will not hurt you."

The boy stopped moving, but his one green eye glimmered with intense distrust.

"What is your name?"

"Anahera," he answered quietly.

"That is a beautiful name," Erikkson smiled at the boy, who was perhaps twelve or thirteen years of age—not yet grown into a man's body or voice, and yet his eyes revealed he was beyond his years. "My name is Anthony Erikkson. Do you know what happened?"

"Boat attacked. Men take goods, leave us. Fire and water everywhere." He spoke slowly in heavily accented, broken English.

"What were you doing on that ship, Anahera?" Erikkson questioned, though he feared he already knew.

"Many men come to village. Take us." He gestured to the chain around his leg.

Erikkson's heart dropped at the explanation, sorrow washing over him like the waves lapping against the sides of the ship. Clearly, the boy had been on a slave ship, likely bound for the Americas with its cargo. But Anahera's English wasn't the result of a few days at the hands of American slave drivers; it bore the evidence of years of practice. "How do you know English?"

"Men come to my home. Good men. God men. They teach English."

Erikkson nodded, continuing to study the boy. The wheels in his head were already turning, the idea he'd had about building his own biomatons beginning to coalesce with this young survivor they'd pulled from the water. "Well, Anahera," he said gently, crouching down to the boy's level. "What do you say about coming home to England with me? I promise you, no more chains. No more cruel treatment. And when we get there, we will see what we can do about that eye."

The boy narrowed his one good eye, brow creasing. "You will keep me safe?"

Safe was relative, but that could come later. He nodded. "Of course."

The boy bit his lip, and Erikkson noted he was missing his left canine. Strange, but nothing that couldn't be fixed. He was eager to get back to England now. Eager to finally set the plans in motion after considering them for so long.

Anahera rose, moving slowly, as if every muscle hurt him. When he stood at his full height, he nodded, offering his hand. "Yes. I go with you."

Erikkson took his hand and shook it. Yes, here was a boy he could build a movement upon. Erikkson smiled. The first piece of the puzzle had already fallen into place.

CHAPTER ONE

Someone screamed.

The searing cry of pain pulled him from the black void of unconsciousness with dreadful insistency. *Please stop. Let me sleep.*

The sound was smothered a moment later, breaking off abruptly, but sleep was not forthcoming now that he was awake. He struggled to breathe. And it was cold, so cold… Someone had opened a window in his side and let a draft in. *How irresponsible,* he thought, the words slurring in his mind with residual sleep.

Perhaps, if he opened his eyes for a moment, he could see what window had been left open and get up to close it without losing the pleasant drowsiness keeping him at the edge of consciousness. The young man blinked his eyes open, squinting against the bright light beaming down upon him.

Figures hovered above him. They were difficult to make out, backlit as they were, but he counted perhaps four or five people wearing white aprons, hands coated in something red. The boy's eyes drifted closed again, but the images stayed with him. What was happening? Who were these people? He could not remember how he had gotten here, nor why he was surrounded by strangers. He couldn't move. Terror surged through his body, a moan emerging from his lips, low and guttural. He smelled the copper-salt tang of blood—his own.

"The subject is waking. Get more ether." A disembodied voice from far away bounced around his head in an extremely unpleasant echo.

"Wait." Another voice, this one low and oddly familiar.

Fingers forced the young man's eyes open, and he found himself staring up at a man with grey hair, colorless eyes, and a hawk-like face. "You thought you were clever, pretending to be a buyer, did you? You did not anticipate my guards spotting that brand on your arm. No one will miss a privateer returned to piracy. Welcome to the Black Castle, 745." The man smiled coldly.

That is not my name! My name is—is... The boy couldn't remember. He struggled weakly as a cloth was pressed over his nose and mouth, smelling like alcohol and something sweet. His eyes drifted closed, his body going numb even as his mind fought to stay awake, to remember.

Just before he drifted off, an image appeared behind his eyes of a girl with copper hair and one clockwork arm. A girl whose name he could not remember. He knew he'd hurt her, though he could not recall what he had done. He'd failed her, somehow. And as the cold darkness took over his mind, he vowed to himself that he would find her.

IT WAS TIME TO LEAVE.

He'd known for a while that it was time. Since Sedition showed up, in fact. She'd thrown quite the wrench into the workings of the airship, and now with Ace and Emmett gone, Seraphim knew he'd put it off for long enough. His creator would be expecting him back home. If nothing else, it was his role to assist Sedition in relearning the fighting skills she'd lost. Still, the *Dauntless* had become as much a home as any place could be for a biomaton, and he had to admit, there were aspects of the airship he'd miss.

He approached the rail of the airship slowly, gazing at the ground far, far below. It all looked so tiny from up here, like a child's playset strewn across the countryside. He wasn't certain where they were currently (somewhere above York, perhaps), but he had a thick cloak in his satchel to hide his wings, and he knew how to travel without being spotted. The hardest part would be disembarking from this height, but he had a contingency for that in the form of the parachute he'd stolen from the ship's supplies. He wondered if anyone would miss him. Cook, perhaps. And Bolts. But the rest of the crew would probably be glad to be rid of him, particularly the captain. He wouldn't miss her vitriol, that was certain.

"What do you think you're doing?"

Speak of the devil. Seraphim turned slowly, his massive clockwork wings rising a little, an involuntary defense against the captain who stood behind him. Her arms were crossed over the heavy leather corset under her captain's jacket, the wind stirring her dark hair. Piercing blue eyes studied Seraphim.

He kept his features cold. "I have no doubt you'd prefer your airship free of the burden of my kind."

"Are you leaving us, Seraphim?"

"I am afraid so."

"You cannot leave. You belong to this ship."

"Consider this my resignation." His wings lifted and spread, the hundreds of bladed feathers glinting in the sun.

She drew a sword. "You *belong* to this ship. I will not just allow you to leave."

Seraphim's lips quirked, turning just high enough to reveal a shimmer of silver, a flash of steel fangs, normally hidden behind carefully schooled features. "You and I both know how this will go, Captain. I think it is better if you let me leave peacefully."

Her eyes narrowed. "I *bought* you from those slavers because I knew your skills would be useful to me. You were as good as dead if you continued to fight in the ring. You owe me your *life*."

So, she still believed it. The narrative was one Master Erikkson had written for Seraphim, a perfect method of infiltration for his perfect weapon. They hadn't expected Captain Storm to be the one to purchase Seraphim, of course, but as long as he ended up on a Navy ship and could spy for Erikkson, it hadn't mattered. Storm's hatred of biomatons had been an obstacle, but in the end, it wasn't enough to throw off Erikkson's plans. Seraphim slipped long fingers into the pocket of his leather coat, feeling the stiff paper hidden there. His fingertips brushed the wax seal still stuck to the page and he drew his hand back, shuddering.

"Let me go," he said, voice soft but threatening.

The captain stepped closer, brandishing her sword. "I said *no*."

Seraphim had no intention of fighting her. He shrugged, shouldered the parachute he'd stolen from below decks, and stepped up onto the rail of the *Dauntless*; one hand grasped a line of the rigging, the only thing keeping him from plummeting toward the ground.

"Seraphim!" The captain's voice was full of venom. "I am warning you."

He looked back over his shoulder, his long, dark locks whipping across his face. He gave her a calculated grin, one that displayed his fangs to full effect. "Sedition sends her regards," he said, and then he leapt from the rail of the ship, snapping his wings out like a deadly angel.

Taryn awoke to birdsong. She blinked her eyes open, momentarily disoriented at the unfamiliar surroundings. She lay in a large, comfortable bed, its four oak posts rising high above her head. The ceiling was decorated with gilded carvings, dark wood, and frescoes in the Italian Renaissance style. Light poured in from a large window on her right, the long curtains pulled back and the shutters flung open outside.

She sat up, raking her hands through tangled copper curls. Besides the four-poster bed, there was a wardrobe against one intricate blue and gold wallpapered wall, and a writing desk upon which stood a basin of steaming water. The door which led to the rest of the manor was closed, made of the same elegant, dark wood that adorned the ceiling.

The events of the day before returned to her one-by-one: the auction at the Black Castle, Lord Erikkson's sudden appearance, the long coach ride here with Erikkson who proclaimed himself her maker, the late meal, and finally, falling into a deep slumber in this room, the deepest sleep she'd had in a long time.

Elmhurst Manor, she reminded herself. *Erikkson's home.* He had rescued her from a life of slavery, but she couldn't be sure his intentions were any better. She lifted her left hand—the one built of clockwork—studying it in the golden morning light. She was a biomaton: a human augmented with clockwork prosthetics. Lord Erikkson had done this to her when she was just six years old; to save her life, or so he claimed. But over the last few weeks, Taryn had learned the hard way how poorly biomatons were treated. A group of privateers had ferreted her out of hiding and sold her to the Black Castle, the biggest biomaton slavery ring in the British empire. There, Taryn had learned a little about her forgotten past and her creator, but she still had so many unanswered questions, so many gaps to fill. Erikkson wanted her to become a rebel warrior called Sedition, but the idea left a bad taste in her mouth. She wanted no part in someone else's war. What she wanted more than anything was to return to the life she'd had before, but that was impossible.

A knock came at the door. "Miss Roft?" a timid voice called.

"Yes?"

"Master LeBeau requested you."

Emmett. Taryn scolded herself for forgetting her friend. Blinded by the biomechanicks' experimentation during their time at the Black Castle, Emmett was capable, but would need her to guide him in their new surroundings.

"Please tell him I will be there in a moment."

There was no answer, and Taryn guessed the girl had gone. Considering what Lord Erikkson had told her, she rose and washed her face and hands in the basin. All the biomatons who lived here shared the duties required to maintain the estate. No one was "owned" by Lord Erikkson, at least, not in his eyes. He preferred to call them his children.

Taryn went to the wardrobe, opening its heavy doors slowly. The scent of cedarwood and mothballs flooded her nose, familiar and yet utterly new. She peered at the elegant dresses inside, knowing each one was worth more money than she'd ever possessed. She found herself almost resentful of Erikkson for foisting such lavish gifts upon her. She didn't ask for any of this.

Taryn chose a heavy blue cotton gown, one of the simplest in the wardrobe. It had a row of buttons down the front of the bodice that would be easy enough to fasten on her own. As her clockwork arm had to be hidden at all times in her old life, she had long ago learned how to dress in even the most complicated gowns. Still, it took longer than usual to dress in the heavy petticoats, to lace up the corset, and pin her bodice to it. The new clockwork arm the Black Castle had built after her own was smashed still seemed foreign, like attempting to control someone else's movements. Her fingers fumbled with the buttons, tangled in the laces. She cursed the prosthetic.

Exiting from her room, she grabbed her precious birthday pocket watch and slipped it into her pocket, the weight of it in her skirt feeling right. It had come all this way with her, despite the fact she'd thought it was gone for good at the Black Castle, and she was grateful for the reminder of her best friend. Pulling her long copper hair into a braid as she walked, she wondered if she'd ever see Royal again, the boy who had given her a home and a purpose. He'd never known what she was, of course. But he had always treated her as an equal, despite the fact that he was gentry and she was not. She moved down the long wood-paneled corridor to the room she recalled from the night before. She knocked, one hand still tangled in her skirt.

"*Oui?*" Emmett's now-familiar French lilt came through the door.

"May I come in?"

"*Oui.*"

She pressed the door open, entering a room much like her own, only wallpapered in yellow. A mirror hung on the wall opposite Emmett's bed, useless and dim, the silver backing tarnished with neglect.

Emmett sat on the bed, wearing a thin white nightgown that was too big for his narrow frame. "*Bonjour,*" he said, turning toward her. His useless clockwork eyes looked different in the golden morning light—more glassy, less like human eyes. "Will you help me dress, *s'il vous plait?*"

Taryn's stomach churned. Of course he needed help, but why didn't he ask the maid, or even Lord Erikkson? But she knew she would not have asked them, either. At least Emmett knew her. Just like at the Black Castle, they only had each other in this place.

"I will do my best," she replied. "Did Master Erikkson leave you anything to wear?"

"*Oui*. Look in the wardrobe."

Taryn found clothing there and chose at random: brown trousers, a white shirt, and a dark brown waistcoat. The articles were nothing like the flamboyant, colorful garments he had worn on the *Dauntless*, but she supposed they would do.

"Here," Taryn offered awkwardly, laying the clothes near his hand, so he might find them easily. "Did Lord Erikkson tell you what the room is like?" She turned away, giving him a bit of privacy as he pulled the trousers on.

"Yes." There was a pause and a rustle of fabric. He hummed softly to himself; she recognized the old sailor's drinking song that she'd learned long ago from Royal. The lyrics had been enough to make her blush. "You need not turn away, *chérie*," he said with a smile in his voice, reading the room more easily than she'd anticipated.

Heat came into Taryn's cheeks. "I thought I ought to give you the privacy."

"No need, I am dressed enough that I will not be embarrassed."

She turned. He had pulled the shirt over his shoulders, but he'd not yet buttoned it. The front hung open, his bare chest showing beneath. Taryn's eyes widened in surprise. She knew she should not be looking at him like this, half dressed in the early light of morning, but she could not tear her gaze away from a round white scar just above his hip, the skin puckered around the old wound. There was a story behind such a scar, and it couldn't be a nice one. She opened her mouth to ask about it but decided against it. There would be time enough for painful stories.

"How did you sleep?" she asked instead as his nimble fingers began to fasten the buttons, hiding the scar from her prying gaze.

"Well enough. It is a new place. It is always hard to sleep at first." He hesitated. "And I felt lost, all alone."

Taryn handed him the waistcoat as he finished with the buttons. "I did not sleep very well, either." Too many nightmares had danced through her head. And too many lost memories taunted her from the dark corners of her bedroom. It was a like an itch she couldn't scratch, phantom pain pricking from her missing arm. But this was worse, a dancing familiarity at the back of her mind with nothing behind it, just missing time. Just questions.

"We will adjust," Emmett answered.

She nodded as he completed his wardrobe. She wondered whether he was putting on a strong front for her sake, or if he truly believed this place was better than where they had come from. She had not yet decided herself. Erikkson had plans, that much was very clear, but whether they were good or not, only time would tell. He was an enigma, his true personality and his intentions for her were locked away along with the history he had stolen from her. She would need to be cautious around him.

Emmett pushed one sleeve up to his elbow and began to slowly unwind the white bandages around his forearm. Taryn watched silently, with her heart in her throat, as he revealed healing red welts, like the lash marks she'd seen misbehaving students receive at Grafton's. "What did they do to you?" she murmured, almost afraid to ask.

He hesitated, his head tilting so she could not clearly see his expression. He pulled his sleeve down and began to unwind the bandage on his other arm, revealing more red welts. "I do not want to talk about it, *chérie*. It is over now."

Her stomach twisted into a painful knot, but she remained silent until he had finished removing the bandages. If he did not want to talk about it, she would not press him. "Come, Emmett. Shall we find out if there is any breakfast?"

They left the room together, Emmett holding her elbow. Taryn knew their path by intuition. The manor's halls were like stepping into a dream. She shut off her mind and let her feet lead, her subconscious carrying her through the strange halls.

They passed a young biomaton girl with a load of laundry. She shifted the basket to her hip so she could curtsy. "Good morning, Sedition."

Taryn's jaw tightened. "I am going to kill him," she muttered.

They entered a dining hall and Taryn froze in her tracks, anger momentarily forgotten. "Oh..." she breathed, awestruck.

In the center of the room sat a table piled high with food. There were cold meats and cheeses, fruit, breads, and pastries. Jams and jellies shone in the sunlight streaming through the regiment of tall, narrow windows. Taryn spotted hot sausages, bacon, and eggs. Pots of coffee, tea, and hot chocolate, and jugs of orange, grape, and apple juice stood amongst the platters of food.

"*Qu'est que c'est?*" Emmett asked. "Is something wrong?"

"No, I—" Taryn stammered. "There is a table laden with breakfast, Emmett. I do not know when I last saw so much food."

"Please, help yourselves," a deep voice interrupted from behind them. Taryn's shoulders tensed uncontrollably at the sound of their new master's voice. Yes, he seemed kind enough, but still. He *owned* them. "I would hurry if I were you. The soldiers normally eat around eight, and there will hardly be anything left after that."

Erikkson placed a hand upon both of their shoulders, ushering them inside. He was tall and narrow, a figure which might, in his younger years, have been described as lanky, but time was beginning to catch up with his frame and the best description for him now was *gaunt*. His wavy red hair was beginning to grey at the temples, and the dark auburn beard showed hints of silver. He wore dark colors, all in silk, with a cream-colored cravat, the look making him seem all the more authoritative and mysterious.

"Please, sit. Eat. You must be starving after suffering so long at the hands of Bellham's hospitality." He seated himself at the head of the table, giving Taryn a smile that made the corners of his forest green eyes sparkle.

Taryn served Emmett first, keeping a wary eye on Erikkson who, though he seemed content enough to sip tea and watch them eat, felt like a venomous snake, ready to strike as soon as she let down her guard. Emmett enjoyed the bitter coffee, while Taryn drank orange juice. They both savored the pastries, which Emmett proclaimed were authentic. In particular, he loved the little square choux puffs called *"La Religieuse,"* explaining with a mischievous grin that the name meant "The Nun" before devouring it whole, custard cream smearing at the corner of his mouth. It was good to see him smile after all they'd been through.

As soon as she began to feel full from all of the good food, Taryn turned her attention to Erikkson. He inclined his head to her. "In case you do not remember, I do this for my children each day. Breakfast is made available to anyone who wishes to partake. Luncheon is laid out similarly, whilst supper is eaten either with me or in groups in the west wing. On Sundays, we all dine together on the lawn, weather permitting."

"How many biomatons do you have here?" Taryn questioned.

"Seventy-one, including you and *Monsieur* LeBeau. It is a pleasure to have you back with us, little one. Elmhurst has felt far too empty without my Sedition."

Her stomach twisted at the number. So many? Taryn scowled. "I am not *your* Sedition. Have you told everyone here to call me that? They treat me like I am some hero."

"Ah, but you are. You are the one who shall lead them to freedom."

Her lip curled in disgust. "That is a suicide mission."

"Perhaps." Erikkson's gaze drilled right through her.

Emmett touched her arm. "*Chérie*, there is no need to get upset."

Taryn took a deep breath to steady herself. "Please ask them to stop. It makes me uncomfortable."

Erikkson nodded. "When you are both finished, perhaps a tour around the manor is in order? I am afraid my apprentice is away and will not return for another two days, or else I'd have him take you about the place. He is around your age."

Taryn had no interest in the apprentice. In all probability, he was just some rich boy with too much time on his hands, forced to learn a trade by a father who'd decided idleness was not good enough for his son. He would doubtless be stuck up and arrogant, and hate her for being a biomaton, despite being apprenticed to such a radical biomechanick. No, she was glad he was away. She was not ready to meet such an individual.

"That is all right," she answered stiffly. "We would rather have you give us the tour anyway."

CHAPTER TWO

THE MANOR HOUSE halls continued waking long-dormant feelings within her. Had Taryn not known she was incapable of such emotion, she might have said she was *nostalgic* for the place.

Erikkson showed them everything but the west wing, which he said they'd see soon enough. He implied that perhaps Taryn was not ready to meet everyone at once, and she had to agree. For the most part, she dreaded meeting the others. She didn't want them to look at her the way the few she'd met already had: like she was the solution to all the hardship they'd faced.

The tour ended in the gardens behind the manor, the rare sun warm on their faces. The air smelled of roses and grass, fresh and crisp and cleansing. Taryn breathed in huge gulps, allowing it to clear her lungs of the dense, oppressive Black Castle miasma. Emmett, still on her elbow, smiled into the rays. Everything seemed just the tiniest bit brighter.

After walking the garden, Erikkson gave Taryn a pointed look, his eyes going to her new prosthetic. "If you are comfortable, I would like to examine your prosthetic more closely. Perhaps *Monsieur* LeBeau would like to stay here in the garden, and we may go to my study?"

Taryn's throat tightened, but she nodded. "Will you be all right out here on your own, Emmett?"

"Show me to a bench, *chérie*. I will happily enjoy the sun."

Taryn knew how he felt. They had spent too long in the dark, haunted halls of the Black Castle. She led him up the path, their feet crunching over the gravel, to a stone bench nestled between rosebush hedges. "Here you are. I will be back as soon as I can."

Emmett squeezed her hand. He seated himself, facing into the sun. The cool breeze ruffled his ashen curls.

Lord Erikkson touched Taryn's shoulder, guiding her silently back to the manor. She had so many questions for him, from how he had kept watch over her all the years they had been apart, to why he thought she would make a good leader. But they stuck in her throat, too many to choose where to start. She eyed Erikkson, his large hand still resting lightly on her shoulder. This stranger knew everything about her. Even the darkest parts of her mind seemed to be an open book to him. And yet, she knew nothing about him. She could not even really bring herself to trust him. In spite of everything, Taryn could not shake the knowledge that this man owned her, no matter how he wanted to frame it. He had chosen to pull her back from the edge of death without asking her permission, torn her apart and rebuilt her with clockwork, and then taken every memory she had.

Erikkson's study was on the first floor with wide windows overlooking the gardens. Blue flowered wallpaper covered the walls, and a dark rug hid most of the stone floor. An elegant limestone-mantled fireplace was built into the left wall, though no fire burned. The right wall was covered floor-to-ceiling in small drawers, similar to a card catalogue. Taryn suspected that those drawers held all the clockwork and tools Lord Erikkson could desire; it was what she would have used such a system for, had she become a mechanick. A huge drafting table stood near the windows, replete with blueprint paper and fountain pens, ready for new biomaton plans. Several leather wing-back chairs sat around the room, and a wooden workbench stood slightly off-center, gouged and chipped. In all, the study made a cozy workspace, revealing something about the man who worked within it. It smelled of tobacco smoke, machine oil, and India ink, the strange mix stirring old emotions in Taryn's chest.

Lord Erikkson turned the gas lamps mounted on the walls to full strength, augmenting the light coming in through the windows. "Can you take your arm out of your sleeve for me?" he asked, pulling a jeweler's glass from a drawer.

Taryn carefully did as he asked, holding the front of her dress up so very little of her undergarments showed. Her chest tightened at the glimmer of lamplight on metal; it wasn't so long ago that she'd kept her arm secret from everything and everyone. Putting it on display still triggered a sharp, heart-rending fear.

Erikkson moved closer, lifting her clockwork prosthetic so he could examine it from every angle. Taryn stood as still as she could. He wasn't going to like the clockwork. It wasn't his. It had been built by mechanicks who worked for a man he detested. And yet, Taryn wanted him to be pleased with her. All of her. The thought caught her off-guard, left her fumbling for a reason she might feel that way. It felt as though her mind wasn't her own.

"It is even more crude than I expected. Lord Bellham has hired poor quality mechanicks in order to keep up with the quantity of biomatons they push through the Black Castle. It is an unfortunate trade. How are the motor skills?"

It took her a moment to realize he intended her to answer. "It is clumsier than my first arm," she admitted. "But that was more stolen replacement parts than original clockwork by the time I boarded the *Dauntless*. It was just as bad as this."

His eyes met hers. "Did you fix it on your own?"

"Yes. No one could know about me."

A wide, genuine grin broke across his face, his green eyes crinkling at the corners. This close, Taryn noticed his long lashes were auburn like his hair. "That's my girl!"

Taryn's expression turned to stone. She turned away from him, pulling her sleeve back over her clockwork arm. She could not look at him. "You are all the same," she growled.

"What?"

"You take every opportunity to remind us we are nothing more than your property." She could barely speak through her clenched teeth. The violence within her rolled in her gut, awakening.

"Little one, that is not what I meant. I was expressing how proud I am of you."

"Yes, but you *do* own me, after all," she muttered. Her clockwork fingers rubbed across the numbers etched on her arm in black ink, placed there by the Black Castle. 743. That was all she'd been to them. A number.

"Do you truly think that is how I see you?"

"You expect me to become your pawn in a fight I do not want. You say it is what you built me for, as if I am just a machine you can order around as you please." She turned and stared at him. "Did you really think I would not know you are just like the rest of them?"

His face wilted, as if looking at her was unbearably painful. "Taryn, I told you I would not force you to become Sedition. I only hoped you would see she is necessary."

"Choose someone else to lead your suicide march."

"There is no one else."

"There is always someone else! Build another perfect warrior for yourself," she spat.

"I cannot." He paused. "No. I *shall* not."

"What?"

"I swore I would not build any more biomatons after I built you, Sedition. I refuse to bring anyone else into this world of cruelty, until the biomatons' freedom has been won."

All the air rushed from the room. She couldn't breathe. The whole world weighed upon her shoulders, but she was not Atlas. She could not bear the weight. "You should not have so much faith in me," she muttered. "I will only let you down."

"May I show you something?" Erikkson asked, a note of unfamiliar tenderness in his voice.

"What?"

He went to the drafting table, pulling a thick roll of blueprint papers from a drawer. He unrolled them upon the work table, beckoning her over. Taryn approached cautiously, her stomach twisted into knots.

"Here are the blueprints I used to build you," he said, smoothing them with his hands. "And below are the blueprints for Sedition."

Taryn stared at the detailed pen and ink drawings, her heart in her throat. The page held a drawing of a little girl, her clockwork enhancements added over the top in copper ink. Taryn recognized the left arm immediately; how could she not? She had worked on the arm hundreds of times. Included in the blueprint was the control panel on the back of her head, and the leg enhancements she had not known about until the Black Castle. Clockwork within her legs worked to assist with muscle strength and flexibility. A few notes hung scribbled around the margins in Erikkson's dense, spidery hand, notations of what he needed to change. Taryn's head spun.

She turned the page, expecting more detailed drawings of the same little girl, but what she found turned her heart to stone. On the next page, a drawing of a grown woman gazed up at her, similar to the first set of blueprints and yet utterly different. The woman's left arm was fierce, all angles and armored. Her control panel was the same, as were the changes made to her legs. Changes Taryn did not understand were drawn onto her shoulder blades. She touched the title at the top of the blueprint. *Sedition.*

She turned the page again. The next contained a detailed drawing of the armored prosthetic. It had hidden compartments for throwing knives, spikes on springs, and reinforced armor plating for combat. Taryn struggled to catch her breath over the lump in her throat. She flipped through the rest of the prints, barely noticing them. "This is *sick,*" she growled. "Did you think this would convince me?"

"I thought perhaps it would help you understand."

She scoffed. "I understand." Her voice cracked like a wildfire. "I am another weapon in your war with society. And when you are done with me, you will discard me, just as you did before."

"This is for *you.* This is for every biomaton who has ever hated the way they were treated. The world *needs* Sedition." He gestured at the table.

"No, *you* need Sedition."

He stared at her. "Do not tell me your experiences at the Black Castle left you heartless."

"No," she answered, voice rough. She locked eyes with him. "*You* did."

He fell silent for a long time, shuffling papers about on the table. Finally, he nodded. "I can see there is no convincing you. Very well."

Despite herself, Taryn's curiosity got the better of her. Erikkson had left a blueprint of Seraphim on the top of the pile. Taryn studied the drawing, unable to breathe. There were the enhancements, all done in copper ink, but her eyes locked on just one mark. "This—is this accurate?" she stammered.

"Yes. That is Seraphim. I believe you met him aboard the *Dauntless*."

Taryn rifled through, trying to find the proper page detailing what she'd spotted. In her frantic efforts, she crumpled the sheets, her clockwork fist uncouth and clumsy.

"What are you looking for?"

"The detail!" She shoved Seraphim's blueprint in his face, crunching it in her fist. "For Seraphim's eye!"

Calmly, he pulled it from the pile, handing it to her. She traded him for the pages she was holding. He smoothed the wrinkles she had made, realigning them. Taryn's chest heaved. A perfect clockwork eye stared up at her, an elegant design of clockwork, glass, and wire.

"Can Seraphim see?" she questioned breathlessly.

"In a sense, yes. Not as you and I see, but—"

Taryn didn't wait to hear the explanation. "Could you do this again?"

"Yes."

She shoved the page toward him, unwanted tears coming into her eyes. "Help him."

Lord Erikkson shook his head, his lips pressed into a thin line.

"Please," Taryn begged. "You have to help him!"

Erikkson just shook his head once more.

Taryn squeezed her eyes shut. She knew what he wanted. She knew exactly what it would take to convince him to help Emmett. And she hated it. She hated that she knew he was manipulating her and there was no other way she could think of to help her friend. She hated him for forcing her into this thing she did not want. But perhaps... Perhaps she did want it, just a little. Perhaps she wanted it just enough that she was willing to agree to his manipulation. She did not know. All she knew was that if she wanted to help her friend, she would do what Erikkson wanted. There was no way out of this one. "If you do this for him, I will do it."

"You will do what?"

"I will become Sedition."

CHAPTER THREE

Taryn approached Emmett where he waited in the garden, at once excited and filled with trepidation at the news she had to share. She settled herself beside him, gently murmuring his name so as not to startle him. A layer of clouds had blown in, hiding the sun from view, but the chill in the air remained pleasant, especially after spending so long confined indoors.

"How was it?" Emmett asked, inclining his head toward her.

"It was better than I anticipated," she admitted. "Though Master Erikkson and I argued far more than either of us expected, I think."

Emmett's brow furrowed. "Why do you call him that?"

Taryn's expression darkened. An icy fist grasped her heart. This time, she had not even realized she'd called him "Master." "It is automatic. It must be something from before, something I cannot remember."

It may even be in my programming, she thought, but did not dare to say such a thing aloud. Though she could not fully trust Lord Erikkson, she wanted to believe he was good, or at least benevolent. The last thing she wanted to believe about him was that he had programmed her mind in ways she could not even remember.

"There is no need to call him Master, *chérie.* He has not asked us to."

Taryn nodded. "I know." She knotted her fingers in the folds of her sky-blue skirt. "Emmett, I have news for you."

He tilted his head. "*Qu'est que c'est?*" His hands tightened on his knees.

She took a deep breath. "Do you remember Seraphim's left eye? It is a slightly different color, duller and glossier..."

"*Oui. Pourquoi?* Why do you mention it?"

"Because that eye is clockwork. And Seraphim can see, Emmett."

His face drained of all its color. He struggled to speak. "You mean— You are saying I do not have to be blind?"

"No. Lord Erikkson said he would have to hurry if he is to fix your eyesight; the longer we wait, the more likely it is that the damage will be permanent. But he is working on it as we speak. You shall have your sight back."

He reached for her, palms out and open. Understanding the gesture, she gave him her hand, and he pressed it to his forehead, his eyes closed, entire body trembling. "*Merci, chérie. Merci!*"

"It will not be as it was before," she answered, throat dry. "You will see, but not as we do. Master Erikkson said it was more like detecting waves of sound to build a picture of your surroundings. As a bat does."

Emmett bit his lip, head cocking to the side as he tried to picture it. Then he shook his head. "If it is good enough for Seraphim, it is good enough for me. I will adapt. Thank you, *chérie,* for granting me this gift."

Taryn nodded to herself, trying and failing to be happy for him. All she could think about was that awful second blueprint, the one labelled *Sedition.* She knew it meant she would have to face Erikkson's knife once more, that she would have to place herself utterly in his hands and at his mercy. She did not know if she could. She had sworn to herself to never allow anyone to control her again. And here she was, sacrificing her autonomy for a friend, because she owed him a debt.

"What is wrong, *chérie?*"

Taryn brushed her copper hair over one shoulder. "Nothing is wrong."

"Do not think just because I am blind I cannot tell. Something is not right."

It would be better to tell him. She released a shaky breath. "I made a deal with Lord Erikkson. In exchange for your sight, I will become Sedition."

Emmett's brow furrowed. "*Quoi? Chérie,* why would you do that?"

"I got you into this mess," Taryn muttered miserably. "I will do whatever I can to ease it for you."

"*Belle,* I do not need my sight if it is an exchange for your life."

The conviction in his voice shook her. "I *must* do this, Emmett. I could not live with myself if I knew I could help you and yet did nothing." She folded her hands carefully in her lap. "You will see again. And I shall become Erikkson's perfect weapon."

"Weapon?" Emmett repeated incredulously.

Her throat tightened until it became difficult to speak. "I am like Seraphim. I am a weapon. I am simply...incomplete." The word tasted bitter on her tongue.

"What do you mean?"

"There is more Master Erikkson must alter within me before I can be what he wants."

"Do you mean he shall operate on you?"

A wry smile touched Taryn's lips. "Yes. He must change me."

"Does that not bother you?"

She scoffed, rubbing the number etched into her forearm. He had one to match, the numbers 744 carved into his muscled wrist. "What can he do? I am already inhuman."

Emmett reached for her again, fingers brushing her cheek cautiously before cupping her face. "*Non, chérie.*"

Taryn pushed him away.

"You do not have to do this thing *pour moi. Je ne le veux pas.*"

"I know. But I need to do it. Please. Do not make it any more difficult than it is."

Emmett touched her shoulder tenderly. "And you are positive about this?"

Taryn began to say yes, she was fine, but the lie weighed heavily upon her. "To tell the truth, Emmett, I am frightened. I am utterly terrified. But perhaps Master Erikkson is right, and Sedition can make a difference in this world where Taryn cannot." She fell silent for a long moment, watching the clouds drift across the sky. A storm was blowing in, the thunderheads huge and threatening on the horizon.

Emmett took her hand. "If you feel you must do this, *je comprend. Mais...* Promise me something, *chérie.* Promise you will not lose yourself to this cause."

Taryn took a deep breath, nodding. "I shall do my best, Emmett."

He squeezed her hand affectionately. "*Merci, belle. Merci.*"

THAT EVENING THEY WERE INVITED TO DINE AT Erikkson's table. Taryn wanted to refuse, exhausted from the strangeness of the day and the anticipation of the future, but Erikkson insisted, saying there would only be one other guest joining them. Taryn had conceded, that overwhelming desire to please him once again turning her will to clay, molded by what he asked of her.

Unsure how formal Erikkson's private dinners were, Taryn selected a lacy black and white dress with a high neckline and semi-bustled skirt as her evening attire. She found silk gloves in the wardrobe, which she pulled on, hiding her prosthetic for the first time in weeks. She helped Emmett dress for dinner in a fine black suit with an indigo cravat. She described both their outfits to him as they made their way to the dining hall, and Emmett smiled at her.

"*Vous êtes plus belle, chérie.*"

Taryn chose to pretend she did not understand.

The dining hall was transformed in the evening light. Elegant candelabras lined the long table, the cream-colored candles casting a warm yellow glow about the room. Erikkson sat at the head of the table, wearing almost the exact costume he'd worn earlier in the day, but this time with a black dinner jacket. He gestured for them to sit on his right.

Only after she'd seated herself did Taryn notice the other man in the room. Seraphim. He had been concealed half in shadow behind a vase of flowers, but now his stoic face came fully into view. Something sharp and sour flooded Taryn's mouth at the sight of him and the memory of what he'd done.

"Hello, Taryn. Hello, Emmett. I heard what happened. I am sorry." Seraphim had made an effort to clean himself up for this meeting, with new clothes and his long black curls pulled back from his face, though Taryn thought he still looked out of place. His dark skin glowed in the candlelight, but Taryn had eyes for only one bit of Seraphim: his left eye, clockwork encased in glass. The design that would allow Emmett to regain his sight.

"Seraphim?" Emmett's face lit up as he recognized the voice of his former shipmate.

"Fat lot of good your sorry does for us," Taryn growled. "You did not even *try* to stop them from taking us."

Seraphim's expression did not change. "You know I was powerless on that ship."

"You have a pair of bloody wings made from blades!"

"Sedition, please," Erikkson's deep voice cut in. "There is no reason to blame Seraphim for what happened. Let us at least *try* to have a civil dining experience. Ambrose has prepared a celebratory meal in your honor. Do not argue and ruin it."

Taryn scowled across the table at Seraphim but said nothing. She would not forgive him so easily for his inaction, no matter what excuse he used.

"I came when Lord Erikkson summoned me. Do you know what happened to Ace?" Seraphim asked. "He left the *Dauntless* in London, and no one has heard from him since."

"Ace left *la Dauntless*?" Emmett questioned.

"Yes, he showed up at the Black Castle, the last day we were there," Taryn snarled. "He came with some insane notion he could break us out."

"Ace came back?" Emmett sounded incredulous. Taryn almost regretted not telling Emmett before, as she knew he'd been friends with the privateer, but so much had happened, she hadn't found the chance. And despite herself, despite the fact that he'd come back for them in the end, she still had not quite brought herself to forgive Ace. It had been his inaction that landed them in the Black Castle in the first place. His cowardice had cost Emmett his sight.

"What happened to him?" Seraphim questioned, leaning forward.

Taryn waved a hand. "Master Erikkson showed up. I assume Ace left."

Seraphim scowled. "If anything should happen to him, we shall have Storm to contend with."

Taryn shook her head, though her stomach twisted at the

mention of her name. The privateer captain was cruel, cunning, and hated biomatons. If Taryn was lucky, she'd never run into her again. "He is fine, I am sure of it. He posed as some collector. No one knew he was a privateer." It wasn't entirely true. Ace had revealed who and what he was to Lady Sara Bellham, the proprietor's wife. But she'd been kind to Taryn, and she doubted the woman would have said anything.

Seraphim looked thoughtful but said no more. Two young men—perhaps fifteen or sixteen—entered, carrying bowls of steaming soup. Erikkson visibly relaxed.

"Not a moment too soon. Thank you, George, Mark. Give Ambrose my compliments." The two boys nodded. Taryn studied them for clockwork enhancements, but found no obvious changes in the boys, save for the silver plates on the backs of their heads, signs their brains had been altered by the biomechanicks who built them.

"Now, my children, in honor of our newest family member, Emmett LeBeau, and our dearest Sedition returned to us at last, I say *bon appétit!*"

They ate in silence, first the creamy mushroom soup, rich and earthy, and the next course was fresh-caught fish with lemon and butter, a bright, summery morsel that set Taryn's tongue ablaze. It seemed so long since she'd eaten good food, let alone something as rich and decadent as this. It was only as George and Mark cleared their plates from the second course that Lord Erikkson spoke to her again. "Why do you hide your prosthetic?"

Taryn had almost forgotten the glove. She hesitated, unsure of how to answer.

"There is no need for that in my house," Erikkson said, without waiting for her response.

Shame swelled in her throat. She opened her mouth to speak, but she could not find the words. She could not explain to him that after five years of disguising what she was, she felt naked without the glove. She could not explain how her heart still skipped a beat every time she caught a glimpse of the silver in her periphery, terrified the glove had torn and exposed her secret until she remembered she was not in disguise. It did not matter that she was no longer in hiding here, the fear had nevertheless followed her.

She spoke none of what she felt, just stuffed it all deep inside, pulling the glove off with shaky fingers. She moved to set it in her lap, but Lord Erikkson held out a hand.

"Give it to me." His tone left her no choice. Taryn set the black silk glove in his palm, and he pocketed her crutch. "You ought to be proud of who you are."

"So far, I have been told I am either a slave or a museum piece. Which is it I should be more proud of?" The words came tumbling out in a heap, words created by anger and shame. Words she did not mean but could not take back.

Erikkson frowned. "Your quick tongue is not a virtue."

Vehemence flamed inside her chest. "Then why do you not just program me to be docile like everyone else?"

George and Mark reentered then, carrying bowls of fresh lime sorbet to cleanse their palates before the next course. Taryn turned the sorbet over in her mouth, holding it on her tongue until it burned with the cold and melted into liquid against her teeth. She stared down at her detested new prosthetic, folded in her lap, and considered leaving the table in protest before the meal finished. She decided against it, the weight of Erikkson's opinion of her like an anchor in her chest.

Emmett spoke up to fill the uncomfortable silence. "Taryn told me about your agreement, *monsieur*. I thank you for your generosity."

Lord Erikkson inclined his head toward Emmett. "If it is possible to restore your sight, I shall do so. I must warn you, though, it shall take some getting used to. Seraphim knows. It's not sight as you know it. It is more like echolocation made visual."

"*Merci, monsieur.* I am certain I will adapt." Emmett seemed to have little difficulty dining without his eyesight, his table manners almost perfect, though occasionally he leaned over and quietly questioned Taryn about which course they were on. She had not expected such refined etiquette from a man she'd met aboard a pirate airship, but she supposed he would have an explanation for that, too. If she had to guess, it would probably have something to do with his French heritage.

The sorbet dishes were cleared, and the main course emerged smelling of garlic and spices, striking a chord deep in the darkness of her mind. The dish was roast leg of lamb, drizzled with a French sauce and crusted with spices. Along with the roast, there were steamed vegetables and silky mashed potatoes, but Taryn found she only had eyes for the cut of meat on her plate. The scent of it was intoxicating and comforting, like waking from a dream. And as soon as she took a bite, she *knew* this was her favorite meal. This was a meal she'd eaten for birthdays and Christmases; a meal that made her ache at the core of her being. She closed her eyes, savoring the way the meat melted on her tongue. The flavor was a memory all its own, a taste sparking joy and sorrow at once, and yet still leaving her past in the dark. The new knowledge made Taryn's chest hurt.

"Do you recognize the dish, Sedition?" Erikkson questioned.

Taryn looked up at him with tears in her eyes, unable to speak.

He smiled. "I thought you might. I requested it specifically. Welcome home, Sedition. It has been too long since you were last here."

CHAPTER FOUR

Taryn spent the next morning wandering the halls of Elmhurst manor, her mind in a fog of memories that refused to return. Each time she wandered into the path of a stranger, she ducked down the nearest hallway. She climbed up and down stairs, avoiding the enraptured stares of Erikkson's other biomatons and wrestling with the reality of what she had agreed to do. She was going to become a weapon. A soldier, leading a rebellion. Just days—or weeks?—ago, she had been a schoolgirl, whose biggest battle had been chauvinist bullies and the risk of being discovered. Now, she was to be something entirely new. She realized she hadn't any idea what the date was, nor the day of the week. She'd left Grafton's School of Mechanicks on Monday night, January 25, 1864. By Wednesday morning, they had been sold to the Black Castle. But how many days had they been there? Four? Five? It felt like a lifetime.

"Ah, Sedition! There you are. I have been looking for you."

Taryn turned fiery green eyes on the man who built her. "Should you not be working on Emmett's new eyes?" she hissed.

Erikkson smiled. "They are complete, save for a single part

my apprentice is bringing from London. I came to take your measurements."

"My *what?*"

"You do not seriously expect me to be able to accurately complete your new mechanicks without taking your measurements, my dear?"

Taryn scowled. "Very well."

He walked beside her as they traversed the corridors to his study. He kept his hands in the pockets of the maroon brocade smoking jacket he wore. Taryn had not seen him smoke, and supposed the jacket was his equivalent of leisure wear. "So, tell me. How are you adjusting to life back here at Elmhurst Manor?" he asked.

Taryn did not look at him, suddenly too aware of the clink and whirr of her clockwork limb. "It is not *back*. Not for me. For you, it may be as if I have come home, but I am merely in another strange house amongst strangers."

Erikkson sighed. "Taryn, I promised you to do all I can to get your memory back, and I shall—"

"But I ought not to dwell on it, I know," she interrupted wryly.

"I did not say that. I understand it is difficult for you here, especially because you have no memories of this place, but I do hope you shall not allow it to taint Elmhurst for you. I have done my best to make my home a refuge from the scorn of the world, and I hope you shall come to see it as one."

Taryn narrowed her eyes, but said nothing. Lord Erikkson was complex, at once kind and domineering, fatherly and manipulative. She hesitated to trust him, and yet the way she had agreed so readily to become his weapon was an utterly trusting decision. Her interactions with him terrified her all the more for their undercurrent of familiarity. He was a stranger, but not. He knew her intimately, and she knew him not at all.

He steered her into his study.

"If you would undress to your undergarments, it will help me to get the most precise measurements."

Taryn shook her head, crossing her arms over her chest. "Absolutely not."

"Now, Sedition, do not be like that. Do you think I care what your undergarments look like? I need my measurements to be as accurate as possible, which means they cannot be impaired by four layers of crinoline and cotton."

Taryn scowled, but turned her back on him, slowly peeling away her red satin dress. She let it fall to the floor, keeping her cotton shift on over her undergarments. "Your measurements should be accurate enough now," she muttered, stretching her arms out.

Erikkson did not argue, working quickly and carefully. He took incredibly detailed measurements, from the length of her arms to the circumference of her fingers, scribbling them all down on his sleeve cuffs. Taryn could not help but smile inwardly at that. Royal had the same bad habit when they first met, endlessly scribbling notes to himself on his cuffs, much to his mother's chagrin.

"May I ask you a question?" Taryn spoke after several silent minutes had passed.

"Of course."

"If we are your children, why did you build us to be weapons?" She could not hide the edge of bitterness in her voice.

He stayed quiet for a long moment, scribbling another number on his cuff. "Believe me, Sedition, if I could protect you from the world, I would do so."

She jerked away from him, dropping her arms by her sides. "Then why do you force me into a role I do not want? You seem to have built an oasis here. Why do you have to alter me more? Why do I have to fight?"

"Because if you do not fight, there will be thousands more

like Emmett and I cannot fix them all," he barked, his voice growing hard for the first time. He would not look at her.

Taryn's throat constricted. Guilt gnawed at her ribs, threatening to consume her from the inside out. She shut the door on the monster inside her. She would not take responsibility for the suffering of every biomaton. It was too much. "And if I fail?" she asked hoarsely. "How many more six-year-old children will you tear apart and rebuild in your quest for the perfect soldier?"

He did not speak for a moment, his eyes trained inwardly, as if examining something only he could see. When he finally spoke, it was slowly, as if the words were being drawn from him one by one. "You shall not fail."

Taryn closed her eyes, unable to express the frustration and weight she felt at his confidence in her. There were times in these last two days that she regretted his ever finding her. Before, she had known she had some terrible purpose, and had expected never to understand, yet perhaps that was better in some ways than having her purpose spelled out and knowing it to be hopeless.

"I am finished," Erikkson said. "You may dress."

She did, sullenly, her eyes anywhere but on him. "Do you really believe you can help Emmett?"

"Yes," he answered. "Of course, it all depends on how much damage Bellham's sorry excuses for biomechanicks did during his original operation—I shall not know until I am operating on him myself—but if there is anything left of his optic nerve, I will be able to give him a new prosthetic. I do not imagine his eyes can be as bad as Seraphim's was when I found him."

Taryn's ears perked up at the opportunity to learn more about the mystery that was Seraphim. "Where did you find Seraphim? What was he before you changed him?"

Erikkson moved to the drafting table near the window,

snatching up a piece of scrap paper and beginning to copy down her measurements. Taryn wondered how she had not noticed before that he was left-handed.

"Seraphim was aboard a slave ship bound for America when pirates attacked. He lost his eye in the ensuing explosion. The pirates stole the best of the cargo and left the rest to perish as the ship burned and sank. The ship I was traveling aboard came across the wreckage several hours later. Seraphim was the only survivor we found." Erikkson did not even look up from his note-taking.

"He was already a slave?" Taryn questioned numbly.

"Yes, he was already a slave, eleven years old and left for dead. And since I know you will ask, yes, he consented to the clockwork adaptations I created for him." Erikkson raised his eyes to her.

"Adaptations?" Taryn scoffed. "You made an eleven-year-old boy into a weapon."

"Better that than allow him to continue as a slave." Erikkson ruffled a stack of papers. "That is the trouble, little one. There has always been slavery, and no matter what abolitionists like myself try to do, it is likely human beings will always exploit and traffic other human beings."

"Then why are you building weapons to fight a hopeless battle?" Taryn's frustration turned the question into a snarl.

"Because slavery is illegal in England. It has been abolished for more than thirty years in this glorious country, and yet people content themselves with the ownership of biomatons by saying you are not human. That is the trouble. They are taking away your personhood, and it does not seem to bother anyone."

CHAPTER FIVE

TARYN SPENT the next morning in Elmhurst's library. The room wasn't large, but it was well-stocked with everything from books on mechanics and anatomy to recent novels. She ran her fingers along spines, pulled books down and flipped through them, replaced them as something new caught her attention. She'd risen to find Emmett missing from his room, already beneath Erikkson's knife for the long, complicated surgery that would, hopefully, help him. She hadn't had the stomach for breakfast, too caught up in memories of the last time Emmett had been taken from her. So, she traced her fingers along the dark wood shelves instead, in the hopes of distracting herself.

A knock came at the doorframe. "Yes?" Taryn asked, barely looking up from the book on African wildlife she'd discovered, filled with fascinating illustrations.

Lord Erikkson entered, a slight smile on his face. He wore a special pair of mechanick's glasses, which had several lenses for magnification that could be adjusted to fit his eye. "I am sorry to disturb you, little one, but I thought you would like to know: we finished Emmett's surgery. He should be waking soon."

Taryn snapped the book shut. "Did it work?"

"It is too early to tell. We will know when he wakes."

"Is he in his room now?" Taryn asked, clutching more tightly at the book. Her heart rate picked up; her pulse throbbed in her palm.

"Yes. If you like, you may wait there for him to wake. I will bring you a pot of tea and a few breakfast things."

Taryn nodded. "Thank you. Oh, thank you for helping him!"

Erikkson smile turned to a grimace. "My dear, I must know you are going to keep your end of the agreement."

A chill traveled down her spine. "Yes. I gave you my word."

"Then I shall fetch you later today. No point in postponing the inevitable, is there?"

Taryn bit down hard on the inside of her lip. "No, there is not. I said I would be your weapon. And I shall." She shut her eyes. "*I shall.*" She repeated the words, as if convincing herself of the truth of them.

Erikkson came and took her hand, his eyes intense and face earnest. "Sedition." He paused. "Taryn. I know this is frightening for you. I know there are times when you will feel defeated. Members of your army may be killed. You may lose those closest to you. But you must remember one thing: you were built for this. *This* is why I saved you. There is no one in this world better suited to this purpose than you, Taryn. *You.*"

She stared at him, tongue-tied by the gravity of his words. He really, truly believed in her and her abilities in this role. Though that knowledge did little to ease her terror at the prospect of allowing him to operate on her again, she did find his confidence reassuring. She reminded herself that he was considered to be one of the best biomechanicks in the world. She would be all right, despite the changes this new surgery would make. She nodded silently, too petrified to say anything.

"You look hungry," he observed, squeezing her hand

tenderly before releasing her. "I shall bring up a tray in, say, fifteen minutes?"

"Thank you," Taryn answered, but he was already leaving the room. She stretched, rolling her left shoulder until the clockwork beneath her skin strained against her muscles. She clenched her clockwork fingers one-by-one, the mechanism still clumsy and uncouth to her experienced eye. She shelved the book in its place, fingers trailing down the spine for a moment longer than necessary, and then left the library, heading for Emmett's room, a fog of anxiety clouding her chest.

The door was open, and Taryn crept inside silently, gaze transfixed on his sleeping figure. White linen bandages covered his eyes, and she marveled at how peaceful he looked, lying there. The late morning light poured through the windows and hesitantly set its front paws on the edge of the bed, as if afraid to wake him. Taryn settled herself in an armchair by the wall, thoughtlessly chewing her thumbnail. She prayed the surgery had worked, prayed he would wake to find his eyesight restored. It seemed futile to lose her own autonomy and independence only to discover it had been worthless.

Erikkson entered with a tray of breakfast things, though the time at this point was nearer to luncheon, including a bowl of cut fruit and a small silver carafe which wafted steam and the delightful smell of continental hot chocolate. Taryn stared at the tendrils pouring from the spout in wonder.

Three summers before, she had traveled to Paris with Royal and his mother, Lady Stokker. They had lived blissfully in a small penthouse suite with a balcony that had a breathtaking view of the Paris skyline. Her favorite ritual had been one invented by Royal's mother, who delighted in French cuisine. She had talked them into drinking the rich hot chocolate with breakfast, and it had become a joke between them. She had not tasted it since Lady Stokker's death.

"How did you know?" she questioned.

"Know what?" Erikkson asked.

Taryn shook her head, unable to explain.

"I have always found a cup of cocoa to be a delightfully restorative beverage." Lord Erikkson set the tray down on a table beside her chair. He began to pour the steaming drink, careful not to spill a single drop. "And you looked as if you needed something to bolster your courage."

He handed her a cup, topped with a dollop of fresh whipped cream, and, because the drink was so thick, a small silver spoon. Taryn sipped it hesitantly, but found it was just hot enough to avoid burning her tongue. She glanced over the other breakfast things he'd brought: a plate of pastries, a few cold meats and cheeses, and some hot sausages.

"Thank you," she said, her voice subdued.

"You are very welcome, little one." He looked to Emmett. "When he wakes, he may remove the bandages, but he ought to be resting his eyes. It will be very disorienting at first. He will need to wait a day or two for the clockwork to bond before he can get up and exert himself."

Taryn glanced back to Emmet. "I will tell him."

"Good. I shall be back to fetch you this evening, when I am ready to perform your operation."

Taryn shuddered, her jaw clenching tightly. "Very well," she muttered.

He hesitated, as though about to say something more, but he simply nodded. "I will be back." He left the room, running one hand across his short auburn beard thoughtfully.

Taryn watched him go in silence, trying to turn her thoughts to anything other than what she would be undergoing that afternoon. Today was her last day as Taryn. Tomorrow, she would be Sedition. A warrior. A weapon. How would she change with such a different role? She would not be the same, that much was certain. She would never be the same.

HE AWOKE SLOWLY, DRAGGED FROM THE DEPTHS OF A DEEP, dreamless sleep. Everything ached, every bone in his body screaming for attention. Slowly, he forced himself to sit up, bewildered, his eyes adjusting to the swollen darkness surrounding him.

He did not know where he was. The air was damp and chilled, and the hard ground beneath his hand grated against his skin. He pressed himself upright. His right arm had gone numb, as though he'd slept on it the wrong way and blocked the blood flow. He reached across his body with his left hand, shaking fingers searching for flesh into which he could rub life.

He found nothing but cold, hard metal.

He froze, his hand jerking away from the unexpected bite as quickly as if he had been stung. *What?* Hesitantly, his fingers moved up to his neck, his shoulder, finding the exact spot where warm flesh transitioned to frigid steel. Horror flooded his still foggy mind. He had not had a prosthetic arm before, as far as he could remember. The trouble was he *could not* remember. Anxiously, he searched his bare chest for more metal, fingers traveling frantically over his familiar form. He found it, across the right side of his torso. Each rib had been encased in metal, exposed over the skin that stretched between them. His breathing came in ragged gasps as he began to understand what had happened. He'd been turned into a biomaton.

Who had done this to him? And why? He wished the fog in his head would clear so he could remember. He focused on the prosthetic, and after a moment of concentration, found he could move the fingers. He lifted his new hand and touched his cheek with steel digits, shuddering.

Footsteps echoed from somewhere in the dark, and the boy froze, irrational terror racing through his chest. His clockwork hand fell to his side, the metal clanging against the stone floor.

He winced as the noise rattled through his already throbbing skull.

A glow appeared, far down the hall to his right, and bloomed as the footsteps drew steadily louder. The boy's eyes stung, adjusting to the light, revealing his surroundings. The floor was damp, pockmarked stone. Caging him in on three sides, heavy iron bars rose from the stone and were embedded in the ceiling, shrouded in shadow above his head. Across the narrow hall outside his cell, a similar cage stood empty. He huddled on the floor, unable to find the strength to rise, making himself small, working to become invisible.

A man appeared outside his cell, carrying a lantern that burned like the sun to his sensitive eyes. The stranger was tall and narrow, his face sharp and hawkish. His intense, colorless eyes examined him. "Ah, 745, you are awake at last. After everything, I thought perhaps you never would."

The boy frowned. *That is not my name! My name is... My name...* He could not remember. How could he forget his own name? He shifted, his prosthetic scraping across the floor, the sound setting his teeth on edge. "Who are you?" His voice emerged soft and hoarse, tasting foreign between his teeth.

"I am your new master." He examined the boy, nothing escaping his scrutiny. His gaze touched the boy's right arm. "It may take you a while to get used to the graft. Do not worry. You should be fully functional in no time."

The boy stared at the man who had just declared himself his master, horror flooding his ice blue eyes. "Why am I here? What have you done to me?"

The man just shook his head, clicking his tongue. "You do not ask questions here, boy."

He frowned, shaking, abject terror flooding his chest, irrational and impossible to ignore. He hadn't any idea *how,* but he knew this man could inflict immense pain without batting an eye if he was displeased. He could not risk that. He turned his eyes away, swallowing his questions. Everything hurt. He wanted to sleep.

"Good," the man sounded pleased. "You learn quickly, 745. Rest now. Allow your graft to heal. Then we may begin your training." He turned away, taking the lantern with him. The warm yellow light was quickly swallowed by the hungry darkness, leaving the boy alone and shivering on the stone floor. He struggled with the spinning of his fractured mind, trying in vain to recall something, *anything* of who he was. His mind remained a void, an empty darkness within himself. He curled into a ball as the earth tilted around him. An image appeared in his head of a red-haired girl with a metal arm like his own. He did not know who she was, but as soon as he remembered her face, he knew he had to find her. She knew who he was. She could help him, if only he could find her.

CHAPTER SIX

EMMETT DREW himself from the darkness of unconsciousness. Sensation returned slowly, like being pulled from the depths of a tepid sea. An intense, burning pain throbbed in his forehead and cheeks, an ache worse than any migraine. The pain was familiar to him, the sharp sting behind his eyes the same as it had been when he woke in the Black Castle without his sight. Emmett took the time to recall where he was, and with it, Erikkson's promise to help him. Though he had not truly believed the man, he'd allowed Erikkson to operate, knowing Taryn blamed herself for his blindness. He harbored no blame for her; no, he cared for her too much to hold any of their unfortunate circumstances against her. But he had agreed to try, for her. She'd sacrificed so much just to give him this fragile hope.

Emmett lifted one hand to his brow, his eyes still closed tightly, finding a cloth bandage over them.

"Emmett, you are awake at last!" Taryn's beautiful, musical voice came to him out of the stillness. He loved the slight rasp in her throat that showed her concern, the way her voice still had the slightest touch of a Cockney accent, despite her attempts to mask it. Emmett smiled.

"*Bonjour, belle.*"

The bed shifted as she sat on the edge of it; he could smell the sweet scent of her hair. He reached out a hand, groping a little, until his fingers met hers.

"Can you see?" she questioned breathlessly.

"I do not yet know." His heart lodged itself firmly in his throat. "Shall we find out?"

He felt her nod, her nearness making her every movement easy to detect. Steadying his hand, Emmett sat up, pulling the wrap away. He whispered a silent prayer, his eyes shut tightly. Everything was darkness. Could he really open his eyes and disappoint Taryn? Did he have any choice?

Emmett blinked his eyes open, anticipating the absence of sensation he had become so accustomed to. Strange, swimming lines poured into his mind, everything red and throbbing and *too much*. Emmett squeezed his eyes shut again, overwhelmed by the images.

"Is something wrong?" Taryn questioned, barely masked terror edging her voice.

Emmett shook his head, unable to speak. He blinked his eyes open again, this time allowing the sensations to bombard him without blocking them out. Everything swam with an unearthly red glow, bubbling and moving in a sea of changing borders, like a topographical map with the lines made of crimson snakes, writhing together on a background of thick black felt. But as he focused, shapes became clearer, the edges of things resolving out of the mass of writhing shapes. That length of straight lines was the edge of the bed. The splash of yellowish lines, the warm sun pouring through the window. And then he could see her, all at once, drawn in outline instead of the way he remembered, but still perfect, still *her*. The lines of her face, the long sweep of her braid. "Oh," he breathed, words failing him for a moment.

Taryn's voice kept its worried undertone. "You can see?"

Emmett nodded. "But it is not like anything I have ever experienced." He raised a hand in front of his face, watched the lines trace the outline of it, create the hand he remembered so well in a hundred winding lines of red and orange. A grin grew on his freckled countenance.

"*Monsieur* Erikkson was correct that this shall take some getting used to." He could tell this new kind of sight had *some* depth, but it wasn't easy to tell how far away things were. "I shall have to relearn my fighting methods."

"I am so thankful it worked. I was half afraid—" Taryn hesitated, and he watched her features shift, the circles that defined her brows and mouth tipping downward. "But no, there is no need to even say such things."

He reached out and gently took her hand. "*Merci,* Taryn. For this gift." He hesitated, surprised to find his heart in his throat, but then he asked before he could stop himself. "Would you—would you describe them to me?"

"I can fetch you a looking glass, if you like."

He shook his head. "I am afraid reflections will not be something I can interpret." He gestured, tracing lines in the air with his hands. The red lines shifted around them, trailing behind and ahead. *Oh,* this *was* like sound waves. He could use this when he got used to it. It might even make him a better fighter than before, because now he could not only see where his opponent was, he could see where they had been, and where they were planning to go. "Describe them for me."

She nodded, shifting on the bed beside him. "They are glass, with very delicate golden clockwork inside, and some sort of lens where your iris would be. When you focus, the cogs spin."

He smiled uncomfortably. "I never thought gold an appropriate color for eyes."

"I think they are very fine. And I am thankful it worked."

He leaned back against the heavy oak headboard, watching

her outline shift. "It is only because of your self-sacrifice, *belle*. I was learning to manage."

She turned her head away, staring out the window. "I could not have lived with myself. Not after I knew I could help."

He reached out and touched her hand. "*Merci beaucoup, belle.*"

She glanced at him. "You ought to be resting your eyes. Master Erikkson said it shall be a day or two before you can spend long looking about."

"Very well." He closed his eyes, his limbs suddenly heavy with exhaustion. "Will you promise to be here when I wake, *chérie?*"

Taryn froze. He waited, wondering what he'd said wrong. Finally, she shifted. "Emmett, Lord Erikkson is coming back for me this evening. He is going to perform the operation tonight." Her voice shook. "Tomorrow, I shall be Sedition."

"*Non,*" Emmett gasped, opening his eyes again to stare at the girl he'd only known for a handful of days. Already, she'd become his world. "You do not have to let him do that."

"I do. He helped you. He kept his side of the bargain, and now I must play my part." She pressed her fingers to the bridge of her nose. "I am frightened, but perhaps this shall be for the best. I have a purpose outside of being a slave. Surely, that is a good thing?"

"*Peut-être.*" He touched her shoulder. "Whatever happens, *belle*, I am with you."

She smiled. "*Merci,* Emmett." She pushed his shoulder. "You ought to be resting. Close your eyes, I shall read to you. Master Erikkson gave me this new novel to pass the time. He said it is very good."

"What is it called?" Emmett asked, leaning back against the pillows and closing his eyes. Her suggestion of reading was more than he could have hoped for; it would allow him to enjoy the musicality of her voice. The sounds of a leather binding being cracked and the rustle of pages turning, like dry leaves across cobbles, drifted to his ears.

"*The Woman in White*, by Wilkie Collins," Taryn began, her soft voice filling Emmett's mind with the images of the story. She read well, though not perfectly, at times stumbling over her words or stopping to sip her hot chocolate. Still, the story was enough to draw them both in, and for an hour or two, they forgot themselves and the ugly world they lived in.

A QUIET KNOCK AT THE DOOR INTERRUPTED TARYN mid-sentence, and she closed the book, reluctantly raising her eyes to the threshold. Erikkson stood with one hand resting upon the doorframe. The other hand gripped the doorknob, the palm wrapped in a white linen bandage.

"How is *Monsieur* LeBeau?" he asked.

Emmett sat up, blinking his new eyes open, the irises twisting as he focused on the man. "He has new sight, *monsieur. Merci.*"

Erikkson nodded. "*De rien,* Emmett. I am glad to know it worked." He gave the Frenchman a mockingly stern glare. "You ought to be resting."

Emmett blinked at him. "I will rest when you go, *monsieur.*"

"We are going now. Come, little one," he replied, turning to Taryn. "It is time."

She rose, leaving the book near Emmett's side, though she knew he could not read it with his new eyes.

He reached out to her as she passed, giving her hand a gentle, comforting squeeze. "*Bonne chance, belle.*"

Taryn nodded mutely. She barely felt Emmett's fingers against her own, so focused was she on Erikkson's summons and what it meant. Her feet carried her to the door without her permission.

"Oh, before I forget—" Erikkson left the door jamb and dimmed the gas lamps that hung on the walls. The frosted glass, which had glowed so cheerily, now dulled to a sullen orange flicker. It was only then that Taryn noticed how dark it had grown outside. Though the day still had hours of light left, thick thunderclouds had swept in, coating the landscape outside in blues and purples. The gloomy clouds mirrored her inner turmoil. "There. Someone will bring you supper shortly, but you ought to rest your eyes as much as you can."

Emmett nodded. "I am resting."

"Excellent. Come, Taryn." Erikkson took her firmly by the elbow. A little shudder slipped down her spine. "We are wasting time."

She wrenched herself from his grasp as they left the room, flickers of Lord Bellham's skeletal fingers dancing through her mind. She reminded herself that he and Erikkson were nothing alike. But what did she really know about Erikkson besides what he'd told her? She followed him silently, through the east wing of the house, moving westward. They took a flight of stairs down and crossed through the part of the manor Taryn recognized from their formal supper a few evenings before.

"How did you hurt your hand?" she asked, unable to bear the silence. The manor seemed deserted.

"I cut it on a bit of the clockwork required for your new prosthetic." Erikkson smiled wryly, turning his hand over, as if examining it. "It has been a long time since I built anything so complex, and I am not as young as I once was."

Taryn had no reply. Her eyes caught on his temple, where streaks of silver and white showed in his auburn hair. Had his hair been all dark when she'd known him before? She could not remember.

"This way."

Erikkson guided her through a massive stone kitchen to a heavy oak door that Tayrn supposed led to the wine cellar. Erikkson tugged on the door, which gave way with a groan, swinging outward on creaky leather hinges. Inside, a narrow stone staircase unfurled itself before them. A draft swept up the stairs, smelling of must and iron. The prospect of walking down those steps turned every bone in Taryn's body to ice, but she steeled herself and stepped down.

The ceiling hung so low Erikkson had to stoop a little in their descent, which left the room below to become visible only by degrees. The room had been converted from a wine cellar to an operating theatre, more intricate and gleaming than the laboratory Taryn had seen at the Black Castle. If the labs at the Black Castle had been designed for utility, this one had been designed to inspire. The stone walls were disguised by rows of books and bottles of ether; gleaming high-beam gas lamps illuminated the entire space thoroughly. A large metal sink with a water pump stood in the far corner. In the center of the room, a metal operating table patiently awaited its next victim.

"Everything is prepared, sir," a familiar voice said from their left. Taryn turned, heart pounding, instantly recognizing the blond hair and big brown eyes. Her mouth fell open.

"Royal?"

CHAPTER SEVEN

Royal's mouth dropped open. "Taryn?"

She spun and tried to dash back up the stairs, hugging her clockwork arm to her chest so he would not see it. Erikkson caught her shoulders, stopping her mid-flight.

"What are you doing, Sedition?"

"He cannot see me this way," she gasped. Her body trembled like a leaf. Royal could not have missed her arm. Her deepest secret had at last been revealed to her best friend, and she could not bear the shame. She didn't want him to find out this way. Not like this.

Erikkson shook her a little by the shoulders. "Think, Taryn. This is who you are. Are you ashamed of that?"

"Yes," she mumbled, staring at her feet.

"This is what you were hiding?" Royal questioned, his voice clouded with hurt.

Taryn turned slowly, fists clutching handfuls of her skirt. She could not meet his eyes. "Aye."

"You are a biomaton?" Royal's face went from white to red, his brow knitting into a scowl. He squeaked on the last word, the break in his voice belying how young he really was.

Taryn nodded weakly. She held her hands out to him: one real, one clockwork, both trembling. "I had to hide it. I am sorry, Royal." *I am so, so sorry. I never wanted you to find out,* she thought, her voice failing her.

"There is a screen in the left corner of the room," Erikkson interrupted, touching her shoulder. "Please go and change into the gown hanging there, so we may begin."

Taryn moved mechanically, obeying his order, but her mind remained on Royal. What must he think of her? Her lies? They had known one another for so long, even lived in the same household for a time, and she had never been brave enough to tell him... She was certain he must hate her. What was he doing here, anyhow? This was the last place she had expected to see him.

Behind the screen, Taryn donned a thin cotton shift with laces down the sides, designed so Erikkson might perform his surgery while still allowing her to keep most of her modesty intact. She paid little attention to the garment. She stepped out from behind the divider, dressed and nervous, only to find Royal waiting for her.

"This way," he said flatly, leading her toward the metal operating table. A small, wheeled metal cart had been pushed to the side of the table and Taryn recognized both surgical and mechanick's tools upon it. She rubbed her right hand on her shift, her palm clammy.

"I am really, truly sorry, Royal," Taryn began. Her tongue was so dry it stuck to the roof of her mouth.

Royal's normally bright eyes clouded over. His jaw clenched tight, the muscles in his neck standing out beneath his skin. "Get up on the table, please," he said tautly.

Taryn followed his orders, the gruff, impersonal edge to his words stinging as badly as if he'd slapped her. "I wanted to tell you," she said, her voice barely more than a whisper. "I did not know how. We had all those horrid arguments over what biomatons were like, and I was afraid..." She shook her head. "Please say you understand. Please, say something."

"Shut up," Royal snapped. "Just—just let me think, please." He toyed with a tool lying upon the metal cart, unable to look at her. Taryn's stomach flipped. She clamped her mouth shut against all the things she wanted to say, all the excuses she wanted to offer him.

"I knew you were hiding something," Royal continued slowly, "but this... Gor, Tiger, I do not know what to think. What else did you lie about?" The old nickname for her hurt like a knife in her heart. His eyes searched her face. "Why are you here?"

"Lord Erikkson rescued me from the fire that killed my parents and replaced my arm with clockwork." Taryn chewed the inside of her lip, struggling to find the right words. The metal table was ice cold where she sat upon it. "I lied when I told you I had been offered a job. A group of privateers discovered what I was and forced me to go with them. Erikkson kept me from being sold into slavery."

"And the boy we operated on earlier?"

Taryn nodded. "It is my fault he is a biomaton."

"Ah."

"But what are you doing here?" Taryn questioned. *I thought I would never see you again.*

"This is the apprenticeship I took when you left school. Tony—Lord Erikkson is teaching me all he knows about biomechanicks—and about biomatons." He picked up a small metal rod, about the length of her pinky finger. "Lie down, please." He pushed her shoulder, not hard, but firmly enough that she knew he hadn't yet forgiven her. Taryn lay flat against the cold metal, trying to keep the memories of the last time she'd been in a situation like this from flooding her mind. The number etched into her forearm burned with remembered pain. "Turn your head," Royal instructed.

Taryn turned, allowing him to click the small plate on the back of her head open. He slipped the metal rod into the controls, then released her, his fingers lingering momentarily in her copper hair.

"What did you do?"

"I disabled your prosthetics, to ensure nothing goes wrong." He hesitated, and some of the sharpness drained out of him. His gentle brown eyes crinkled at the corners. He touched her hand. "I missed you, Taryn."

The lump in her throat dissolved. "I missed you, too, Royal. Can you forgive me for hiding what I am?"

Royal took a long, deep breath, then nodded. "Even a fortnight ago, I do not think I would have understood, but now I think I do. Tony has taught me much."

"Yet I still have more to teach you, it seems," Lord Erikkson interrupted, appearing on Taryn's left. "Go wash your hands, Royal, and get the ether. All this chatter is delaying our work."

Royal gave Taryn a look, rolling his eyes, but stepped away. Erikkson began to secure leather straps around her wrists. Terror and violence began to well up inside her chest, clawing its way up her throat like an animal. She tugged at the straps. Her left arm hung heavy, immobile. Unbidden flashes of the last time she'd been strapped down and broken blinked behind her eyes. Taryn shut her eyes and swallowed hard, forcing herself to breathe through the fear and red animal rage. She was stronger than this. She was *Sedition.* Or she would be all too soon.

Erikkson seemed to take note of her fear and patted her hand. "The straps are for your safety and ours. Do not be afraid, little one. I shall not let anything happen to you."

Another deep breath brought the cloyingly sweet scent of

chloroform into her lungs, stinging her eyes and throat. Tears welled in her eyes, sharp as needles. She did not want this. What had she been thinking, allowing him to operate on her again? She did *not want this.* The stone walls and ceiling pressed in on her.

"Breathe deeply," Royal said, pressing a white cloth over Taryn's nose and mouth. Her eyes widened.

"Shh, it is all right, Sedition," Erikkson insisted.

He will not let anything happen to me, she told herself, though the words felt thin against the ferocious beating of her heart. *I chose this. I will do this.* The chloroform fumes tasted sweet on the back of her tongue, and already her mind was fading, her vision growing foggy at the edges. She forced herself to look at the man who was her master, her creator, her surgeon. He smiled softly, and the image almost felt like remembering.

"Hush now, little one. You are in good hands. When you wake, you will be a warrior."

Taryn tried to speak, but her tongue stuck to the roof of her mouth. There was something else she needed to say, but her mind spun when she tried to put words together. Her eyes drifted shut.

"Good. Now we can begin."

"You can do better than that," the man shouted, punctuating his words with the crack of the whip he held in his fist. The boy—745 to his captors, though he could not bring himself to accept the number in place of his name—ducked his head, struggling with the heavy plough. His new clockwork limb strengthened him, but he was still healing from the invasive surgery, and the work his handler forced him to perform seemed designed to break him down physically and mentally.

Somewhere in the back of his head, he was engaged in a battle for his mind and autonomy, but after just a few days as a biomaton, he'd found it easier to lower his head and be obedient than to fight them.

Still, he resented the loss of all his memories, and missed the sense of touch in his arm. His own mind felt too vast, as though he'd been diminished and could no longer fill the space vacated by the person he'd been before. Instead, he focused on his immediate surroundings: the freshly churned earth beneath his bare feet, the loamy scent of the soil he tilled, the gentle misting of rain on his neck and face, and, of course, the sharp lick of the whip against his legs or back when he displeased his handler.

"I believe that is enough for one day," Master Bellham's voice interrupted, and the boy breathed a sigh of relief, turning to see his new master standing beside his handler, beckoning him.

"Yes, sir," the boy answered, leaving the plow and crossing the field to where they waited.

"You are learning more quickly than I expected, 745," Bellham murmured, and the boy glowed with the simple praise. "With that little insignia, I thought you would be much more brutish and stubborn. But you are smart, boy. You understand your place, far better than 743 did. You liked her, did you not?"

The boy's brow furrowed, and he looked down at his hands, rubbing at the dirt encrusting his palms. "I—I do not remember."

"Oh?" Bellham smiled cruelly, his colorless eyes shining. "You do not remember the pretty young biomaton you so foolishly came here to rescue?"

Again, the boy shook his head. "No, sir." He scuffed one heel in the grass. "What was her name?"

Bellham's eyes flashed with disgust. "You do not have

names until you are purchased. Then your masters may call you whatever they like. Her tag was number 743."

A flash of electricity flooded the boy, beginning at the base of his spine, some emotion he did not understand sweeping through his soul. 743. Only two numbers behind his own. And yet, he could not remember her. He could not remember anything. He ducked his head. "Yes, sir." He paused, then asked hesitantly, "May—is she—may I see her?"

"She is no longer here. Her creator claimed her." Bellham glanced over the boy, studying his new silver prosthetics. Harper had done a fine job, and the clockwork was integrating nicely and healing well. This was one of their better hybrids, almost as detailed as Erikkson's strange warrior biomatons. *Almost.* He suspected the boy would be ready with a few more weeks of training. Not fighting ring ready, not like Harper kept pushing for, but ready for sale. He'd be glad to make something off the boy, as he'd been quite the irritant in Bellham's perfectly oiled machine.

It had almost been too easy, catching the boy off-guard after Erikkson had taken 743, knocking him out, and performing the operation. He'd protested so much in the hours before they changed him, insisting he would be missed by his crew; and with that privateer's brand on his arm, Bellham had almost believed him. The boy even slew one of the guards before they managed to sedate him. That was when Bellham elected to wipe his memory. It worked; perhaps too well. 745 was utterly compliant now, pleasant to work with and quite teachable, even with little force. Bellham still anticipated a raid—someone must be missing him somewhere—but as the days passed and no one came looking, he began to wonder if there had not been some quarrel that caused the boy to go rogue, leaving his crew. Most likely, he had come alone because of his feelings for the girl. 743 *was* sort of pretty, Bellham had to admit, if you liked that sort of thing.

The boy was still patiently awaiting orders. "Back to your quarters, 745," Bellham commanded.

"Yes, sir." 745 turned and trudged back toward the Black Castle, expression utterly devoid of humanity. Bellham smiled to himself. Yes, this boy was a job well done. He'd fetch a good price.

CHAPTER EIGHT

TARYN AWOKE in a flood of crimson agony. She blinked her eyes open, groggy and disoriented, staring at the ceiling until she could recall where she was. Everything came flooding back to her in a rush. Erikkson's house, her agreement, the surgery, Royal... *Royal.* She groaned. What was she going to do about Royal?

What was she going to do about the pain?

Her head throbbed, her back ached, her shoulder burned, and her hips *hurt.* She closed her eyes, her vision red with agony. She moaned again, pressing her right hand to her forehead. Her left arm seemed heavier than usual and refused to move even as she focused on lifting it. Taryn blinked her eyes open once more, staring down at the new prosthetic lying atop the blankets.

It was like staring at some dead machine beside her, and not her own arm at all. It took several moments for her mind to begin to register the prosthetic. It was a far cry from the one she'd grown up with; her first prosthetic had delicate gold filigree and mesh, curved and molded to look as much like a real limb as possible. This new arm was all angles and armored steel plates, solid and strong; no fall would damage or destroy this prosthetic. It maintained the anatomical shape though, despite its enhancements, and Taryn supposed in the right dress it could be concealed well enough to pass as real. Still, it was clear just looking at it that it had not been designed to be hidden. It was even beautiful, in a strange way. The interior workings were entirely hidden by solid, interlocking steel plates. Was this what she had seen in Erikkson's blueprints? It looked similar, though not identical. She flexed her fist, watching solid, half-inch spikes emerge from her knuckles. Taryn's stomach flipped.

"Oh, you are awake."

Royal stood in the doorway, carrying a basin of steaming water. His face had gone pale, and he stared at her with big brown eyes, as though she was a ghost.

"Aye," she croaked, her throat dry and crackling like a forest fire. "Is there a problem?"

He shook his head, finally remembering his feet and stumbling into her room. "No. Of course not. Why would there be a problem?" His words all tumbled out in a heap, and she, who knew him so well, knew he was lying.

She decided to let it go as another wave of scarlet pain washed over her. "Everything hurts, Roy. Should everything hurt this much?"

He set the jug of water upon a table beside her bed, concern painting his cheeks pink. "What hurts?"

"Everything." She pressed her head deep into the feather pillow, her body stiffening with a wracking wave of agony.

He touched her forehead hesitantly, his scarred mechanick's hand fluttering against her skin. "Your temperature feels normal. I— I ought to get Lord Erikkson. I do not think you were meant to wake so soon..." He trailed off, studying her intently. His eyes leapt down to her new steel prosthetic.

A tiny, horrified understanding struck her. "I am still the same person," she whispered. "This prosthetic makes no difference, Royal. I am still the same urchin you pulled off the streets." Her lip curled into a weak expression of bitterness. "Whatever that girl was worth to you."

His cheeks colored. He turned away, chewing the side of his thumb, as he always did when he was anxious or upset. "I know. I just—it shall take some getting used to."

Taryn wanted to say more, to somehow *convince* him she was the same person, but the pain was rapidly becoming unbearable, and she surrendered to it. "I think you ought to get Master Erikkson," she moaned. She squeezed her eyes shut. "Please."

His eyes widened. "Oh. I am sorry, Taryn. I am going."

He hurried from the room, and she wondered briefly if he would ever truly forgive her. Would *she* forgive him, in the same position? She didn't know, but she did not think it would be easy. She understood his reluctance, however much it hurt.

She clenched her new, solid metal fist, watching the lethal spikes slide from her knuckles. The craftsmanship was exquisite. Despite herself, she felt a little awe at Erikkson's skill and attention to detail. Even the time it must have taken to shape the armored plates covering her forearm was mind boggling. The metal fit together nearly seamlessly, allowing for the perfect rotation and movement a real limb would offer. She could only imagine the intricacies of the arm's inner workings. When she was feeling better, perhaps she could ask for permission to take it apart.

The pain washing over her intensified, and she laid her head back down, trying to breathe slowly. She prayed Erikkson would come quickly. If only she could go back to sleep, she would be able to escape the pain, even momentarily.

"Sedition, I am here now," Erikkson's voice broke through

the ringing in her ears. Taryn blinked her eyes open, staring up at him.

"Everything hurts," she whimpered.

He brushed her copper hair back from her forehead. "I am sorry, little one. You were meant to sleep through this."

She scowled, her temper spiking along with the heat in every limb. Surely, there was something he could do for her?

"I can help you return to sleep, and numb your pain for a while, but I need your permission to access the control panel in order to help you," Erikkson said.

Taryn shook her head. "No. Not again."

"Then you will have to endure the pain on your own, little one."

Taryn noted Royal leaning in the doorframe, silently observing. "No," she repeated firmly. She hated the panel on the back of her skull, and all it meant to her tenuous humanity.

"Sedition, I know you do not like it, but I am only trying to help you." He touched her shoulder, gently but firmly. "I promise, I will do nothing to harm or alter your mind."

Still, Taryn wanted to refuse him, to deny him the right to even touch her. She found anger in the pain, and she held on to it, like a wounded animal snarling at its rescuers.

"Do you not see," Royal burst away from the threshold, "that Tony is trying to help you? This is the only way, Taryn."

She stared at him silently, her eyesight swimming with tears of pain. Chewing at the inside of her lip, she closed her eyes again. "I give in. Do what you must."

She turned her head so Erikkson could access her control panel. She squeezed her eyes tighter, a whimper welling in her throat. Erikkson moved her long copper hair away from the plate on the back of her head. He carefully opened the small hatch, and Taryn felt something *click*. Her mind relaxed, the sharp, tight portions of it unwinding. The pain began to fade away, slowly at first, and then faster as a wave of cool calm spread through her body. Taryn breathed a sigh of relief. At last, she could rest.

"Is that any better?" Erikkson asked tenderly, touching her cheek with his thumb.

She nodded, eyelids suddenly heavy. "Thank you," she breathed.

He smiled, the corners of his eyes crinkling. "You ought to go back to sleep, little one. The world can wait while you heal. Rest now."

She breathed a heavy breath of relief, letting the tension drain from her chest. Her fists relaxed on the blanket, spikes sliding back into her new knuckles with the hiss of metal on metal. Erikkson tenderly brushed her hair back from her face. "Good girl," he murmured.

Erikkson rose, glancing at his young apprentice, who had retreated back to the doorframe, as though afraid to fully enter the room. He steered Royal out, closing the door gently before speaking. "There is no need to be frightened of her," he said firmly, though he smiled a little as he said it. "I promise her condition is not contagious."

Royal chewed the side of his thumb, eyes anywhere but on the biomechanick. "I know, sir. But... You do not understand what it is like to realize the girl you considered your best friend has lied so completely to you." He shuffled his feet against the hardwood floor. "I thought I loved her."

"And now you do not love her because she has a clockwork prosthetic?"

"It is more than just a clockwork prosthetic, Tony. I saw the extent of the changes you made to her body—I *helped* you make some of those changes." Royal's face flushed, thinking of the surgery he had assisted Erikkson in performing. He had seen more of Taryn than he had ever expected to see, even in his wildest dreams; her pale white skin, the brutal scars from the fire she'd survived, and the broad, yellowing bruises from the abuse she'd suffered at the hands of the Black Castle. Worst of all, though, were her grafts; the places where metal met flesh, marked by ropy pink scars and the gleam of copper. Royal could not have said why, but the sight bothered him. There remained a cognitive dissonance to Taryn's biomaton identity which he could not shake.

"She is just the same as you or I, Royal. Her only difference is a bit of clockwork helping her along."

A shudder ran down Royal's spine. It had been all well and fine, converting to Erikkson's doctrine of biomaton equality when it had been no more than an intellectual exercise. He had even felt a little rebellious, like he was taking part in a movement outside the mainstream, something privileged and special. But the bombshell Taryn had dropped upon this new worldview had brought old, ugly, ingrained thought processes back to the surface. Though he knew his friendship with her should have convinced him of the biomaton's equality, it had the opposite effect. He found a kernel of hate and hurt under his tongue each time he imagined her prosthetics gleaming under the lights of Tony's surgical lab.

"You do not understand the societal implications my friendship with her will have," Royal muttered lamely.

Erikkson chuckled, the corners of his eyes crinkling. "I thought you did not care about your high-born status?"

Royal scowled. "I cannot hide this from my father forever. It was bad enough to tell him I was taking this apprenticeship and dropping out of classes. It is another thing entirely to tell him the girl he had been sponsoring for nearly four years is a biomaton."

"Then do not inform your father. From what I understand of your relationship, that will not be difficult. Allow him to continue to believe she took a job and has disappeared from your life. It is not exactly a lie. The girl you helped me operate on is no longer Taryn Roft. She is Sedition of Erikkson. And I can guarantee that you have never met someone like her before."

TARYN BLINKED HER EYES OPEN. SHE WAS NOT SURE HOW long she had been asleep, but the strange numbness had worn off, leaving her a little sore, but not nearly as agonized as she had been.

"*Chérie!* You are awake at last," a French lilt came from her right. Taryn glanced over to see Emmett rise from an armchair near the window. His golden clockwork irises spun, adjusting as they focused on her face. "How do you feel?"

"A little sore, but not too bad. Should you be up already, Emmett?"

"*Monsieur* Erikkson said I could get up. You have been sleeping for nearly two days."

Her eyes widened. "Two days?"

"They gave you something to help you sleep. He said it would help you to heal."

Taryn winced. "Two days," she breathed in shock.

"*Oui.*" Emmett smiled at her. "But you are awake now. I am to tell *Monsieur* Erikkson." He headed for the door, walking with more confidence than she'd seen since the Black Castle, only reaching out once to brush his fingertips against the door-frame. Her sacrifice had done some good, it seemed. At least Emmett appeared happier than she'd seen him in a long time.

Taryn shoved herself into a sitting position, sighing. Two days lost. She wondered what she had missed. Her new armored prosthetic glinted in the light, and she glared at it out of the corner of her eye, almost afraid to know all it could do.

She was truly an Erikkson now, through and through, and though her grafts were not as obvious as Seraphim's, she would be unable to hide what she was. Her life as a schoolgirl was over. Someone new was rising from the ashes.

Erikkson entered with Emmett and Royal. He smiled at her. "Welcome back, Sedition."

She opened her mouth to protest, but the heavy new prosthetic in her periphery seemed to wink at her. She closed her mouth. "Good morning. Or...is it afternoon?"

"It *is* afternoon. How do you feel?"

"A little sore, but much better," Taryn replied honestly. Her stomach chose that moment to grumble about its recent treatment. "I *am* hungry, though."

"I am sure you are. Ambrose is preparing something for you as we speak."

Taryn nodded, sensing Royal's eyes on her. She looked at him, and he shifted uncomfortably, directing his gaze elsewhere. She sighed. "If what I am bothers you so much, you can stay away."

"N-no, Tar— That— That is not—" Royal stuttered, his face turning beet red.

"Then why do you hover in the doorway as if I have some disease you could catch if you come too close?"

Royal shook his head and took a few hesitant steps into the room. "I am not."

She snorted, a hint of a smile crossing her face. "I promise you, I shall not bite."

He gave her a painful, forced smile in return.

A biomaton Taryn recognized from her dinner with Erikkson entered the room, carrying a tray bearing a steaming bowl and a spoon. Taryn thanked him as he set the tray on her knees. He gave her a thin smile.

"Chef Ambrose says to just call if ye need anything else," he said in a quiet Scottish brogue.

Taryn eagerly dug into the broth as the biomaton left. It was heavenly, scented with herbs and not too salty. Though she wished for something more substantial, some vegetables or meat to sink her teeth into, she savored the broth, sipping it delicately from the spoon. As it cooled on her tongue, new flavors struck her, until it seemed Ambrose had performed some kind of magic, cramming a thousand different tastes into a single bowl of broth.

"Is Ambrose a biomaton?" she asked, glancing up at Erikkson.

He smiled. "He is. And he is the best chef this side of the English Channel."

Taryn sipped her broth again. "I can agree with that."

"He is French," Emmett interjected. "But of course he is the best. You English accept the most tasteless dishes and call them food."

Royal turned a deadly glare on Emmett. "At least we do not eat frogs and snails."

"Even our most unappealing dishes are better than your English *drivel*."

Taryn held up her hands. "Now, boys," she interrupted, a smile playing at the corners of her lips, "there is no reason to argue over such a trivial subject."

Erikkson nodded. "Actually, would you both fetch a tea tray please? Ambrose knows how I like it."

"Surely you do not need us both to go," Royal said, shooting a haughty look at Emmett.

"It shall require all your hands. And I should like to have a few moments to speak privately with Sedition."

Royal grumbled but left the room with Emmett following silently behind.

Taryn sighed, frustrated by Royal's petulant actions. "He can be such a child sometimes. Do you think those two will find a way to get along?" she asked over the rim of her bowl.

"Perhaps," Erikkson answered with a chuckle. "They will learn. Give them time."

Taryn nodded and set her soup bowl aside. The broth had been delicious, but not completely filling, and she found herself wishing once more she had more to eat.

Erikkson came and sat on the edge of her bed, his face turning hard and serious. "We need to discuss your training."

"Training?" She didn't look at him, feeling the sharp edges inside herself suddenly rising to the surface once more.

"You are a warrior, little one. You demonstrated that in the Black Castle when you broke through your programming."

Taryn remembered the incident all too vividly. Her mind had been shut down by the biomechanicks in the Black Castle, her free will eliminated so she was more machine than human. It had taken a moment of danger and violence to break through that programming, and most biomatons never managed it. Most biomatons *could* not manage it, but her creator had given her a way out. If her mind was strong enough, it could break free. Apparently, it had been.

"You *must* train if all that instinct is to be of any help. Much of your previous training will return, with practice, but we must also ensure you are comfortable with your new prosthetics. As soon as you are healed enough to get up, we will begin."

She chewed her lip. She had known becoming Sedition would require more than a simple surgery, but combat training still came as a surprise. Looking back, she should have seen this coming. She was meant to be a weapon—of course there would be training involved. So much of her mind had been focused on the surgery, that she'd forgotten there was an *after*. Something had to come next. She ducked her head, nodding her assent. "Very well," she replied, voice sticky in her throat. "I agreed to this. I suppose I must follow your plans. But you are quite mad if you think I shall be any good at this combat training."

"You may surprise yourself," Erikkson replied. "At any rate, you must make an effort to heal first."

A wry smile grew on her lips. "What is it you think I am doing?"

"Yes, well, hurry up."

CHAPTER NINE

Royal took a few steps from Taryn's room and turned to glare at Emmett. "If you have something to say, I suggest you say it."

Emmett stared at him, his clockwork eyes spinning to focus on Royal's face. "I do not know what you mean."

"I made Taryn a promise years ago to protect her from any man who grew too forward with her. And you are most *certainly* too forward."

"Ah, so now it is about me," Emmett smirked. "Here I thought you cared about Taryn."

Royal hated the way her name flowed off the Frenchman's tongue. "Of course I care about her. She is my best friend."

"Then why do you look at her as though she may give you some incurable disease?"

"I do not," Royal spat. "And I do not like the way you look at her."

"How do I look at her, *monsieur?* Like a friend? Perhaps more? You do not understand what we endured the past few weeks. I will not hide the fact that our experiences have made us close."

Royal's lip twisted. "You think you know her, but you do not. Not as I do."

"Ah, *je comprends*. You are jealous. I promise you, *monsieur*, I shall not come between you." Emmett shoved past Royal, muttering beneath his breath, "*Vous faites que vous-même.*"

In an instant, Royal grabbed Emmett's shoulder and shoved him backward. He pinned the smaller Frenchman to the wall, his forearm pressing against Emmett's throat. Emmett's hands rose to Royal's arm, but the apprentice was taller and stockier than the wiry Frenchman.

"Let me go," Emmett hissed through gritted teeth.

"Not until you take back whatever you just said." Royal pressed harder on his arm.

"Release me," Emmett hissed again. "This is your last warning."

"Warning?" Royal scoffed. "*You* are warning me?"

Emmett's expression did not change. He brought the heel of his foot down on Royal's instep, then rammed his knee hard into his gut. The boy stumbled backward, gasping for breath, his face beet red.

"I did warn you," Emmett said with little emotion. "If you touch me again, you will have more than a few bruises to show for it."

"How dare you—" Royal spluttered.

"Now, *monsieur,* this is all very immature. Lord Erikkson gave us a task. I think we will have better luck fulfilling it than brawling in the hall."

Emmett turned and moved away, toward the stairs. Royal stood there, mouth gaping, watching his rival go. He muttered a curse. That bloody Frenchman thought he could just step in and take Taryn? Not if Royal had anything to say about it.

For a moment, Royal considered forgetting all about Tony's orders and allowing Emmett to handle it all on his own. But no

—Erikkson would be furious to learn they'd been fighting, and Taryn... Taryn... Royal straightened, following Emmett down the hallway.

"AH, HERE THEY ARE AT LAST," ERIKKSON SAID AS ROYAL and Emmett entered the room. Royal carried a tea tray with an assortment of sandwiches, biscuits, and other delicacies on it. Emmett bore a second tray with the teapot, cups, saucers, sugar bowl, and creamer. Erikkson gestured to the small bedside table. "Set it there, and I shall pour the tea. Feel free to help yourselves, gentlemen. There is more than enough here for the four of us."

Erikkson rose, pouring tea for Taryn. "Do you still take milk and sugar, little one?"

She nodded, tongue-tied as the earthy scent of English breakfast tea filled the air. The juxtaposition of this scene to her "training" at Black Castle struck her harder than a fist to the gut. It was meant to be the other way around. She was the biomaton, the one considered less than human by law and by most of the country, and yet, here he was, serving her with a smile. An unfamiliar thrill crowded her chest and throat. Maybe *this* was what equality really meant.

The thought filled her with purpose, and she sipped at her hot tea in an attempt to wash it away. She'd agreed to become this thing she did not yet fully understand: a leader, a warrior, a martyr, perhaps, if that was where this road led. But this was the first time she'd seen a picture of equality and wanted it, wanted more than just her past life. Maybe this man understood better than she thought. Maybe his purpose could mean something.

Royal handed her a small plate with a few of her favorite tea delicacies on it: a scone slathered with clotted cream and marmalade; a shortbread biscuit dipped in lemon glaze; and a small, white cucumber sandwich. She smiled. "Thank you, Royal."

He nodded, but the muscles in his jaw tightened. It might have been imperceptible to anyone else, but she spotted it immediately. He had not yet forgiven her.

Royal and Emmett found places to settle about the room with their own teacups. Erikkson resumed his seat at her bedside. Taryn turned her eyes into her cup, self-conscious with so many eyes directed her way.

"So, Emmett," Erikkson spoke, filling the silence. "I do not know much about you. How did you come to be aboard the *Dauntless?*"

Taryn's ears perked up. It was the question she'd held since she met Emmett, but was too afraid to ask. She wondered if his story had anything to do with that livid scar she'd seen on his hip.

"It is a long story, *monsieur,*" Emmett replied. His clockwork eyes focused somewhere past Taryn's shoulder.

"We have time."

Emmett's expression twisted and he nodded. "I do not like to talk about it. *Mais...* I suppose if anyone deserves to know, it is you and *mademoiselle* Taryn for saving my life." He paused, shifting on the windowsill where he was perched, one knee up, one foot on the floor.

"I have studied combat since I was very young. I can read an opponent like a book, predicting their movements even before they happen. Or..." He hesitated, face twisting. His fingers drifted to his cheek. "Or I could. I became very famous for this in the French aerial navy. Too famous, it seems."

Emmett stopped, taking a sip from the teacup in his left hand. Taryn studied him. In spite of the time they had spent together, she barely knew him. "I sailed aboard the airship *La Triomphe.* We were attacked by a bigger English warship—*la*

Dauntless. My shipmates fought valiantly, but to no avail. I remember watching *mon capitaine* fall under an English blade." Emmett's right hand moved to his hip, where that ugly scar was hidden beneath his shirt. "I did try to help him, but I was shot and collapsed. I believe I fell unconscious.

"When I came to, there were strangers standing over me, a man and a woman." Emmett gave Taryn a strange smile. "Ace and Storm. I am not the only one with a special ability; Ace is the best shot with a pistol I have ever seen. I spoke no English, but Ace translated in passable French. Storm gave me a choice. Die aboard *La Triomphe* or swear fealty to the English Queen and board *la Dauntless.* I chose life."

Taryn looked away from him, shocked by the violence of his story. So that was how he had come to be aboard the *Dauntless.* Storm had forced him into service, nearly killing him in the process. The woman knew no compassion. Just thinking about her cruelty left a bad taste in Taryn's mouth.

"I am sorry for what happened to you," Erikkson said, "but I am thankful you were aboard that ship to protect my Sedition."

Emmett smiled, raising his head. "*Merci, monsieur.* I am thankful also."

A knock came at the doorframe. Seraphim stood there, his skin glowing gold in the waning light pouring through the windows. "It is good to see you awake at last," he said, nodding to Taryn. "Our rebellion draws nearer to completion all the time."

"What is that supposed to mean?" she snapped.

"It means Seraphim is eager to begin training," Erikkson chuckled. "She needs a few more days to heal. Then we shall begin."

"If she is half as good as she was before, we shall win this war in mere weeks." Seraphim shuffled his wings, flashing a hint of his silver fangs with an expression Taryn supposed passed for a smile.

"Which reminds me—" Erikkson rose, setting aside his empty dishes, and reaching out for Taryn's cup and saucer. "Royal and I are due to check your incisions again. Is that all right?"

She nodded, though her stomach had twisted itself into knots. "That is fine."

Erikkson helped her sit up, directing her to lean forward. Taryn was still wearing the thin cotton shift she'd donned for the surgery, and Royal looked on, chewing the side of his thumb as Erikkson unlaced the sides of the dress. He opened the back to reveal cotton bandages covering her shoulder blades, stuck to her upper back with some sort of mild adhesive. Erikkson peeled the bandages away ever so gently. Taryn waited in silence while the two inspected her incisions. A twinge of pain shot down her spine. She winced.

"This is healing nicely, Sedition," Erikkson said after a few moments.

Emmett rose from his place on the windowsill, his brow furrowing. "What have you done?"

The hairs on Taryn's neck stood on end. "Is something wrong?" she questioned, a cold sweat breaking out on her forehead.

"No, nothing is wrong," Erikkson answered, too quickly.

She raised one hesitant hand over her shoulder, only to find Erikkson's fingers in the way.

"Now, little one, I would not do that."

Her heart stopped. "Why? What have you done?"

Erikkson hesitated, then released her hand, allowing her to run her fingers over her shoulder. Where she expected to find flesh and perhaps a neat row of stitches, Taryn found metal. Clockwork had been embedded over her shoulder blades. She gasped, jerking back as something sharp caught her fingertip.

Blood seeped from a shallow cut on her finger. Taryn sucked at the cut, her vision blurring red with the salty iron tang of blood.

"You lied to me," she growled.

"Do not forget, you gave your consent," Erikkson replied, moving so he could meet her eye.

"What have you done to me?" Her voice had a pleading tone to it, but the awful violence welling inside her refused to be ignored. "How am I supposed to live this way?"

"You will get used to the new grafts, in time. Your training will teach you to use them."

Taryn leapt from the bed, cursing his training, stumbling on legs weak from their enhancement. Every incision protested her sudden movement. Seraphim caught her and held her back, one strong arm around her waist, his other hand restraining her right arm as easily as if she were a child. She fought him, ignoring the pain, overwhelmed by the deadly instinct to kill *kill KILL*. An animal snarl tore from her throat.

"Enough!" Erikkson cried, locking eyes with her. Taryn glared at him, growling, unaware of the others in the room. Royal and Emmett backed toward the door.

Erikkson moved closer, until he stood just beyond her clawing hands. "Taryn, listen to me. What you are feeling right now is the fault of the violence switch Dr. Harper changed in the Black Castle. This is not you. You must *not* allow this to control you. Control yourself."

A tiny voice inside her head urged her to keep fighting, to slay this man for what he'd done to her, but she forced herself to breathe. She hung her head, recognizing all the moments she'd allowed violence and anger to get the better of her in the past week. It *was* controlling her. She could not even trust her own mind.

Seraphim released her, and Taryn slumped to her knees, shaking. She pressed her palms into her eye sockets. Her body ached with her mistreatment of muscles that still needed to heal. Her hair hung like a curtain, obscuring her face.

"Come now, little one, do not cry." Erikkson gently touched her shoulder.

She was not crying. She detested herself too much for that. "Forgive me," she whispered.

He sighed. "Friends, I believe Taryn could use some time to rest. You may come to see her again tomorrow, but for now it would be best if you gave her space to breathe."

Taryn listened as her friends' footsteps faded away, too ashamed to raise her eyes and watch them go. She wondered if any of them would be too afraid of her to return. She would not blame them. She feared herself.

Her creator brushed her copper hair back from her face. "Get up, little one. You should not be out of bed so soon."

A short, hiccupping breath left her lungs. She allowed herself a second, deeper breath, and rose. Her legs would barely lift her weight, and before she was fully upright, she collapsed heavily on the edge of the bed. She kept her eyes down, unable to meet her master's gaze. "I— I am sorry," she whispered. Shame burned across her cheeks. "I have acted like a fool these past few days."

He sat beside her. "You are forgiven."

An icy hand ran its fingers down her spine. "I could have killed you."

"Seraphim would not allow that." Erikkson brushed her hair away from her face, tenderly smoothing it behind her ear. "You mustn't think this is a weakness. It will become a strength, but you must learn to control it first. Next time the fury comes over you, remember what it is. Breathe first and consider your actions. Then, use it to your advantage."

She nodded, closing her eyes. "I am sorry."

"No need to apologize. I should have warned you about the blades. I knew it would be a shock."

"Blades? You mean, the new graft is like Seraphim's wings?"

"A little. You will learn more about your new weapons with time. For now, I think I ought to let you rest."

Erikkson helped Taryn lie back and squeezed her hand tenderly. "Rest, little one. Let your body and mind heal. Your destiny can wait for that."

Taryn's eyes drifted closed, and despite her aching limbs, she fell asleep almost at once.

CHAPTER TEN

Taryn spent the next week confined to her bed, save for the few minutes she was allowed to exercise her legs each day. Her brash leap had torn more than a few of her stitches, and Erikkson warned her against any more actions like it; he would rather chain her to the bed than see her lengthen the healing process anymore. She knew he was joking but followed his orders anyway. She was eager to learn to control her new prosthetics, and more so, her mind.

She spent much of her time reading, or chatting with Royal and Emmett, as the boys took turns delivering her meals. Things were still awkward with Royal, but he seemed to be warming to her true identity, bit by bit. The air continued to turn frosty whenever he and Emmett met, and Taryn could not understand why. Never in her wildest imaginings would she have guessed the tension between her friends had to do with herself.

At the end of the week, Erikkson checked her bandages, clicked his tongue, and gently peeled them away, handing them off to Royal, who had brought a basin of warm water to her bedside. Drawing a wet cloth from the basin, Erikkson gently bathed her shoulders around the new prosthetics. "You've healed well enough to begin your training, I think."

She pulled her knees to her chest, a tightness around her ribcage that had nothing to do with the undergarments she was wearing. "Good," she said in a voice that betrayed none of her mixed emotions. "I am tired of lying here while the world moves on without me."

"Nothing moves without you, little one. Not where this rebellion is concerned."

She choked on the pressure of his words, the confidence he imbued in her abilities. Her fists clenched handfuls of the sheet. "May I get up?"

Deft fingers finished tying the laces of her shift the moment she said the words. "Dress, then come to my study. I need to oil your prosthetics. Then you may want breakfast before we get started?"

She wasn't sure she could eat with the tangled knots her stomach was making, but she nodded anyway.

"Good. Five minutes. My study." He rose, snapping a quick gesture toward the door as he made his way out. "Come, Royal."

Royal gave Taryn an eyeroll that was becoming all too common, then hurried out with the basin of water. She took her time getting dressed, languidly stretching her legs like a cat waking from a long nap. Though she didn't know why, she wanted to draw these moments out. She wanted to spend as long as she could dressing, allowing the linen against her skin to wake her from the stupor of days spent idle in bed. She'd allowed Erikkson to operate on her, yes, but this, here, felt like the true turning point, and it wasn't even marked by any great fanfare or excitement. She'd thought her acceptance of this role would come with something more, some world-ending explosion as she agreed to commit treason in the biomatons name. Instead, the world kept turning, everything outside her little bubble moving on as if her decision meant nothing, weighed nothing. Becoming Sedition felt like a birthday: everything had changed, and yet she felt exactly the same.

As she walked through the halls to Erikkson's study, she noticed the others who lived in the house for the first time. It was not as if they had appeared out of nowhere; rather, it was like something had opened her eyes to them. Young men raced from one doorway and through another ahead of her, laughing. A pair of girls about her age carried baskets of laundry up the stairs, their freckled cheeks marked with smiles when they passed by. A boy of no more than twelve or thirteen carried a saddle past one of the windows, his back bent with the weight of his load. She couldn't help but compare this place to the Black Castle, the last place she'd seen biomatons in such abundance, where her kind were hollow-eyed, numbed to the world by the control panels in the backs of their heads, or scarred and feral from the fights they were forced to take part in. Maybe there was something to this place, oasis or training ground or sanctuary, she was still deciding. But better, oh *so much better*, than where she had been.

She arrived at Erikkson's study and stepped inside, finding him poring over a set of blueprints with Royal. Seraphim sat backward in a wooden chair nearby, his wings draped half-open behind him, like a bird of prey mantling over its nest. He looked almost content, arms folded atop the back of his chair, chin resting on his hands, but he had a gleam in his eye that indicated the shrewd observation she'd come to understand was his nature. Taryn suspected it was hard to put anything past him.

"You said you wanted to oil my prosthetics?" she asked tentatively.

"Actually, I think Royal will be able to handle that just fine," Erikkson answered, not looking up from the drafting table.

"I can do it just as well on my own," she said. "I have done it for most of my life."

He raised his head then, looking at her with something sharp in his green eyes. "I am sorry. I forget you are not the young girl I once had to help with these things." He took a bottle of mineral oil from the desk and brought it over to her, offering a soft rag from his pocket. "Will this be enough? We can assist you with the prosthetics on your back if you wish."

"This is fine," she replied. After a week of letting them wait on her hand and foot, she was eager to take back any small piece of autonomy she could. "I will manage."

Her left fist clenched tight as she reached out with her right to take the bottle, and something inside her prosthetic clicked. A dagger that had been concealed in her forearm dropped out, hitting the floor with a thud. She stumbled back a step, staring at the knife.

"You can leave that here," Erikkson said with an uncharacteristic smirk. "Go, take care of your pieces, eat, and find me when you are ready."

TARYN ALLOWED ROYAL TO LEAD HER FROM THE ROOM. Erikkson watched them go, a look of tenderness crossing his face. Seraphim rose, fingers dipping into a pocket as that watchful expression he'd worn hardened into something like resolve. "Master Erikkson, I would like to speak with you."

"Of course, Seraphim," Erikkson said, turning back to his sketches without meeting the biomaton's eye. He drew a quill from its inkwell and began scratching notes in his spidery left-handed slant. Seraphim's stomach churned as he watched the familiar script take shape.

Crossing the room, Seraphim closed the door. Sedition was gone, but he didn't want to risk her overhearing what he had to say. Despite himself, he wanted the girl to like their creator, to take up his cause as her own. There would be time enough for her to learn of his failings later.

"It's that serious, is it?" Erikkson raised himself from his bent-over position at the drafting table. "Very well. Speak." The older man settled into one of the leather wingback chairs near the windows, looking at Seraphim expectantly.

The winged biomaton paced, trying to settle the tension in his stomach. He'd known this man a long time. Most of his life. Erikkson had rescued him from drowning, made him these grafts so he could defend himself, and given him a place to live and a family to call his own. But somewhere along the way, Seraphim had realized that Erikkson's methods were not entirely benevolent, and though he thought they wanted the same thing, he wasn't so sure they agreed on the best methods to achieve it.

"You sent me to spy for you on the *Dauntless*."

"Yes, of course," Erikkson chuckled a little, crossing his arms loosely. "But as we discussed before you took that position, it did not matter which ship you ended up on, as long as you were on a ship and could report back to me."

"You knew it would be Captain Storm, though."

Erikkson blinked. "I knew she attended those fights regularly, yes, but so did a dozen other high-ranking officers from other ships."

"But you wanted me on the *Dauntless*," Seraphim pressed. He didn't know why, but this was important. This was significant. If Erikkson had planned this from the start... What did it mean? He didn't know.

"It *was* a strategic placement for you, especially with Petrichor's entanglement with the ship's commanding officers. But I would have been happy with your placement on any ship."

"But you used my position on the *Dauntless* to force Sedition out of hiding."

Erikkson's smile dropped. "What?"

Seraphim drew the letter he'd taken from Storm's desk out of his pocket, holding it so Erikkson could clearly see the red wax seal on the front, the stylized *E* ornamented with cogs. He'd considered keeping this to himself, but he had to know the truth. "This is your seal, is it not? And this *is* your handwriting. I know that left-handed slant as well as my own hand." He released the letter, dropping it in Erikkson's lap. The biomechanick lifted the paper.

"Where did you find this?"

"Storm's cabin aboard the *Dauntless*. Please tell me I am mistaken. Please tell me that is not your hand."

Erikkson's face had gone pale. He skimmed the letter's contents with all the speed and nonchalance of someone re-reading something they had written. Seraphim's heart sank as his suspicions were confirmed. "You were not meant to see this," Erikkson muttered.

"Why? Why would you send them after her? You knew how much Storm hates our kind. I was more than clear on that point."

Erikkson shook his head, folding the letter slowly. "I knew you would not understand, Seraphim."

"Then explain it to me."

The biomechanick raised his eyes, studying Seraphim for a moment. "Sedition was doing too well in hiding. She had not learned what I needed her to learn. And the war cannot wait forever. So, I pushed her in the right direction."

"You pushed her into the Black Castle! Biomatons do not come back from there."

Erikkson shook his head. "I must admit, I did not foresee Storm having direct connections with Lord Bellham. I thought she would find some private biomechanick, and you would be able to bring Sedition to me directly from the airship. But it all worked out in the end. She is here with us now."

Seraphim shook his head, speechless. Erikkson had gambled with Taryn's life. He had forgiven his master for many things, but he did not know if he could forgive him for this. "Someday, your meddling is going to backfire on you," he muttered.

Erikkson nodded. "You know, Seraphim, it may even get me killed. But that is a risk I am willing to take."

Seraphim took Sedition's dropped dagger from the floor, turning the deadly blade slowly in his hands. "And now you've turned her into another Petrichor."

"I provided her with the tools she needs," Erikkson answered dismissively.

"She did not need your weapons. Her heart is big enough. It is a shame you still feel the need to mold her to your will."

Erikkson blinked, staring at him. "Are you questioning me, Seraphim?"

The winged biomaton slammed the blade down into the drafting table. The biomechanick didn't even have the decency to flinch. "If you continue to treat Sedition as you treated Petrichor, you may lose her also. Petrichor went mad after the way you punished them both."

"She did not go mad. She ran away because she could not handle the truth. And she will return to us, before this war is over."

"Petrichor would rather die than come near you." Seraphim's usually soft voice rose to a growl. He'd seen this happen before. *This* was why it had been so important for him to be here. He had to temper his creator's more destructive tendencies. Before it shattered his family again. "Taryn has much of the same fire Petrichor had before you lost her. I only warn you not to break her the same way."

"Sometimes a thing must first be broken in order to achieve its full potential," Erikkson responded coolly.

"Such as?"

"Do you know what a shepherd does with a wandering lamb?" Erikkson returned the question with another.

Seraphim shook his head.

"A shepherd takes a wandering lamb and breaks one of its back legs. Then he carries it on his shoulders until it heals, teaching it to listen to his voice. When it is fully healed, it never wanders again."

"We are not sheep," the winged biomaton snarled.

Erikkson waved a hand. "It is a metaphor. The point is, sometimes a creature must endure pain in order to be brought into good. Why do you think there are consequences for our actions?" He turned the letter until it caught the light coming in the window, illuminating the heavy cream paper. Standing, he raised his dark green eyes to the winged biomaton. "I think we both agree that Sedition must not know about this."

Seraphim nodded his head. "I think it is the surest way to drive her away." He hated saying so, but he agreed with Erikkson. If Taryn ever found out Erikkson had been the one to ferret her from her hiding place, she'd abandon them. She'd never take her role as leader. They needed her if they were going to have a chance at freedom.

"Good. Then we are agreed." Erikkson took the letter and held it to the flame of a gas lamp for a moment, letting the paper catch. He held the page, watching it burn, and then dropped it into a metal waste basket. He nodded and left the room, leaving the lingering scent of smoke and an unsettled feeling in Seraphim's gut.

His body was still, but his wings shuffled, the metal feathers rasping against one another. He was not sure he agreed with Erikkson... And yet, here he was, ready to fight for the man. He supposed a family was like that sometimes. He remembered Taryn's first training well. She'd grown so much since then. But she had no memory of it, and he worried

Erikkson's harsh training techniques would destroy her, despite the mechanick's confidence.

⁂

Emmett looked up from his plate as Royal and Taryn entered the dining room for breakfast, smiling his broad, welcoming smile. "*Bonjour, belle!* It is good to see you up!"

"*Bonjour,* Emmett," she answered, settling herself in a chair near him. Royal glared daggers at the Frenchman. She did not notice, piling her plate with eggs, bacon, and pastries. "I have been so hungry since the operation. I do not understand it."

"You may thank Tony for it," Royal replied. "He said your new grafts would require more energy to operate and boost your metabolism. Just wait until you have begun your training."

She smiled at him. "Well thank you, mister expert."

He returned her expression with his own trademark lopsided grin. "It is all this new information Tony throws at me. I feel quite knowledgeable, but sometimes I sound as if I am spouting drivel."

"But very clever drivel," Taryn remarked. "I could not make such things up."

"Yes, but you have the imagination of an egg."

Her mouth dropped open in mock offense. "How dare you! I shall have you know I am very creative. I excelled at both embroidery and watercolors in finishing school. I received top marks."

"Now, Taryn, it is no shame to be unimaginative. Your destiny is to be a soldier, after all, and that role requires little imagination."

Taryn began to laugh, a full, throaty, genuine laugh, almost bordering on the hysterical. She pressed her hands over her face, shoulders shaking with laughter. "I am sorry," she exclaimed, struggling to swallow the hiccupy laughter bubbling from deep in her gut. "It just seems so absurd..." She took a deep, calming breath, blowing it out of her lips in a stream of cool air. "I cannot remember the last time I laughed like that."

Royal stared at her, his fingers tangled about his silverware. "I missed your laugh," he mumbled.

Taryn rolled her eyes. She busied herself by pouring a cup of hot coffee, a delicacy she'd learned to like when they lived in Paris.

Emmett stood abruptly, glancing briefly at them both and then striding toward the door. He left his breakfast practically untouched.

"Where are you going, Frenchie?" Royal's voice was edged with contempt.

Taryn called out, "Emmett, wait!"

He did not answer, speeding up his pace to leave them behind. Taryn groaned, pushing her chair back from the table. Royal shook his head. "Let him go, Tiger. He will be back."

"Roy, he is upset—"

"There is no need to coddle him. He will be fine. Besides, you need to eat. Training shall require everything you have."

Taryn sat back in her chair, frowning. Royal could see her thinking, the wheels turning behind her emerald eyes. Finally, she turned her piercing gaze on him. "Why do you do that?"

"What?"

"Call him names. Why do you call him names?"

Royal shrugged, turning guilty eyes away. "I do not mean any harm by it."

"You have been acting like a child since we got here. I am sick and tired of seeing you lash out at Emmett. If you have a problem with me, direct it at me." She pointed at herself with two metal fingers. "But do not take it out on my friends who have endured torture you cannot even fathom."

"I thought I was your friend," he muttered.

"You are my *best* friend, Royal, but I do not understand why you are behaving this way."

He shook his head, hands clenched into fists on the table-cloth. "I am trying to wrap my head around all of this. You lied to me for so long, you cannot expect me to accept it all in a day!"

She narrowed his eyes. "It has been a week."

His lips flattened into a thin line and he gave half a shrug, narrowing his eyes.

"Besides, is this not what you wanted? *You* signed on to work with a man with a reputation for building dangerous, illegal biomatons. And yet you cannot accept me as I am? What kind of hypocrisy is that?"

He covered his face with his hands. "I know, I know. But when I saw you on that table—" He stopped speaking when Taryn thumped a fist down, rattling the dishes.

"Here is what Erikkson changed in me," she said, standing up without pushing her chair back, so the legs made an ear-shattering *shriek* against the stones. She held her arms wide. "My left arm is clockwork and now it is a weapon. I have shoulder blades that are actual blades, and apparently my legs are enhanced as well. My mind has been manipulated, dampers put in place that I cannot get rid of. I cannot love, but I feel every other emotion just as strongly as you do. Is that enough?"

Royal's mouth fell open.

"Whatever you thought you believed about biomatons being the same, forget it," she said dryly. "I am incapable of love, so you may as well forget I am human entirely."

"Taryn—"

She shook her head, turning away. "Like you said, I am meant to be a soldier. I shall not need love." She left the room, her legs still weak but her head held high. Erikkson had been right: if she took the time to breathe, she could control the violence in her head.

EMMETT GLARED AT THE SHAPE OF THE MIRROR ON HIS bedroom wall, the dead rectangle impossible to read. He turned away, tight-lipped, struggling with his emotions. Taryn's lemon-bright laugh echoed through his mind again, as vivid as a ghost haunting him. He took a deep breath, then spun and smashed his fists into the mirror, yelling wordlessly. The mirror shattered, hundreds of fractal lines streaking away from the impact point of his fists, toppling across the floor, shattering his vision with hundreds of fractured, jagged edges. His knuckles split, blood running down the backs of both his hands. He closed his eyes, breathing heavily.

"That is no way to treat a mirror," Seraphim's voice came from the door to Emmett's left. "You know it is seven years bad luck."

"You should have seen the way he made her laugh," Emmett muttered. "That was the first time I heard her laugh." He glanced at the bigger biomaton in the doorway. "It is the most beautiful sound in the world."

Seraphim watched him, silent. He did not move, save for a slight bob of the head.

Emmett stared at the shape of his bloodied knuckles, feeling the blood drip down his fingers without seeing it. "I know she cannot love, but perhaps there is some way she might learn to?"

Seraphim shook his head. "Our love is gone for good, Emmett. That is not something we can bring back. Nor is it something you should blame her for. It is not her fault."

Emmett bowed his head, shrugging. "*Regardez-moi*," he

muttered sourly. "I fell in love with the one girl who could not love me back and look what it has earned me."

"But is she worth it?"

"Oh, she is worth all of this and more, *mon ami*, simply to be in her presence. I only wish she could understand the way I feel about her."

Seraphim shuffled his wings. "Come, my friend, let us take care of those cuts, and get someone to clean this mess. It is pointless to dwell on impossibilities."

"*Mais oui*, Seraphim. You are correct. *Je suis désolé.*"

Seraphim smiled at his former shipmate. "No need to apologize. You are not the first man to be driven mad by a beautiful woman, nor will you be the last."

As Emmett followed the winged biomaton, a question leapt to his lips. "How do you do it, Seraphim?"

"Do what?"

"See like *this* and naturally." Emmett gestured to his prosthetic eyes. "It was disorienting enough for me at first without the added trouble of trying to bring color and depth into it."

"I think perhaps it is easier for me than it is for you," Seraphim answered thoughtfully. "The effect of my eye lays a kind of grid on everything, helps me see shape and depth, as two eyes do. But I still see color and detail and texture." He paused, closing his right eye, so only the left stared at Emmett, glassy iris turning almost imperceptibly. "This makes it much more difficult. You are adapting quickly, my friend."

Emmett smiled a little at that. "And yet not fast enough. I itch to hold a sword again."

"We should bandage those knuckles, then we shall see what we can do about the sword."

CHAPTER ELEVEN

Erikkson caught Taryn in the hall. "Finished already, Sedition?"

She nodded silently, supposing she was as ready now as she ever could be. She nursed an ugly, dark spot of anger in her heart for Royal. Despite herself, his words had hurt. She had never seen this side of him before; this ugly, prejudiced side, but she should have expected it. The aristocracy were all the same when it came down to it. It had just taken longer than usual to show in Royal. Then again...they were all a little prejudiced at heart. Some people were just better at hiding it. And Royal had always been the kind of person who wore his heart on his sleeve, for better or worse. She only hoped that, given time, he'd come to see the error of what he'd been taught. Despite what she'd said, she didn't want to lose his friendship. They'd known each other for so long. But even so, she recognized that he needed to do better. She was finished making excuses for him.

"Excellent. If you will follow me..."

Erikkson led her swiftly through the corridors, into the west wing of the manor. It was a later addition to Elmhurst, and it showed. Despite being two stories high (with a basement beneath), there was only a single door that led to the wing, keeping it isolated from the rest of the house. It wasn't that those who dwelled in the west wing were prevented from entering the rest of the house, it was simply that they kept to themselves and preferred it that way. The differences in the wings were immediately obvious upon entry: the walls and floor were bare stone, and candles, not gas lamps, lit the hall, hung in great iron chandeliers from the ceiling. There were no windows. This was the barracks and the training ground, the place where biomatons were transformed from slaves to warriors, and all Taryn could think as she entered the barren hallways, was of her time in the Black Castle. Her stomach lurched into her throat.

Erikkson led her down into the basement, to an immense room with a variety of weapons hung along the walls. Six biomatons paused in their sparring, some with rapiers, others with bare fists, and stared as they entered. As soon as they glimpsed Taryn, the biomatons stood to attention, saluting. Taryn's cheeks warmed. She turned her gaze to the floor until they left the training room behind.

Beyond the large room was a hallway with wooden doors, all closed against prying eyes. Taryn frowned, finally speaking up. "Where are you taking me?"

Erikkson smiled enigmatically and said nothing. He led Taryn to a door near the far end of the hall on the left, pressing it open with his palm. Inside was a brightly lit room, much larger than Taryn had expected. Reams of fabric lined one wall, like bookshelves for textiles. Numerous dress forms stood side-by-side, each wearing a garment in progress, both masculine and feminine. A long, patterned silk screen hid one corner from view. A girl sat at a narrow table near the front of the room operating a sewing machine. She looked up as they entered.

"Gennifer, I would like to introduce Sedition," Erikkson said.

The girl rose, a smile splitting her cheeks. She wore thick, round glasses, and her long, strawberry-blonde hair was tied back in a knot at the nape of her neck. She half walked, half limped over to them, lifting the hem of her pale blue skirt just enough so Taryn could see her left foot was made of clockwork. From the way she walked, Taryn guessed her leg was a heavy prosthetic.

"Sedition, it is so good to meet you at last," she exclaimed, extending her hand. She spoke with a musical Irish accent. "I have heard so much about you."

Taryn took her hand, pleasantly surprised by the willowy girl's firm grip. "All good things, I hope."

Gennifer nodded. "Master Erikkson could hardly say a mean thing about you if he wanted to."

Taryn smiled, despite herself.

"I believe you know why I brought Sedition here," Erikkson urged.

The girl's bright hazel eyes flickered to him. "Yes, sir. Of course."

"Very good. Sedition, meet me in the training room when you are finished here," Erikkson said, indicating the room they had passed through on their way.

"Yes, sir."

And then he was gone, leaving her alone with Gennifer. Taryn looked at her, clearing her throat. "You know why I am here, but I do not. Do you mind explaining?"

"I am your seamstress." Gennifer limped to another door set in the wall. Inside, a giant walk-in cupboard was filled with clothes and uniforms of all kinds. "That is my job in this war: to make uniforms and armor for you and your army."

"You will not fight?"

"Dear me, no!" Gennifer laughed, patting her left leg good-naturedly. "This old thing slows me down too much. I would only hinder you."

"I am sorry."

"Do not be sorry. *I* am only too sorry to be unable to contribute more." Gennifer rummaged about for a moment, then came up with a pile of folded clothes. "Here, try these on." She held them out to Taryn. "Master Erikkson gave me your measurements. I ought to take them again, but in the meantime, here is something to get you started."

Taryn took the pile, one eyebrow quirked. "What is this?"

"A training uniform. You did not expect to train in a whale-bone corset and petticoats, did you?"

Taryn glanced down at her bustled dress. "No, I suppose not."

"Please, try it on. I want to see how it fits," Gennifer urged, pushing Taryn toward the screen in the corner.

She stepped behind it, removing her dress and petticoats, and hung her frock over the top of the screen before turning her attention to the uniform. First, she pulled on a pair of supple leather breeches, their shape fitted at her hips, but loose around her thighs before cinching about her calves. Next, she donned a soft linen blouse, thin enough to be breathable without becoming translucent. The sleeves had some contour to them and gathered at her wrists. The neckline drooped down in an open V. Atop this, she pulled on a fitted vest, dark blue, lacing down the front like a corset while still allowing her to move freely. Finally, she donned a black military-style jacket, its long tails falling to her knees like a skirt. Taryn stepped stiffly from behind the screen, feeling almost naked in these new, fitted clothes. "Well?" she asked rigidly.

"You look wonderful!" Gennifer clasped her hands together. "But I think..." She took up a pair of scissors, beckoning Taryn over. With a few swift snips, she cut off the left sleeve of both Taryn's blouse and jacket. "There. That fierce bit of mechanicks ought not to be hidden."

Taryn rubbed her metal shoulder. "You said you needed my measurements again? It seems you have very precise measurements already."

"Aye, but I do not want to get anything wrong," Gennifer replied, setting aside the scissors and taking up a measuring ribbon.

"Wrong?"

"Aye. Your armor must be very precise. The smallest error could mean a difference between life and death. I cannot allow that."

Taryn nodded, though her stomach clenched at the mention of life and death circumstances. She certainly hoped it would not come to that. "Please, take any measurements you feel are necessary."

Gennifer took down her measurements quickly and easily while Taryn held still, her eyes tilted up to the rough stone ceiling. The measurements she took weren't what Taryn had expected; she ignored her height, bust, waist, and hips, instead focusing on the circumference of her wrist and forearm, her neck, her ankles and the size of her feet.

"I am finished. You may go now, my lady," Gennifer said, smiling. "If there are any problems with the new uniform, just let me know."

"Thank you," Taryn replied. She left the room, following the route Erikkson had led her down earlier. Her new clothes were surprisingly comfortable. Her black heeled boots felt a little out of place with the rest of her outfit, but she supposed she would change them out for something more sensible when she got a chance. She smiled a little to herself, imagining how Royal would react to her new outfit. She thought perhaps they would have to invent a whole new shade of red just for him. Still smiling, Taryn pressed the training room door open.

She stopped dead in her tracks, her smile falling away. Perhaps twenty-five people waited in the room, all fresh faces Taryn did not recognize, save for Erikkson and Seraphim. The people—biomatons, every last one, and most of them remarkably young—stood to attention as she entered the room. Twenty-four hands rose as one in salute. Taryn's mouth went dry.

"Sedition, meet the first regiment of your biomaton army," Erikkson announced in a voice like a ringleader introducing the audience to the man-eating lions. Taryn grabbed his arm, pulling him aside.

"I am not ready for this," she hissed.

Erikkson gave her an enigmatic smile and turned to face the gathered biomatons. "Say something to them," he urged.

Taryn's mind felt as vacant as if her memories had been wiped again. "Hello," she said lamely, her voice barely audible. Her tongue stuck to the roof of her mouth. Every biomaton eye watched her with scrutiny, picking out her flaws from a mile off.

"That is it?" a voice called from somewhere in the crowd.

A ripple of murmurs followed the cry. Taryn cringed inwardly. She might have known this would be their reaction. She was not one of them. Not even close. But her eyes scanned the crowd, despite her misgivings, and she was surprised to see the faces looked less like hardened soldiers and more like the ragtag street gangs she had encountered in London. About half the group was female, and a few were older than Taryn, but most were around her age. She was surprised to spot a few young faces in the group as well, no older than twelve or thirteen. It was the rattiest regiment she had ever seen.

"She is nothing but a schoolgirl," someone else shouted.

"Do I hear a challenge?" Erikkson questioned the crowd. "Please, step forward if you feel Sedition is an unfit leader. You may fight her for the role."

The color drained from Taryn's face. She turned stunned eyes to Erikkson. Was he out of his mind? She had as little hope of defeating a trained fighter as she had of growing her arm back.

A young man stepped forward. He had a mop of curly, vividly red hair (which made Taryn's hair look practically auburn by comparison) and freckles so dark and thick it was as though a pointillist had begun a painting across his cheekbones. He stood head and shoulders above Taryn, his tall, lean frame canting to the left. "I challenge her," he spat. "No soft girl should be allowed to lead this army, no matter how tough her arm looks."

Taryn studied him, her chin held high, the violent monster within already fighting to break free. "Two clockwork fingers hardly makes you a biomaton," she retorted.

Erikkson held up his hands. "Now, both of you save it for the challenge." He beckoned to the other biomatons in the room. "Form a ring. You all know how this works."

Seraphim began to trace a large circle of white chalk on the stone floor. A pair of biomatons with warm, nut-brown skin, so alike they could have been mirror images, stepped up to Taryn's challenger, muttering encouragements and strategic tips. Erikkson helped Taryn shrug off her new jacket.

"Now is a good time to use that violence," he whispered. "Do not stop to think. Your body will know what to do even if your mind does not."

"I cannot fight him," she hissed, desperation edging her voice.

"You can." He clapped her on the shoulder. "This is what I built you for."

Taryn tried to protest, but Erikkson was already moving to the center of the chalk circle, his arms outstretched. The biomaton soldiers surrounded her on all sides, creating an impenetrable barrier of bodies. Taryn kicked off her shoes, gripping the stone floor with her stockinged toes. She bounced on the balls of her feet, flexing her hands, trying to calm the storm raging in her head and chest.

What am I doing? She didn't know the first thing about fighting. This boy was going to beat her solidly and then she'd lose her role. *And maybe that would not be so bad,* she thought. Maybe she could let him get a few good jabs in, concede her place, and go back to being Taryn. Taryn the schoolgirl. Taryn the mechanick. Taryn who had gone under Erikkson's knife twice, who had survived the Black Castle and the *Dauntless* only to fail here, in front of the man who'd built her to change the world. *Gor,* she'd be nothing again. Everything she'd gone through would be for nothing. *He built you for this,* she repeated his words from moments before back to herself, and though the thought terrified her to death, she thought it might just be enough to break through the walls she'd built around Sedition in her mind. She loosened her death grip on the violence inside her. If there was any moment to let it out, this was it.

"You know the rules of a challenge," Erikkson cried, holding out his hands for silence. "The fight will continue until one participant yields, either verbally or by loss of consciousness. This shall *not* be a lethal battle. Do not attempt to kill your opponent. Anything else is legal." Erikkson strode around the circle as he spoke, stopping in front of Taryn. He gave her a silent nod, meeting her eyes, then stepped over the chalk barrier. "Begin."

Taryn's body tensed, becoming a bundle of kinetic energy. Her mind raced. What could she do? She had no fighting skills and few instincts. She raised her fists in front of her chest. She was making a fool of herself. She wasn't a warrior. The last man she'd fought had been half-crazed, his mind shattered from too much tinkering, and he'd still nearly killed her.

Her opponent came forward, his own hands in loose fists.

He moved like a cat, all lithe, controlled muscle. He circled her slowly, bright blue eyes searching for a weak spot he could exploit. Taryn knew he was toying with her. Still, she kept her eyes on him, her paces matching his as they rounded the perimeter.

His attack came so quickly she did not see it, just reacted viscerally. He feinted with a jab at her jaw, and when Taryn raised her arms to protect her face, his foot came up, striking her just below the ribs. Taryn doubled over, gagging on her own breath. She did not see her opponent's fist until it smashed into the bridge of her nose. She blacked out momentarily, her vision going dark with the pain and shock of the blow. She came to a moment later, flat on her back. Tears streamed from her eyes, though she was not crying. She expected the crowd to be cheering or yelling insults, like boys at a brawl, but the room was eerily still. Violence bubbled in her gut, sending sparks of electricity through the ends of her fingers. Taryn kicked out, catching the back of her opponent's knee, buckling his legs. Her vision blinked crimson, bloodlust singing in her ears. She gave in to the thirst for blood.

The redheaded biomaton weighed twice as much as Taryn, and even her strike to his legs did not take him down completely. He caught hold of her ankle with an iron grip, and she used the leverage to lift herself into a sitting position, kicking him hard in the shoulder with her heel. Hot blood ran down her chin, but she ignored it. The bloody fury coloring her vision blocked the pain in her skull, turning it to little more than a dull buzzing in her mind.

Her opponent fell back, releasing her ankle on the second strike from Taryn's heel. Bone crunched beneath her foot. In a flash, she was up and pinning her opponent to the floor, one knee pressed to the base of his throat where she knew it would hurt but would not cut off his air completely. She raised her spiked fist in warning. "Yield," she hissed.

He refused, struggling. Taryn put more weight on his throat, slamming her spiked fist into the side of his head. He retaliated with a punch to her side. She grimaced and struck him again, harder. "I said yield!"

He hesitated for a moment, and she prepared to strike him a third time. Then, reluctantly, he tapped the floor with his clockwork fingers.

"Sedition is the victor," Erikkson announced from the sidelines, his voice brimming with brass. He sounded almost *smug*.

Taryn rose, somewhat shakily, breathing hard. Every bruise her body had sustained made itself known. Her body ached. Seraphim silently held out a handkerchief to her, but she waved it away, allowing the blood to stream down her face, preferring to look as if she did not care. She held her arms wide, turning in a slow arc to meet the eyes of the onlooking biomatons. "Would anyone else like to challenge me?" she cried. When no one spoke up, she sneered. "Please, step forward. I am only a schoolgirl, after all."

Taryn's redheaded opponent met her eyes. He was bleeding from a series of cuts at his temple, his cheek swelling. Slowly, he raised his hand, saluting her. "My lady Sedition."

One by one, the other biomaton soldiers followed suit until they all stood with their hands raised, even Erikkson. Taryn nodded to them. "You are dismissed."

The soldiers scattered, and Taryn sagged, panting. She turned toward Erikkson, ready to berate him for throwing her into battle like that. He wore a wide, proud grin.

"You are ready," he said.

"Do not *ever* make me do that again," she snapped, her adrenaline dissolving into fury.

"I am afraid you shall have to do that many times before this war is over. But I shall never again force you to do it without preparation." He offered her a white handkerchief, and this time she took it, wiping away the blood that streamed down her chin. "You did well, little one."

"How did you know I would win?" she asked, at last finding the violence beginning to ebb.

He smiled enigmatically, refusing to give her an answer. "Are you ready to meet everyone and begin your training in earnest?"

Narrowing her eyes, she nodded her agreement. Whatever had just occurred, whatever she had become in those few moments, she knew she needed to learn to control it. Sedition was waking within her, and she would not be denied.

"Excellent. Let us begin."

"Ye think she will be any use as a soldier?"

Seraphim kept his eyes on the chalk circle he was wiping off the floor, now spattered with blood, but his ears pricked as he heard the other biomatons in the room discussing Taryn.

"That waif? Of course not."

"But she beat Rylan in a fair fight."

"She got lucky. I can beat Rylan in a fair fight, too."

Seraphim recognized the rolling Scottish brogues of the twins, Ari and Rorin. They were relatively new additions to the army, only here since he'd joined the *Dauntless,* but Erikkson trusted them enough to make them commanders, so that had to mean something.

He finished his task and got up, dusting the chalk off his hands. He let his wings stretch, articulating the razor-sharp flight feathers one by one, ensuring he was in fighting condition. The barest uptick at the corner of his mouth indicated his pleasure. It would feel good to get some practice in, to stretch his limbs and swing a quarterstaff, his weapon of choice. Given the option, he preferred diplomacy to violence, but even

Seraphim had to admit the last few months on the *Dauntless* had been remarkably quiet, and without the exercise a good fight provided, he felt rusty and out of shape. None of the sailors had been willing to spar with him; they were too afraid of what he was. But here he fit in as well as he could hope to, and he knew many of the soldiers looked up to him. Plus, it would be good to get his mind off of all the secrets he was keeping.

"Seraphim," Emmett spotted him from halfway across the training room and approached, golden eyes spinning as he studied the stone basement that had been retrofitted to provide the biomatons an indoor training ground. Emmett's knuckles had been bandaged, and he looked back to his chipper self, but Seraphim could read the Frenchman's days in the Black Castle on his face, and he knew they hadn't been kind.

"Hello, Emmett," Seraphim answered. "Feeling better?"

"*Oui, merci,*" Emmett replied. He took up a rapier from one of the weapons racks, swung it a few times, the blade whistling through the air. "Ah, *mademoiselle,* I have missed you," he murmured to the weapon.

"Are you going to be a part of our little rebellion?" Seraphim asked, realizing he didn't know Emmett's plans. He knew the Frenchman was smitten with Taryn, would probably follow her to the ends of the earth if she asked, but still, asking him to join a potential suicide mission was a risk. Emmett had a strong survival instinct; Seraphim admired that in him. But it also meant he might choose himself over the cause.

"But of course!" His golden eyes flashing in the candlelight. "After what Taryn and I experienced at Black Castle, how could I not?" His bright features darkened, and Seraphim caught a glimpse of the warrior behind his cheerful gaze. "I would like a chance to repay their cruelty."

The corner of Seraphim's mouth turned upward. "I would be glad to assist you."

Emmett swung the rapier again and performed a perfect lunge, his foot slapping the stone hard as he landed. He gave Seraphim a grin. "This is a good weapon."

"Only when it is wielded by a good swordsman," Seraphim answered, lifting a quarterstaff from another rack and weighing it in his hand. It was iron tipped and well-weighted, but after so long aboard the *Dauntless,* it felt wrong in his hands. He would have to get back into practice. "I was about to do a little sparring. Would you like to join me? We can see just how well you've adapted to your new eyes."

Emmett grinned. "Of course, *mon ami.* It would be an honor."

They stepped into the middle of the circle to spar. As they moved, Emmett frowned at a spot on the floor, puddled with blood from Taryn's earlier fight. He crouched, tracing the damp stone with his fingertips. He sniffed at them, grimacing at the scent of blood. "This is fresh," he murmured. "What happened?"

"Sedition won her first skirmish. I am surprised you spotted it," Seraphim answered, a chill running down his back as he remembered the savagery with which she'd beaten Rylan. The more he saw this new version of Sedition, the more it worried him. She was too much like Petrichor. She'd lost too much of her memory, and the more he observed, the more certain he was that she would become exactly what Erikkson wanted her to be.

"Liquid has a strange, rippling quality. I would not have recognized it had I not split my knuckles earlier today." Emmett wiped his bloodied fingers on a handkerchief. "A skirmish against another biomaton?"

"Yes. Someone who thought she wasn't worthy of the title Master Erikkson has given her."

Emmett shuddered and rose. "She has a difficult path to tread."

"She always has," Seraphim answered. "But she has always risen to his expectations."

"And tell me, *mon ami*," Emmett murmured, drawing into a fighter's stance, "is that a good thing?"

"For the cause, yes," Seraphim answered honestly, easing his hands into a comfortable position on the guard of the quarterstaff. "But only Sedition can tell if it is good for her soul."

CHAPTER TWELVE

"Are you paying attention?"

Taryn winced, drawing her back even straighter. Not that she had poor posture to begin with; there was just something about the stocky woman screaming in her face that made her feel as though she was slouching.

"I do not think you heard me. I said, are you paying attention?" the woman yelled again. The short, square-framed bundle of muscle strode down the rank of biomaton recruits, all standing stick-straight and doing their best not to make eye contact.

"I am," Taryn answered. The violent part of her pressed against her ribcage, but she kept it under control. Barely.

"I do not care that you are Erikkson's prodigy. When you address me, you will say madam or Officer Belchick, understood?" The woman turned catlike dark eyes back on Taryn; one real, one made of glass. It was rumored she really *had* been in the military, a biomaton designed to train soldiers, and most of her bones had been repaired with clockwork over years of sparring. She was perhaps fifty years of age, and wore her dark hair cropped at her chin. She had the dark, red-clay skin tone of the Punjabi, and spoke English with a heavy, rolling Indian accent. She carried a riding crop under one arm and gestured at the biomatons with it when she addressed them. Her other arm remained tucked tightly behind her back.

"Yes, Officer Belchick." Taryn glared daggers at the woman for singling her out.

Belchick did not even acknowledge Taryn's assent. She stalked down the row of biomatons, eyeing them skeptically. "You are the sorriest lot of biomatons I have ever seen. How am I to make you into soldiers? You are nothing but ladies' maids and footmen, not warriors." Taryn's chin rose a little with silent pride. The woman turned toward her. "And you are the worst of the lot. Do you think you are better than the rest of us because of your education?" Inside, Taryn wilted. "Well? Answer me when I speak to you."

"No, madam."

"No, madam," Belchick mocked. "Everything Erikkson does will make you believe you are superior to us. Therefore, everything *I* do shall ensure your head does not grow too large."

A few of the other biomatons snuck glances at Taryn. She nursed a kernel of resentment for each and every one of them; she would show them, of course. She had been chosen for a reason, and she *would* prove to them all that she was worthy to be their leader. It was all a matter of finding that worth within herself.

"Have any of you lot held a weapon before?" Officer Belchick questioned.

A young boy, about fourteen years of age, raised his hand timidly.

"You? Pah! A rifle would knock you backward the first time you tried to shoot it."

"I *have* held a rifle, madam," he protested in a soft, sweet Yorkshire accent. "I attended my former master on his hunting sessions." A bloom of red blossomed on his freckled cheeks.

Officer Belchick shook her head. "That is not what I meant, boy. But not to worry. I shall have you all in shape before long." She gestured with the riding crop, pointing down the long stone hall where the biomatons had assembled for inspection. "Outside. March!"

The biomatons paraded down the hall and out the door, leading from the west wing onto the grounds of the manor. This section of the grounds had been converted from gardens to training ground, with large fields for the soldiers to spar upon, and an obstacle course for physical conditioning. There was a shooting range tucked into the edge of the forest surrounding Elmhurst, keeping it secluded from the rest of the training grounds. The entire space was framed by a high hedge, disguising it from prying eyes. In fact, all of Erikkson's designs ensured his biomaton army was as secret as possible; he had few friends outside his biomaton "family," and rarely attended any of the high society events he received invitations for. He chose to be a social recluse in order to protect the little family he'd built.

A soft drizzle fell as Taryn and the other biomatons emerged from the house. Taryn grimaced; she would have to treat her prosthetic with oil that evening to prevent it from rusting. The grass squelched with mud beneath her feet.

"Madam, the rain shall ruin our prosthetics!" a girl with a simple clockwork arm protested. Pieces of her arm were built of wood, and her pink skin had lost all its color with the cold. Taryn knew the girl had probably never had her prosthetic treated for rust—whomever had constructed her had only rudimentary biomechanickal knowledge. Most likely, she had simply been warned against moisture of any kind. Taryn wondered how she bathed.

Officer Belchick gave the girl a bloodcurdling sneer. "If you are concerned about a little rain, Petunia, you may return indoors and report yourself unfit for duty."

The girl blinked, then hung her head and slunk back to the house. Taryn was surprised to discover she agreed with Belchick. The girl would be useless as a soldier if she could not even endure a little rain.

"This is your last chance," Belchick cried. Rain poured down upon them, the skies opening as if even they could not bear the idea of slaves training to be soldiers. "Would anyone else like to display their yellow belly and return to the warmth of the house?"

As one, all ten biomatons left standing answered, "No, madam!"

Belchick nodded and pointed her crop at the obstacle course, quickly turning to mud in the rain. "A reward to whomever finishes first!"

The biomatons scrambled over one another to get to the course. Taryn joined in, the leader inside her refusing to surrender even as the soft parts of her begged to be allowed to give up. She received elbows to the ribs and returned them with blows of her own. She struggled through the mud and the rain, her breath steaming in the cold. The others cast her glares and insults, but she persevered, focused on the pounding rain against her back and the rush of blood in her veins. And, despite it all, she finished dead last.

SUPPER, THE EVENING OF THAT FIRST DAY, WAS A DISMAL affair. Taryn knew Belchick had reported her poor performance to Erikkson; she was exhausted, and just wanted to collapse into her bed and perhaps have a good cry; she had barely had enough time to bathe and oil her arm before supper; the dining room was eerily silent, just herself and Erikkson, alone. Taryn kept her eyes down as their first course was delivered, fidgeting with her skirt. She could sense Erikkson watching her, silent, waiting for her to speak. Finally, she clutched at the tablecloth, laying her silverware down.

"I failed, I know. You may stop staring at me so. I am quite aware of my poor performance today. I am sorry I did not live up to your expectations of me." The words came tumbling out in a heap, and she stared at them where they'd piled up on the table before raising her eyes.

Erikkson was laughing.

She stared at him. "Is this amusing to you? I am meant to be your perfect fighting machine, not the girl who gets beat into the mud during training."

"It is your first day, little one. You must not be so hard on yourself." Erikkson raised his glass of wine to his lips and drank before continuing. "It will take you some time to grow accustomed to the new grafts and the training style. Be patient."

Chastened, Taryn lowered her head again. Her outburst stung in her cheeks. "Officer Belchick singles me out," she muttered. "Because I am your chosen leader, and because I am so soft." She stared down at her right hand, studying the fresh pink blisters from swinging the wooden sword she'd been given.

"Then you must show her you deserve the title. After supper, you and I shall have a private training session. It is time you learned the intricacies of your new prosthetics."

Taryn scowled. "I have been training all day. I do not need *more* training. I need to sleep."

"Nevertheless, we *shall* do some more training after supper, my dear. You did not think this would be easy, did you?"

Taryn glowered, selfish resentment souring the meal in her mouth. She forced herself to slow down, take a few deep breaths, and relax. It was only the difficult day getting to her. And it wasn't fair to take out her own shortcomings on Erikkson.

"May I ask a question?" she ventured as the next course was delivered.

"Of course, little one."

"In the Black Castle, I saw biomatons with no other visible grafts than the control panel on their heads. Is that something you have seen?"

"Interesting, is it not?" Erikkson gestured with his fork. "They have begun building biomatons with no other graft than the control panel and the mental dampers that allow full control of the person."

The color drained from Taryn's cheeks. "That cannot be."

Erikkson nodded. "Worse, it is mostly children subjected to this sort of graft, as their elastic minds are so much easier to control than an adult's. The twins, Ari and Rorin, whom you met yesterday, share a story like this one."

She nodded, remembering the two biomatons with nut-brown skin. They were officers in her army. Rorin seemed to have an easy-going manner, but Ari had given her a glare that could have soured milk when they were introduced after her challenge with Rylan. "The twins are physically whole?"

"Ari is. Rorin has only one lung, and the other is built of a complicated construction of clockwork and leather, housed neatly in a hatch in his chest. He has had it most of his life, and it rarely slows him down." Erikkson shook his head. "They were targeted from birth, the product of a father from Carribea and a mother from Scotland. We are still so intolerant here, though we would like to pretend we are not. We have simply found more 'acceptable' channels for our prejudices; channels like kidnapping a pair of toddlers and operating on them so it is not only the color of their skin that makes them inhuman."

Taryn swallowed hard, her appetite gone. "That cannot be allowed to continue."

Erikkson smiled wryly. "That is why I built you, Seraphim, and Petrichor. You *must* ensure the world understands what they have done. The sooner, the better."

Taryn nodded. "May I be excused?" she asked. "I am finished, and I ought to change before we begin training."

Erikkson nodded. "Go to Gennifer. She has a new uniform for you. I shall meet you in the training room in ten minutes' time."

TARYN STOOD IN THE CENTER OF THE TRAINING ROOM, wearing Gennifer's new uniform. It was much the same as the other ensemble, with two distinct differences: there were holes over her shoulder blades, revealing the clockwork grafted there, and the entire uniform was black as night. Gennifer had also added a pair of soft black shoes for Taryn to wear, the cloth hugging her feet so snuggly she felt barefoot.

Erikkson entered, wearing a pair of leather breeches and a loose-fitting white shirt. It was as relaxed as Taryn had ever seen him, save for the dagger tucked into his belt. Some of her tension slipped away. Dressed like that, he could not be taking this too seriously. She took a steadying breath.

"Black suits you," Erikkson said approvingly. "I suppose I no longer have any right to call you 'little one.' You are a woman now, and I did not have the decency to notice."

Taryn smiled at his compliment. "You may call me what you like. I am quite content with 'little one.'"

Erikkson's eyes crinkled with a smile. "Hold out your hand."

She did as she was told, offering him the prosthetic, palm up. Erikkson caught her wrist, holding her hand still. He pointed with his pinky to a segment at the base of her ring finger, near the gap between her third and fourth fingers. "The controls of your prosthetic's hidden abilities are all contained in the palm of your hand. You are already aware of the dagger hidden in your forearm, which is released with a pressure plate here." He pointed to the small square plate at the base of her thumb. "Now is as good a time as any for you to take this back," he said, offering her the dagger from his belt. "You left it in my study."

Taryn pressed the plate and watched with awe as a hidden spring-loaded hatch in her forearm opened. She slipped the dagger back into the silver prongs that waited to hold it securely within her arm.

"There are also four knives hidden in your forearm, accessed here," Erikkson continued. Again, he pointed to a small hatch on the top of her forearm, spring-loaded and easily accessible with her other hand. "A small razor is hidden in your wrist, in case your hands are bound." Erikkson released her. "To access it, press down first your third, then your first finger." He demonstrated with his own hand. Taryn imitated his movements, and watched a tiny, glittering razor blade emerge from between her wrist and palm.

"A flick of the wrist will retract the blade."

She flicked her wrist, and the blade disappeared. "You have put a lot of thought into this."

"I had five years to perfect it."

She shuddered at the thought, but there was something waking deep inside her that thrilled at the new weapons she possessed. What damage she could do with these hidden blades. She wished she'd had this at the Black Castle. She could have destroyed every one of her tormentors. Taryn swallowed the emotions down.

"Inside your fingertip here"—he indicated her pointer finger—"is a needle packed with enough poison to stop an elephant. Your finger opens, like so." He cracked the tip of her finger open, the sculpted tip hinged to fold back and reveal the tiny needle inside. Taryn folded it closed again.

"Are you finished?"

"Not quite. For the *pièce de résistance—*" He gave her a

mischievous grin. "That area on your ring finger I indicated first. Twist it."

Taryn obeyed, pressing the panel with her thumb until it gave, twisting under the pressure. A spark of electricity ran down her spine, followed by a whirring sound. Taryn turned her head to see metal blades sprouting from her shoulder blades, the sharp steel glinting in the light cast by the chandeliers overhead. Her stomach twisted into knots. "What have you turned me into?" she asked hoarsely, her mouth dry. The blades fanned out in an arc from her spine, like deadly fairy wings. She could not imagine any use for such a strange, horrifying prosthetic. Even Seraphim's wings paled next to this monstrosity.

"Now, Sedition, we have discussed this," Erikkson chided, his voice carrying a patronizing edge.

She backed a few steps away from him, for the first time truly fearful about what kind of man she'd placed in charge of her life. "No. No, we did not discuss *this*. You did not tell me you were going to turn me into another Seraphim." Her breath came in shallow gasps, too fast, and her vision glowed red. She knew this was the violence in her head, knew she should take a breath and control herself, but she could not breathe and the sheer horror turned everything into crimson anger.

"Control yourself," Erikkson warned.

She raised shaking fists. "Make me," she growled.

"If that is how you want it." Erikkson took a quarterstaff from a nearby rack, his face expressionless. He pointed the quarterstaff at her, the heavy wood tipped with iron, making it a formidable weapon. "Do not make me do this," he urged.

In reply, Taryn charged at him, keeping low to minimize his target. She doubted he would really strike her; she wasn't about to be intimidated by an old biomechanick with a stick.

She dodged his first two thrusts, and parried a third with her metal forearm, releasing the hidden dagger and catching it in her right hand as swiftly as if she had been doing it her entire life. Her slash with the blade caught Erikkson's staff on the guard, between his hands. He shoved her back, then swept the butt of the staff down, catching her heel. Taryn stumbled but did not fall. She was breathing heavily, searching for a chink in Erikkson's defenses. She lunged, the blade aimed for his knuckles. He swept the head of the staff around, keeping his hands out of reach, and the iron tip struck her hard in the temple. Taryn stumbled backward, losing her vision for a moment.

"Use your blades," Erikkson ordered. "You are acting too much on conscious thought. Allow your instincts to take control."

She lunged again, snarling wordlessly. A rap on her knuckles sent her dagger flying, but she kept coming, intent on wresting the staff from his hands. As he swung at her again, she dropped to one knee and twisted her shoulders to move her blades into position. She heard fabric tear and raised her head to see she'd caught his forearm with her blades. Blood ran down his arm, staining his sleeve crimson. Taryn hesitated, the sight of her creator bleeding causing every cog in her body to freeze in horror. The butt of his quarterstaff caught her between her shoulder blades, and Taryn fell flat on her stomach.

"Not bad," Erikkson grinned down at her, laying the staff aside. "I am *almost* impressed. But you are still allowing the violence to control you. You must control it. It can only be an asset to you if you know how to use it."

Taryn coughed, pushing herself off the floor. She understood what he'd done now: provoked her into letting the violence out so he could teach her to use it. "That was not fair," she growled, rising.

"Perhaps not, but I hope you learned something just the same." Erikkson raised his arm, studying the shallow cuts she had inflicted. "You will not be Sedition until you stop being ashamed of what you are and instead embrace what you were built to be."

She scowled. "I am not ashamed."

"Would you choose to be human again, if it were possible?"

"Of course I would!"

He nodded. "Then you are still ashamed of what you are."

The furrow in her brow deepened. She wiped an arm across her forehead. "You think it is wrong I would prefer being human to this?"

"Did I say wrong?" He shook his head. "No. But you must find pride in what you are if you are to lead the biomatons."

Taryn chewed her cheek, knowing he was right, hating the admission. But how could she find pride in what she had been ashamed of for so long? It seemed too much to ask.

"Are you ready to go again?" Erikkson asked, holding out the quarterstaff.

Her eyes flickered to his torn sleeve, stained with blood. "I do not want to hurt you."

He smiled. "Then do not hurt me. But *do* try harder to use your blades to your advantage."

She nodded, taking up a fighting stance. A few strands of copper hair had come loose from her braid and hung in her face, but Taryn ignored them, focusing on Erikkson.

"Begin."

CHAPTER THIRTEEN

THE FOLLOWING days were much the same: humiliation during the day in front of Officer Belchick and her peers, then exercise until late in the evenings with Erikkson, honing her skills, developing a fighting style all her own to utilize her prosthetics, and learning to control the violence in her head. She did not manage to form a camaraderie with any of the biomatons she trained with; Erikkson ensured she was set apart from the rest. Taryn slept in her bedroom in the manor rather than in the barracks with the others, took her meals with Erikkson, and was treated as a superior officer, despite her amateur status. Daily, she sensed a growing enmity from her comrades.

Taryn had been certain she would hate every moment of the training, but after the initial shock and resentment, she discovered she *excelled* at whatever she put her mind to. It was not just her former training that helped; Taryn's grafts assisted her as well, making her stronger, faster, and more agile. The early morning run required for each trainee before breakfast (approximately four and a half miles around the perimeter of the manor and gardens) took her less time than any other biomaton, including the fittest young men. And when she arrived in the dining room, she was hardly winded.

And it began to pay off. She grew more confident in herself, more skilled during drills, and more focused. Which was not to say any of it was easy; it continued to be the most difficult thing she had ever done. But she was beginning to transform, the soft parts of her hardening into muscle, and the timid, shy schoolgirl sloughing off to reveal the soldier beneath. And everyone else could see it too.

Left, left, right cross, left. Uppercut, feint, left.

"Again," Officer Belchick intoned from the corner of the training room, watching the biomatons repeat the form she'd given them, boxing with the air. Taryn blew a strand of hair out of her face and performed the set of movements again, nursing a knot of anger in her chest. She was *beyond* this. She'd been training one-on-one with Erikkson for two weeks, with her fists and weapons and her still-secret shoulder blades, honing the skills she hadn't known she possessed, waking up the warrior within. And yet she was still training with these beginners, shadow boxing when she could be sparring with someone who knew what they were doing.

A sharp slap interrupted her angry thoughts, Officer Belchick's riding crop connecting with her shoulder. "Your form is lazy."

"Should we not be sparring with each other?" Taryn asked before she could reign in her tongue.

The crop caught her on the wrist, stinging. She could feel the eyes of the others on her now, even the dozen or so other soldiers in the training room stopping in their sparring to watch Sedition get in trouble. "If you punch someone like that, you will break your fingers," Belchick responded. "That is why you are not fighting each other yet."

Taryn threw the next punch in her set, metal fist missing the officer's ear by mere centimeters. "I am *ready*. I am not like them! I have had training and I *need* to be sparring with people, not repeating the same five strikes over and over."

Belchick's dark eyes studied Taryn carefully. Tilting her head to the side, she spoke in a soft but authoritative voice. "Very well. You think you are better than they are. Prove it."

She stepped back, voice rising so the whole room could hear. "Sedition will fight anyone here who would like to spar." She turned, pointing across the room to where the twins stood, already damp with sweat from their own training session, which they had paused to watch this new lesson. "Ranking officers are welcome to start."

Ari grinned a malicious grin and stepped forward. Rorin reached for his brother, a crease appearing between his brows, but he dropped his hands as the biomatons in the room began to crowd closer, outlining an approximate circle in the center of the room. Taryn swallowed hard as the big biomaton approached, her heart in her throat. Her anger had dissolved, turning to a dagger of fear that pierced her heart.

"That is not—" she started, but stopped at the look she received from Belchick.

"This is what you wanted. Prove that you are ready for more."

Shuffling her feet back on the stone floor, Taryn closed her eyes for a moment, trying to picture Erikkson's lessons. Trying to call the monster up from inside her, let the violence take over. But when she blinked her eyes open again, all she could see was Ari towering over her across the circle and hard faces watching from all sides.

"Begin!" Belchick cried, and Ari charged forward with the force of an elephant.

Taryn dove out of the way, somersaulting and coming up behind the big man. Her foot lashed out, catching his heel, but he was surprisingly light on his feet and turned the misstep into a side kick. She barely ducked out of the way, back flat against the floor as the strike passed inches from her face.

What am I doing? She shoved herself to her feet and came at him head on, fists readied. He danced sideways, lashed the back of his hand out, and struck her hard on the side of the head. Taryn's ear rang, disorienting her.

The next punch hit her right in the gut.

"Are you still convinced you know all you need to know?" Belchick asked.

She stumbled back a few feet, tasting acid in the back of her throat. She reached again for the violence within her, wanting her vision to go red, waiting for the fighter to take over, and still she could not find it, and still she was just Taryn, getting beat up for what?

For a cause she had not asked for? For people who so clearly wanted to see her defeated, to see her hurt and helpless, all those things she'd sworn never to be again.

Where was Erikkson? Wasn't he supposed to protect her from things like this? She ducked the next blow only to catch one to the jaw, stumbling into the biomaton behind her. The boy was one in her cohort, a sharp-faced little weasel named Clarence, and he grabbed her shoulders. "Ye are not ready for this fight," he sneered in her ear. "It would be better for everyone if ye leave and never come back, just as Petrichor did."

Petrichor. The name rankled on Taryn's nerves, ringing a silent bell in the back of her head. Petrichor the assassin. Petrichor the rumored third Erikkson, the one he never, ever talked about. Taryn opened her mouth to speak, but Clarence shoved her back into the circle, and she had to dance out of the way of Ari's flying fists again.

Trying to use her size and her speed against him, she scored a glancing blow off his chin only to receive a powerful hit to her stomach. All the wind left her in a gasp, and she dropped to one knee, heaving for breath.

What am I doing?

"Some legendary Erikkson," Ari spat, his thick Scottish brogue rumbling through the crowd. "She cannot even hold her own against one of us."

Sweat trickled down her brow. Tears burned at the back of her nose, but Taryn forced herself to raise her head, to really look at the faces scowling at her. She expected to see her cohort and the others she had met in passing, well-trained soldiers who were right to resent her, who were right to want her gone so that they could lead this rebellion themselves.

Instead, her gaze found Royal, his brow furrowed, brown eyes watery with concern. Then she saw Rorin, his expression lacking the hatred in his brother's, instead containing compassion and worry. Gennifer stood on the outside of the circle with her hand pressed over her mouth in horror. And Emmett, fury turning his ears red, was restrained from jumping into the circle to protect her by a pair of biomaton boys.

Something clicked inside her chest as she looked at these people, her army, her friends, her *family*. She wanted this. She wanted to belong, to be Sedition, to save the biomatons who couldn't save themselves. If she was honest, she'd wanted it since the very beginning, but fear and anger and cowardice kept getting in the way, convincing her she didn't. This was what she was *made for,* and gor, wasn't there something beautiful about having a purpose? She shoved herself back to her feet.

"You are wrong," she said, the words tasting like steel in her mouth. "I am Sedition. I *will* lead this army. And if you do not like it, I do not care." The violence came to her all at once, then, but it wasn't like before, it wasn't a loss of control. It was a power that lived in her limbs and her feet and her chest. She struck fast and hard, dancing around Ari's strikes, ducking beneath his defenses, blows raining on his face, his chest, his stomach.

She finished the combo with a knee to his stomach and he fell to one knee, gasping. The room watched in silence.

"Who is next?" she snarled.

Clarence stepped into the ring, his fists clenched, his grin sharp. "I challenge you."

Taryn studied the wiry boy. She'd seen him fight in training, all long limbs and fast, wheeling strikes. She nodded, beckoning him with two fingers. "I accept your challenge."

He came at her with the speed and grace of a cobra, all flowing movements, hands moving in a blur. She let her mind go blank, let her own body match the tide of his, but his technique was unfamiliar, and they danced around each other, striking only glancing blows on one another.

"Each opponent is different," Belchick said from the sidelines. "It is not enough that you can fight one. You must be prepared to fight them all, and win each time, win *every* fight. In the real world, you will not be given a second chance."

Anger flared up in Taryn's chest. Who did this woman think she was, turning this fight into a lecture?

The momentary distraction cost her. Clarence found a chink in her defenses, punched her square in the nose. Blinded by the pain and tears streaming from her eyes, Taryn stumbled forward. His foot caught hers and she fell, jaw hitting the concrete with a *crack* that sang through her bones.

"Good, Clarence," Belchick said in that same firm, lecturing tone. "Have you learned your lesson, Sedition?"

Taryn pushed herself onto her elbows, tasting blood. She swiped one elbow across her face and staggered back to her feet. Blood dripped from a split lip, and her eyes wouldn't stop streaming. "Next," she growled.

"Taryn, this is stupid—" Emmett gasped from the sidelines, still held firmly by two of her soldiers.

"*Next*," she repeated. If this was the way she earned her place, so be it. She would fight them all, one by one. She would let them beat her to a pulp. But she would *not* give up the authority Erikkson had given her. "I am not leaving. You cannot scare me away."

The girl who stepped forward struck hard and fast with the sides of her hands and balls of her feet, acrobatically flipping around the ring as Taryn tried to return her blows. She swept Taryn off her feet and gave a graceful curtsy before stepping out of the ring. Once again pushing herself upright, Taryn invited her next challenger.

There was hesitation around the room, for the first time since Belchick announced this challenge. Taryn was panting hard, blood and sweat and tears streaming down her face, staining her uniform. And she still *stood*, swaying, yes, but upright and waiting for her next opponent. Murmurs rippled around the ring.

"I said," Taryn spat a gob of blood and spit on the floor, the inside of her mouth tasting of copper and salt and anger, "*next.*"

"Perhaps that is enough for today," Rorin said quietly from where he stood, watching.

A boy with a fox-like face stepped forward, swinging a blackjack at his side. "I have not yet had a turn."

"That is not fair," Emmett yelled. "Taryn wields no weapons!"

"Let him come," Taryn answered, grimacing a feral grin with bloody teeth. "Let them all come."

The boy took that as his cue to attack. He threw himself across the ring, club raised in one hand, his movements slow but coordinated, like he already had their fight in his mind's eye and was playing it out with each step. Exhausted as she was, vision blurry with tears and blood and sweat, Taryn tried to duck out of the way, first feinting to the right before moving to the left. Or trying to. He let her move around him before striking, waiting for her to reach the apex of her dodge before the club lashed out, catching her on the side of the head.

One moment she was upright, the next she was on the ground, clockwork arm raised to guard against the blows he rained down on her. She heard metal crunch, gears grinding against each other. *I may have taken this too far*, she thought foggily, before a kick caught her in the ribs and she was rolling, conscious thought finally losing out to animal reaction as she tried in vain to get away from the pain. Phantom pain flared up her prosthetic arm, pins and needles striking in a place she knew it was impossible to feel. Another kick drove any remaining air from her lungs. Her scream emerged as a silent gasp for breath.

"That is *enough!*" The voice came to her over a long distance, Erikkson's baritone only becoming audible by degrees as it drove away the fog from the edges of her mind. "Would you treat any other of your fellow biomatons this way?"

Murmurs echoed around the room, accusations and pointed fingers and retorts. Taryn barely heard them, trying to shove herself upright on a prosthetic arm that was no longer functioning properly.

"It got out of hand," Belchick explained, though her voice sounded smug, unapologetic. "It was an exercise to demonstrate that Sedition must be prepared to face all kinds of fighting techniques, not just yours."

"Out of hand is an understatement." Erikkson had reached her now, gently placing a hand on her shoulder. "Royal, get her back to her room and see what you can do about the damage to her prosthetic. I will deal with this."

Taryn grabbed his wrist, meeting his gaze through swollen eyes. "No. I want to handle this."

"Little one, you are in no condition—"

"Tomorrow, then." Her voice was thick with blood. Royal ducked under her arm, gently helping her to her feet. "But I want to deal with this myself. I cannot keep hiding behind you."

Her creator's brow collapsed into a tender expression of concern and worry. "Very well. Tomorrow morning, Sedition will deal with all of you. For now, you are to return to your quarters. If I see a single one of you set foot outside the barracks, you will face both her punishment *and* mine."

By the time they'd reached her room, Taryn's eyes had fallen closed, her feet only moving with the dragging insistence of Royal's body holding hers. It was the closest they'd been in weeks, she realized numbly. Maybe the closest she'd ever allowed him to come, considering the measures she'd taken to hide her prosthetic from him before. His palm was warm on her shoulder through the fabric of her shirt, and she focused on that. It was the only thing that didn't hurt.

"Sit," he said gently, voice lowered to an almost-whisper. "You are all right."

She felt herself lowered to the edge of her bed before she collapsed back against the pillows, eyes shut tight against the light in the room. Her head throbbed. She moaned.

"Come on, Tiger. Open your eyes. I know it hurts. The pain means you are still alive."

Taryn forced her eyes open a sliver, squinting at Royal as he leaned over her. "Everything hurts and I might be dying."

Royal patted her cheek as she attempted to close her eyes again. "You are not dying. I will not allow it."

She blinked her eyes open fully at last, staring up at Royal with a sour expression. With a grimace and a long, deep breath, she managed to push herself into a more comfortable position, sitting against the pillows. Her mouth tasted like blood. "My hero," she deadpanned.

"Show me your arm, and I will see what I can do for it." He knelt on the bed beside her, and for the first time in weeks, he did not flinch at the sight of her prosthetic. That was growth, she supposed. She missed the easy manner with which they used to tease one another, but perhaps this was a step in the right direction. It would do, as a start.

She lifted her prosthetic hand, offering it to him. His cheeks lost some of their color as he took in the damage. He grabbed her metal wrist, examining the clockwork with a practiced eye.

"Taryn, what have they done?"

She smiled wryly. "It is not bad. You should have seen my arm after I fell on the *Dauntless*. It was crushed beyond repair."

Royal took her chin, forcing her to look at him. "Give this up, Tiger. I beg of you. If this is the kind of damage you sustain during training, how much worse will it be when you begin to fight this war?"

Taryn shook him off, frowning. "I know you mean well, Royal, but I cannot stop."

"Why?"

"I made a promise." She hesitated, watching him as he began to lay out his tools. He'd started carrying them in a sheath on his belt, in case something like this occurred. She tried to find a way to put what she'd felt during the fight into words. "And... I do not know quite how to explain it. I feel more like myself than I ever have. This is what I was made to do. And it is not just about me. Every biomaton is relying upon this rebellion. I cannot abandon them."

"Allow someone else to take your place. You are not the only one who can do this job." Royal stopped with his work to meet her eyes.

"It is this or slavery," Taryn replied flatly, lowering her voice. "I do not think you quite understand. I am either Sedition or I am biomaton 743." She touched the place where her identifying numbers were at last wearing away, barely visible beneath her skin. "There are no other options for me."

"We can move away. Even in France biomatons are free. You have other choices."

"I cannot run away from this! If I do not fight, the ideology will spread. There will be nowhere safe to run."

Royal shook his head, but fell silent, bowing his head over Taryn's prosthetic. He began to work in earnest on her fingers. Taryn leaned her head back against the wall, closing her eyes once more. There remained a tension between them despite their easy rapport, a tension that threaded all the way back to those stupid arguments they'd had over biomatons before he knew what she was, and Taryn could not help but sense it in the air. Her head throbbed with the blows she'd taken, muddling her thoughts. The gentle tapping of Royal's clock-maker's hammer seemed too loud in her ears. Her mind began to drift toward the soft darkness of exhaustion.

Royal shook her shoulder. "Taryn, you cannot go to sleep."

"Why not?"

"I am afraid you may have a concussion," he replied, pushing his hair from his eyes. Taryn wondered when it had gotten so long; the blond locks brushed his jaw when he didn't have it tied back.

"Nonsense," she answered with a shrug. "My brain is rein-forced with steel, remember? I am exhausted from training, that is all."

His lips twisted, brown eyes again flooding with that thick concern—the kind that made the violence inside her raise its head. She did not want his *pity*. Taryn glanced away, swal-lowing the emotions. He returned his attention to her fingers. "I can fix this, but I do not think it will look like it did before."

Taryn nodded, looking down at her armored prosthetic, now bent, scratched, dented, and torn apart where Royal was working. "It could not stay pristine forever. I prefer it scratched and dented."

He looked up from his work, surprised. "You do?"

She shrugged. "I do not have to worry so much about damaging it this way."

Royal paused, his deep brown eyes studying her closely. "You are different, Tiger."

She blinked. "Different how?"

He shook his head. "I do not know how to describe it. Just... Different."

"Different because now you know I have a metal arm and my mind is altered?" she snapped.

"That is not what I meant," Royal growled. Taryn blinked, taken aback by the frustration in his voice. "Not everything is about you being a biomaton!"

"I never said it was," she mumbled, crestfallen. Secretly, she wanted to argue. Everything *was* influenced by what she was, whether he admitted it or not. It permeated every part of her life, just as being female in a male dominated society did. She couldn't forget it or leave it behind. There wasn't a place she could go or a life she could live where it wouldn't matter.

"I do not care about your grafts, or how different you are," Royal continued. He would not look at her, his eyes trained on her prosthetic. "What I care about is that you do not get so lost in this revolution that you forget your friends. I care about you, Tiger. I hate to see you hurt. And you have some self-destructive tendencies you are not controlling." He paused, and at last looked her in the eye. "You can do no good for anyone if you are dead."

"What, are you lecturing me now as well?" Taryn questioned, a crooked smile splitting her expression.

"You have not heard me lecture," Royal retorted, but his own crooked smile appeared, mirroring Taryn's.

She eyed him quietly for a moment. "I am honored you

care for me. No need to worry, Royal. Master Erikkson is taking good care of me."

He raised an eyebrow. "And these biomatons who attacked you tonight?"

"Rest assured, they shall be punished." She nodded. "Yes, Sedition shall deal with them."

THE NEXT MORNING, ERIKKSON CALLED FORTH THE WHOLE of Elmhurst's forces on her request. In the first grey hours of morning, Taryn found herself standing before her biomaton army who stood to attention in ranks, one hundred strong. It was the first time she had seen them all gathered in one place, and she marveled to realize the ragtag band *did* look grand, standing there with their hands behind their backs and chins held high. Erikkson stood off to one side, observing as she addressed them for the first time.

Taryn stalked down the ranks of biomaton soldiers, silently studying each one as she passed. She came to Clarence and stopped. "Step forward," she ordered.

The boy glanced at Erikkson, then took a few hesitant steps forward. Taryn moved on, until she reached Ari. He was wearing his best scowl, refusing to meet her eyes. "Step forward," she repeated. "Beside Clarence." Two times more, she ordered biomatons to step out of ranks, until all her assailants stood in a row, glancing at one another when they thought she was not looking.

She held her head high, letting the sun catch on her swollen lip, the bruises across her cheeks and jaw. "Yesterday, I faced the four of you in a training exercise that turned rather violent." Her heartbeat lifted as she sensed the eyes on her, the rapt attention as she spoke these words. She'd thought about this moment all night, barely getting any sleep. Every word was carefully chosen. "You thought you could beat me into submission. You were wrong."

Seraphim stood near Erikkson, his black hair flowing in the breeze. She caught him moving out of the corner of her eye and held up a hand. "I know I am not what you expected. I did not ask for this position, and I have a long way to go before I become the leader I need to be. But what I cannot stop thinking about, what I cannot believe, even now, is how much my experience yesterday felt like being in the hands of our enemy."

A rustle went through the ranks of biomatons, not a murmur of voices but rather a ripple of fabric moving as one hundred shoulders collectively shuddered. She alone held stock-still, only her mouth moving as she continued her speech. "The world is cruel to us. We all know it. We've all experienced it." She pointed at Erikkson. "He wiped my memory and sent me out into the world so that I could know what all of you have endured for myself.

"But when you bring cruelty here, you do their work for them. *You perpetuate* the story that we can only learn through violence. Through suffering. That we are somehow less than they because we have had our minds and our bodies changed with the clockwork they made. Is that not exactly what we are fighting against?"

Someone in the crowd yelled an affirmative. She let the barest smile touch her lips. "There is no room for cruelty here. Let that be your guide the next time a young, inexperienced biomaton comes to us seeking a purpose. Seeking hope. Welcome them better than you have welcomed me."

Another shout—perhaps it was the same biomaton who had called out in the first place, she could not tell—rose from the ranks. Others began to whoop, cheer, and applaud. Biomatons banged their prosthetics together and stomped their feet in the grass. A surge of pride rose in her throat, and for the first time since she'd arrived, she felt something akin to belonging. She raised her hands, waiting until they quieted.

"We still have a long way to go. You may return to your training."

They broke up across the field, dissolving into clumps of four to ten, those she'd singled out vanishing back into the crowd. She didn't know if what she'd said would convince them of anything at all. She'd only known it was the right thing to say.

"You handled that well," Erikkson said, coming to stand beside her.

Taryn tried to keep her voice level and nonchalant, though inside she was shaking. "I felt it was time to address them as myself, not from behind your skirts."

Erikkson turned forest green eyes on her. "My Sedition." He smiled, but the expression did not reach the corners of his eyes as it usually did. "You have always been a fighter, since the day I pulled you from the fire. But you have gained wisdom, too, and that is something I could not teach you."

She glanced away, watching her army returning to their exercises. A question that had haunted her for too long rose to her lips. "One of them mentioned Petrichor during our fight. Why did she leave?"

A shadow passed over his face. "Should you not be with your training regiment?"

"I have been given the day to train on my own. And you are avoiding my question."

"She left. The why does not matter. I lost my best soldier that day, and a dear daughter as well." He stiffened, as though steeling himself against the loss of Petrichor. "When we need her, we will find a way to bring her back."

Taryn frowned, frustrated by the way he danced around the topic. She supposed it would be better to ask someone else —perhaps Seraphim could tell her the truth of what had occurred. "Show me your technique with the quarterstaff again," she requested. "I think I have nearly figured it out."

SERAPHIM WATCHED FROM AFAR AS TARYN SPARRED WITH Erikkson on the terraced field, half-hidden by the rose hedges scattered throughout the vast gardens of Elmhurst. The air was crisp and cold, biting across his cheeks, but it carried with it the promise of coming spring. Spring was his favorite season; the time of rebirth and renewal ignited his blood like nothing else, but this time it felt different. Wrong, somehow. Like the lies festering inside him would corrupt the cycle of life and the things bursting from the ground would be half dead, twisted, and misshapen.

He shook himself. He couldn't think like that. Not now, not ever. Not if they wanted to win. He'd made his choice, for better or for worse. He would keep Erikkson's dirty secrets. And Sedition would fight the war she'd been built for, none the wiser to her creator's schemes.

He turned away. He needed a book to occupy his thoughts for a while. Perhaps that new one on botanical poisons had finally arrived from London.

"Seraphim?" Her warm voice, breathless but euphoric, interrupted his exit. Sedition jogged up to him, red-faced from her session with Erikkson. He turned toward her, schooling his features.

Not now, not now! Not when he'd just been thinking about the one thing he *couldn't* say to her. He excelled at keeping secrets, but Sedition had a way of worming knowledge out of him. Then again, this girl wasn't the one he'd known before. She was older, yes, but she seemed more rounded, too. More whole. She was no longer strictly Erikkson's perfect weapon; she was Taryn. In spite of what she'd endured, he thought perhaps what she'd been through *had* been for the best. Had shaped her into someone who understood the fullness of her purpose, beyond being built to *kill*. Whether that was because of her time away from Elmhurst or merely her time separated from Petrichor, he wasn't certain. "Yes?" he replied, voice cool and even. Composed. He kept walking. She matched his pace.

"I have seen you spar with the twins and Emmett over the past week. I would like you to teach me." She pushed her hands through her hair as she said it, nonchalant and eager. She made it feel like a suggestion, but he saw it for what it was: an order.

He ducked his head, clockwork wings rustling. "Of course, my lady Sedition."

Her expression soured, the oft-repeated words jumping to her lips. "Please, call me Taryn."

She'd asked him the same a handful of times, and each time he gently rejected her. She deserved an explanation, he supposed. "If you do not mind, I will continue to call you Sedition. You are our leader, and you deserve our respect. I fear that if I do not show you the proper deference, your soldiers will take the lead from me and disrespect you as well."

A smirk broke across her face. "I do not think they need any encouragement."

He stopped, now that she'd made it clear that she was not going to let him walk away. "They attacked you." He'd heard about it from the twins—Rorin concerned, Ari furious but cowed—and then again, later, from Erikkson. He'd seen training sessions go wrong before. Throw that many traumatized biomatons together with weapons and things were bound to get out of hand on occasion. And who could blame them? They were angry young men and women. They'd all faced more than anyone should, let alone someone their age. And she'd held her own well enough, though the sight of the bruises across her freckled cheek made his blood run cold. She was their leader, yes, but she was also his younger sister—

She narrowed her eyes. "I suppose you could call it that."

He cursed himself. He'd never been prone to get lost in his own thoughts like this before. But with Sedition returned and memories of their younger years around every corner... "I apologize for my lapse. You handled it soundly this morning. I was impressed with your speech."

"If only words could get me so far in battle." She chuckled, shaking her head. Emmett was right. That was a laugh a man could bottle and get drunk on. "Well, what can you teach me? You are formidable with those wings, but I am afraid that may not help me much."

"Poisons," he said quickly.

"Poisons?"

"And the quarterstaff, of course."

"Ah. Between you and Master Erikkson I shall be quite deadly with a big stick, should that ever be necessary."

This time Seraphim's lips quirked. He quickly turned away so she would not see. "Come. Let me give you a primer."

"You are going to give me a lesson now?" she asked, hurrying to keep up with his long strides. That was familiar, too. He'd always had the advantage of height on her. And he could not help the smile that teased his lips when he recalled her tiny form, barely seven years old and already dogging him through the halls like a shadow. *Teina. Little sister.* Again, he drove the thoughts from his mind. It had been a long time since he'd referred to her in his native tongue. And if she knew what he was hiding, she would be furious.

"No," he said, passing into Elmhurst's extensive library. "I am going to give you a book."

"A book?"

This time he really did smile. He took the narrow green book from its place on the shelf, brushing dust from its cover reverently before handing it to her. "*The Language of Poisons,*" he said, reciting the title from memory. "It was my first introduction. Now it will be yours. I will expect you to have read it before our first session."

She looked up from the title page incredulously. Her copper hair was quickly coming loose from its braid, stray strands dancing around her face. "When am I supposed to find time to bloody *read*, Seraphim? Master Erikkson has me working from sunup to sundown!"

"Then I suppose you will have to read while it is dark," he replied. He turned his attention back to the shelves. "I have no doubt you will manage."

Her footsteps moved toward the door, and then stopped, hesitating. He held his breath, waiting for her to cross the threshold, to leave him in peace.

"Seraphim?"

"Yes?"

"May I ask you something?"

He sighed, the held breath leaving his lungs in an attempt to slow the pounding of his heart. "Of course."

"What happened to Petrichor?"

Her name stopped his heart. He paused, fingers lingering on the spine of the book he'd been about to pull off the shelf. He turned toward her. She clutched the little tome he'd given her to her chest, looking younger than she had any right to. Guilt welled in his throat. She didn't remember. Of course she didn't. "She left."

"Yes, I know that, but why? No one will tell me more than a few words."

He bit the inside of his lip. "Petrichor was...volatile." He chose his words carefully, each one a potential grenade to her constructed worldview with Erikkson at its center. She had to continue to believe she was the hero of their story. A fresh start would do her no good if it was spoiled by tales of the past. "She and Master Erikkson endlessly quarreled from the very beginning. It all came to a head after he lost you. She left." He shook his head. "That is what happened."

She narrowed her eyes and studied him closely with her sharp emerald gaze. He half expected her to press for more, but then her lips twisted and she sighed. "I see I shall not be getting a straight answer from you either. Very well. I shall figure it out myself." She rounded on her heel and left the room.

Seraphim bowed his head, thinking of Petrichor, thinking of the days leading up to the loss of not one but both of Erikkson's best weapons. His family. His sisters. Tears welled in his eyes and he blinked them away, cursing himself for his soft heart. Things would end in bloodshed. They always did. He just hoped that this time, it was the kind of bloodshed that resulted in change.

CHAPTER FOURTEEN

No one challenged her authority after that. Soldiers stood to attention as she passed, saluting or nodding deferentially. Even Officer Belchick respected Taryn during training, singling her out as a good example rather than a failure, though Taryn suspected that had more to do with Erikkson than her own speech. Taryn's muscles began to acclimate, her body hardening into sinewy curves. Her bruises were less frequent; more often, *she* bruised her opponents.

Her days were full from the moment she awoke to the moment she fell asleep. She spent the morning with her training regiment, though she was quickly surpassing her fellow recruits as her technique improved. Her former training *was* kicking in; though she still did not remember it, she could feel the effects of it, like an invisible breeze moving through her. In the afternoons, she trained with Erikkson, Seraphim, or Emmett. Seraphim surpassed even Erikkson's skills with the quarterstaff, and he had an encyclopedic understanding of battle strategy and poisons, which he imparted to Taryn as they sparred. She worked with Erikkson on a fighting style that would utilize her shoulder blades to her advantage. Emmett taught her to fence with the sabre and the foil.

She not only trained her body, but her mind as well. She practiced becoming Sedition before the mirror and before her troops, and the more she practiced, the easier it became. She read the great theorists: Augustine, Sun Tzu, Machiavelli, Clausewitz, and Jomini. She studied human anatomy, learning not only how to kill, but how best to stop a man in his tracks, how to incapacitate without killing, and how to inflict physical and psychological pain in order to extract information. Much of it seemed superfluous, but Taryn filed away every scrap of information, aware any piece of it might be the one thing to save her life—or all biomatons—in the future.

Two weeks passed, then three, and at last Erikkson called a private meeting in his study between Taryn and Seraphim. "You have both been working very hard," Erikkson said without preamble, directing the two biomatons to sit in the chairs placed in front of his desk. Royal stood off to one side, his face a serious mask. Erikkson seated himself behind the desk, facing Taryn and Seraphim. "That is why I believe it is time you began to run missions for me. It is time to put your training to the test."

Taryn leaned forward. "Are you saying you want to begin this rebellion in earnest?"

"Not quite. Seraphim remembers our previous tactics for taking the biomatons from those with reputations for being cruel," Erikkson trailed off and Seraphim nodded. "Think of yourself as a modern-day Robin Hood. But rather than stealing gold, you are stealing human beings."

"Biomatons," Royal corrected from his place near the window. "Please do not steal any human servants. We want to keep our operations here as covert as possible."

Taryn frowned. "Am I to understand you want us to trespass on someone's property, free any biomatons we find, and bring them back undetected?"

"Yes, except for the undetected bit," Erikkson replied, steepling his fingers thoughtfully.

"What?"

"Our enhancements have more uses than just as weapons," Seraphim answered, baring his sharp silver fangs in an unsettling, predatory smile. Taryn's stomach flipped. She swallowed hard.

"Your first target is a man notorious for working his biomatons to death," Erikkson intoned, spreading out a map of the nearby countryside and pointing to an estate about thirty miles from Elmhurst. "Threaten him. Do whatever you can to make him understand what he has done is wrong."

More of his reasoning for their strange prosthetics was coming into focus. Taryn stared at him. "You built us with this in mind. You *want* us to terrify people."

"I want you to win this war."

Taryn glanced at Royal, who was watching her closely. "And what about when we do? Will you then give us new prosthetics that allow us to live normal lives? Or are we to take up occupations fitting to our prosthetics as Petrichor did? I am sure Seraphim and I will make excellent assassins with all your training."

"You agreed to this!"

"Yes, well, you did not give me all the details," Taryn growled. She couldn't explain the pit in her stomach—she *liked* becoming Sedition, but this was somehow different. This was allowing herself to be seen as something monstrous. Didn't they want to be seen as human, like everyone else?

"The man's name is Albert Potter," Royal interrupted. "He quite literally works his biomatons to death. You would understand if you saw it, Tiger. Those poor children."

She perked up. "Did you say Albert *Potter*?"

"Yes." Royal frowned, puzzled.

"He is about six feet tall, thickly built, with dark hair and eyes?" she questioned, almost urgently.

"Yes. How did you know that?"

"He attempted to purchase me." She leaned back, crossing her arms. A pleased expression came into her eyes. "Very well. I am in. How do we do it?"

Taryn pressed a finger to her lips as Seraphim alighted on the roof beside her. She hardly needed to bother, as his tread was as light as a cat's and nearly as silent. She waved over her head to the small air yacht that had dropped them there. Piloted by Royal and propelled with clockwork and steam rather than a traditional combustion engine, it glided through the night with little noise in its wake. Royal would circle the house until they emerged with the biomatons—or it became clear they had been captured. Taryn pulled a black mask over her nose and mouth, so only her eyes showed, bright green and full of venom in the moonlight. She was wearing a new costume from Gennifer, all black with metal buckles, fierce while at the same time disguising her identity. At Gennifer's insistence, Taryn's hair was bound up into a series of elaborate Viking-style braids, the ends cascading into a wave of curls. The effect had left Royal speechless.

Seraphim wore a similar all-black costume, his long black locks tied back from his face. The dark fabric seemed to emphasize the copper and steel glint of his wings and the deep mahogany of his skin. He grinned at her, his silver fangs flashing in the moonlight.

Together, they crept over the tiled roof, moving toward a tower with a window large enough to enter. Fresh midnight dew coated the tiles. Many were loose, clattering as the biomatons put weight on them, but they moved slowly and carefully, relying on one another. Taryn's heart thundered in her ears, and her palms grew slick with sweat, but it wasn't from terror; it was from exhilaration. The night breeze had a distinct chill that sliced through their clothes like butter, and yet neither of them shivered. Their bodies, taut with excitement and kinetic energy, kept them warm from the inside.

Taryn reached the window and drew a razor-thin throwing knife from her clockwork arm. She slipped it into the frame, feeling the tip catch the window latch. A flick of her wrist, and the latch opened, leaving the window to swing freely. Taryn lifted herself over the windowsill and into the room—a dark, wood-paneled study. Seraphim entered after her.

She examined her surroundings, noting the expensive rug and the spotless layout of the room. Not a single sheet of paper was out of place. Taryn crept to the door of the study, pressing her ear against it. Silence reigned through the manor. After she was certain she could not hear anyone moving about, she pressed the door open, moving agonizingly slowly to keep any noise from travelling.

Seraphim followed her closely, his wings folded tightly to keep from striking on something in the dark or dragging on the floor. There would be time enough to leave their mark on this house after they found Potter and ensured he could do nothing to stop them.

The narrow hall outside the study led to a flight of spiraling steps. Taryn dragged the fingertips of her right hand along the inner wall, maintaining her balance by touch as she descended the stairs. She emerged on an upper floor landing and paused, listening. Up ahead, she could hear footsteps from an adjoining corridor. Taryn hesitated, waiting to see if the footsteps would fade.

Instead, they grew louder.

A glow appeared a few doors down, and before long, a man

emerged, carrying a candle, his eyes half-closed with sleep. Taryn recognized him at once. Silently, she gave Seraphim the signal they had determined to mean "that is him." He clicked his wings in anticipation.

Potter did not see them, and turned his back, moving away from where they stood. Taryn leapt swiftly but silently forward, snatching up a heavy iron candlestick as she rushed toward the man who had attempted to purchase her only weeks before.

He heard her when she was just steps away and spun, his mouth forming an 'o' of surprise. Taryn slammed the candlestick against his temple as hard as she could, putting all her momentum into the swing. Potter's eyes widened, and then he crumpled, unconscious. Taryn caught the candle from him as he fell, the flame flickering but remaining lit.

Seraphim stepped up behind her. "That was efficiently done," he murmured.

"No need to waste time waking the rest of the household," she shot back, her voice as soft as it could be without whispering. "Let us get him up into the study before he wakes. That room should be remote enough to muffle any sounds." She pointed to the gold band Potter wore on his left hand. "Let us hope his wife is a deep sleeper. I do not want to frighten her unless we must."

CHAPTER FIFTEEN

"Do wake up already."

A splash of cold water jerked him back to reality. Potter blinked his eyes open, raising his head slowly. His dark eyes made quick work of his predicament: the open window; the skillful sailor's knots tying his arms, legs, and chest to the chair he was placed in; the two shadowy figures in front of him, illuminated from behind by the moonlight. Their silhouettes were *wrong*, somehow, though he could not say why. His head throbbed. He attempted to speak, only to discover a gag in his mouth, preventing him from pronouncing a word. He glowered at the figures.

"So, you join us at last," the figure on the right said. She—it *was* a she, he was sure of it, though her voice was muffled and low. "It is kind of you to grace us with your presence, Mr. Potter. We were beginning to think you would never come 'round." She turned her head toward the second figure, and he caught a glimpse of her face in the moonlight, half hidden by a black fabric mask. There was *definitely* something wrong with these two. He thought he caught a glimpse of metal behind her. He had to be mistaken.

She cocked her head, clicking her tongue. "I know you must have questions. But before we can remove that gag, we have to be sure you will not scream and wake your dear wife. We would not want her involved in all this unpleasantness, would we?"

There came a sound in the dark of metal against metal, slow and deliberate, so Potter could practically picture the singing blade. He shook his head vigorously. Blood thundered in his ears.

"Good. I believe we understand one another."

The second figure came forward and released the gag, leaving it to hang around Potter's neck.

"Who—who are you? What do you want?" the man spluttered as soon as he could speak. The corners of his mouth were sore, and he tasted blood.

"You may call me Sedition," the girl answered. "And this is my brother, Seraphim." She turned to the figure beside her. "Would you be so kind as to provide Mr. Potter a little illumination? It seems he cannot see as well in the dark as we can."

A match flared, momentarily blinding Potter. His mouth fell open. The two standing in front of him were *biomatons,* but the strangest biomatons he had ever seen. The girl had a heavy, armored prosthetic arm, and fierce green eyes above her black mask. Freckles scattered across her pale forehead, freckles nearly the same color as her messy copper hair. There were blades rising from her shoulders, as though they grew from her back. Her brother was even stranger. He had dark skin and long, wavy black hair. As Potter stared at him, the biomaton spread massive metal wings, which reflected the candlelight in strange, fiery flashes. He grinned, revealing silver fangs like some sort of half-beast. Potter twisted his wrists in his restraints, struggling against his bonds in vain. Sweat rolled down the back of his neck, despite the chill coming in the open window.

"We heard recently that you are not very kind to the biomatons in your household," Sedition said. "Seraphim and I cannot allow that to go on."

Potter shook his head. "How *dare* you trespass on my land! What I do with my property is my own business, not some biomaton *freak's!*"

The point of Sedition's dagger slammed into the wooden arm of his chair, a hair's breadth from his fingers. Potter gulped.

"I do not think you quite understand your predicament, Mr. Potter. If you say your house was broken into by two biomatons, who is going to believe you? We are just machines, after all," she hissed, leaning over him. "And yet, here we are."

He spat at her, forcing her to move back. "I am not afraid of you. You *shall* be caught, and when you are, you shall be reprogrammed!"

Even through the mask, he could tell she was smiling. "Shall we make an example of you, Mr. Potter?"

He glanced from her to Seraphim and back again, lost. "What?"

"All of your biomatons are now ours. I am sure you keep the paperwork for your purchases somewhere in here, hm?"

Before he could stop himself, Potter's eyes flicked to the file cabinet in the corner near the window.

"Thank you," Sedition said, tilting her head up. "I thought we might have to drag it out of you."

She pulled her knife from the arm of the chair, leaning against the wall as Seraphim rifled through the cabinet until he found what he wanted: the papers documenting the purchase of each of Potter's biomatons. When he returned, Sedition's knife had disappeared, though Potter could not say where. She took the papers from Seraphim, flipping through them. Her eyes lit up with malice. "You own quite a few biomatons, Mr. Potter."

"They are not all in my possession," he answered, eyes wide. "There are only twelve currently in my household."

She cocked her head at him, holding the papers in her clockwork hand. "No, there are none in your possession." With those words, she held the corner of the sheaf of papers over the candle's flame.

"No!" Potter cried in horror. The documents caught with a burst of light, filling the air with the acrid scent of burning ink. Sedition held the sheaf up, allowing it to burn down around her metal fingers without flinching. Delicate black ashes drifted to the floor, crumbling to dust on the carpet.

"If you mistreat your biomatons in the future, Mr. Potter, rest assured I shall know. And I shall *not* be so kind next time," Sedition said as she brushed the ash away from her palm with indifference.

"The police shall hear of this," Potter exclaimed furiously, leaning as far forward as he could against his bonds. "You shall not get away with this!"

"Please, tell as many people as you like," Sedition answered. "And tell them this: The biomatons are *not* machines to be used. We are human, and we are rising."

With that, she passed him by. Seraphim followed her, and Potter turned his head to watch them head for the door. "Wait! Release me!"

He received no response. The biomatons left him alone, tied to a chair in his study.

THE CHILL AIR SWEPT TARYN'S HAIR BACK FROM HER FACE, but she leaned into it, electrified by the feeling of flying. She clenched and unclenched her left hand, swearing loudly.

"Is something wrong?" Seraphim questioned.

"No. I should not have held those papers as they burned. I know my hand is uninjured, but my brain does not." She gave him a wry smile. "I sometimes still have a sense of feeling in my arm, though I know that is impossible." She shrugged. "Right now, it is telling me I burned my fingers."

Royal stood at the ship's wheel, wearing an old pair of Erikkson's aviator goggles to protect his eyes from the sharp wind. "You held his documents as they burned?" He laughed with incredulity.

Taryn crossed her arms. "If you are not impressed, you may scare the next target on your own."

Royal shook his head, a lopsided grin gracing his face. He turned the ship's wheel, angling the yacht toward Elmhurst. They were still about fifteen miles out, and Taryn glanced back to the stern of the ship, where their new charges huddled: twelve of the poorest looking biomatons she had ever seen. They were dressed in rags, barely more than skin and bones, clutching one another for comfort.

"They need a doctor, not a general," she hissed, leaning closer to Seraphim. "Not one shall make a decent soldier. Why, I believe I could break them as soon as look at them."

"They do not look like much," Seraphim agreed. "But remember you and I did not look like much when Master Erikkson discovered us. It is not hopeless. Give them a few hot meals and a little time to recuperate, and you may be surprised by what is uncovered."

Taryn looked over her shoulder, studying the poor, cowering biomatons who shied away and hid their faces when they saw her looking. "Perhaps you are right. Still, we are going to need true soldiers if we are to ever move beyond guerilla warfare."

Seraphim gave her a strange look. "That is something you shall need to take up with Lord Erikkson."

CHAPTER SIXTEEN

Taryn was allowed to sleep late the next morning because of her nighttime escapade, which meant she missed the early morning training she normally performed with her regiment. Rather than attempt to interrupt their routine halfway through, Taryn rose and ran the track around the manor by herself, enjoying the warmth of the morning sun upon her face as it peeked through the storm clouds building on the horizon. They would be in the midst of a major storm by nightfall, of that she was certain. Still, the sun was breaking through at the moment and she savored it.

After her run, Taryn had worked up quite an appetite and ran into the house, hoping she had not arrived too late. She found the dining room unoccupied, and though the table had been picked over, it was not entirely bare. She chose a pair of hard-boiled eggs, a small sweet bun, and a glass of orange juice. She settled herself at the table, pulling a copy of Paine's *Rights of Man* from her pocket. It wasn't a long book, but it was dense, and she was struggling to work her way through it.

"*Bonjour, belle,*" Emmett's voice came from the doorway, interrupting her reading just moments after she began.

Taryn raised her eyes, setting the book aside. "*Bonjour,* Emmett."

"You are not usually here so late for *le petit déjeuner,*" he remarked, strolling over to snatch up the last of the French pastries Ambrose prepared fresh each morning.

"I was out late last night," she replied, sipping her juice. "I made up for it with a late start this morning."

Emmett nodded, his clockwork irises twisting as he focused on her. "Seraphim told me what you did. I remember *Monsieur* Potter from before. I am glad you did not allow him to get away with his cruelties."

She nodded, turning her eyes away. "As am I."

"I should like to be with you when next you go."

Her gaze snapped back to him. "You would?"

"*Oui.* I was a pirate, remember? I can help."

"You were a privateer," she corrected.

"You may be surprised how similar it is. One is sanctioned by the Queen. Both employ methods outside the law."

Taryn smiled wryly. "You are welcome to come along the next time we go out."

"*Merci, belle!*"

Taryn thought perhaps he was too eager, but she knew if anyone had any right to desire revenge on those who abused the biomatons, it was Emmett. She still did not know what had happened to him at the Black Castle and probably never would. Emmett refused to say a word about it.

He snatched up a slice of orange and sucked on it, waiting for her to say something. A question hung on her lips—a request she'd been considering for weeks but hadn't found the right words for. She could ask him now... But what if he said no? She shook herself, changing the subject. "Have you seen Master Erikkson this morning?"

"He left early for London. There is some kind of auction he said he is attending."

Taryn grimaced at the word. "I know it is better for those he brings back, but I cannot bear the thought of such events. They represent the very worst of humanity."

"*Oui,* but is it not better that men like *Monsieur* Erikkson exist to help those too victimized to help themselves?"

Taryn frowned. "There is no one in the world like Master Erikkson. He is unique." She sighed. "But yes, you are right. It is good that he exists, and that he cares so much about the injustices we face. Still, I will be much happier when the biomatons can fight for themselves. It is our fight, after all."

Emmett watched her thoughtfully for a few moments, eyeing her with those strange golden irises. "Since *Monsieur* Erikkson is not here today, shall we spend some extra time sparring? Your sabre skills are getting better, but you need more practice."

"Is that a challenge?" She rose, a fire igniting behind her eyes, eager to prove her worth against his skill.

Emmett grinned. "I shall meet you in the training room in five minutes."

Taryn nodded her assent. He turned to go, but on impulse, she called his name. He looked at her over his shoulder expectantly. She clutched her book to her chest, taking a moment to steady her breathing. She was a leader now, a warrior, and still the question weighed down her tongue. "Emmett, will you be my advisor? You are the only one of us who still possesses the ability to love, which means you feel pity and compassion on a level I cannot fathom. Will you use that ability to advise me? Will you keep me from going too far?"

His eyebrows drew together in the center of his forehead, his eyes shining with pity. For half a moment, she was afraid he would not answer. And then his gentle, familiar voice trundled across the dining room floor. "*Oui.* I am honored to be your heart, *belle.*"

She smiled at him. "Five minutes. Then I shall prove that I am the superior swordsman!"

He laughed. *"On va voir."*

***

"TOUCHÉ!" EMMETT CROWED, SLAPPING TARYN'S shoulder with the flat of his blade. Mumbling a curse, she abandoned her fencing position. She rolled her shoulders, stretching the kinks from her neck. They'd been fencing for well over two hours now, and she'd scored nearly as many touches on him as he had on her. Still, she was beginning to tire of his gloating exclamations every time he won.

"You are not tired already, *chérie?*"

"Five minutes, Emmett. Then I will be good to go again." She slung her training rapier into the rack on the stone wall, then settled herself on one of the wooden benches set around the wide training room. Regulating her breathing, she let her eyes wander until they caught on the bloodstain that still spattered the floor where she'd fought with Rylan. Taryn tore her eyes away.

Emmett came and sat beside her, smiling. He had his sleeves rolled up above his elbows, leaving his strong forearms bare. The red welts from their time in the Black Castle had long since faded, and if he still had scars, they were too pale to notice in the lamplight. He leaned his head against her shoulder.

"Emmett—" Taryn muttered, feeling something like the violence in her chest rise a little at the touch. They'd kept themselves apart since the Black Castle. Neither had spoken about how near they'd grown in that place, and Taryn wasn't certain she could bear getting into it with him now. Emmett was a dear friend. But what would she do if he wanted more and she could not give it to him? She'd always handled Royal's friends by keeping them at arm's length, and whether it was because of what they'd been through or simply his charm, Emmett had slipped right past her barriers.

"I am only teasing, *chérie*," he reassured, as if sensing her discomfort. He sat up, nudging her shoulder with his own. "I know you have a warrior's reputation to uphold, but this is me saying *je t'aime*."

Her mouth had gone dry. "You know I cannot—"

"You misunderstand, *belle! Aimer* is also *to like*. I *like* you, Taryn Roft, *Mademoiselle* Sedition of Erikkson. Regardless of what you are able to reciprocate. I like you. And you must forgive me if I sometimes express my affections in little touches."

She could not help the smile that crossed her lips. Hesitantly, she reached out and laid her hand atop his. It was not a romantic touch—her heart did no backflips and her body temperature remained stubbornly even—but it was a comforting touch. Like the way he'd held her in the Black Castle. "What did I do to deserve a friend like you, Emmett?" she murmured.

"Nothing at all." He leaned over and kissed her cheek. "Friendship is not something any of us deserves or earns. It is a gift given freely."

"Thank you for agreeing to be my heart," she murmured. "Sometimes I think... Sometimes I think this violence in my head is more than I can control on my own."

"Is that something *Monsieur* Erikkson put inside of you, or something the Black Castle did to you?" he asked gently.

"It is something the Black Castle did. Something Master Erikkson tried to keep at bay. But I think it is something that has been inside me all along."

"I know you, *belle*. You will master this. You are no killer."

But that is what I fear. Perhaps I am a killer, and I have been fooling everyone all this time. She couldn't find the words and ducked her head. "Thank you, Emmett." She rose, dusting off her palms. "Well, are you ready? Shall we go again?"

His smile was bright and immediate. "*Allez-vous.*"

SHE'D MANAGED TO PUT HER CONCERNS ABOUT HER emotional capabilities behind her by evening, taking sundown's signal to cease her physical training and retreat to a warm seat where she could focus on training her mind. But she'd barely gotten comfortable before Emmett burst into the first-floor parlor where Taryn was curled in an armchair, reading *The Rights of Man.* His face was pale, drained of blood, and from the way he was breathing, she guessed he had run a good distance to find her.

"*Monsieur* Erikkson has brought—" he stopped, panting, appearing to reconsider his words. "He has brought a biomaton you will want to meet."

"Why?" she asked, setting her book down. Something had clearly rattled Emmett, and it was unlike him to remain so cryptic.

"Trust me. He is on his way." Emmett paused, fidgeting, glancing over his shoulder toward the door. "Do you have your weapons with you?"

She nodded, tapping her prosthetic.

"And your pistol?"

She frowned and pointed to the mantle where she'd set the weapon; she had removed it from her belt because it was uncomfortable to sit with. Emmett had insisted she wear it after they trained that afternoon, telling her she needed to learn long-range weaponry as well as close. The trouble was, she couldn't hit a target with it. "What is going on?"

Emmett shook his head. "Remember what you asked of me this morning?"

Taryn frowned. "Of course I remember."

"I am advising you now. Do not be rash, *chérie*. Be compassionate."

"Who *is* this biomaton?" she questioned, turning on him.

Emmett's eyes widened, revealing the curve of the glass orbs that had replaced his eyes, but he shook his head. "I cannot tell you."

Taryn scowled. *Who* could Emmett be so afraid of? What would she want to do to this biomaton if she knew who they were? She could not puzzle the pieces together. She was missing something vital. "Leave me," she growled.

"But *chérie*..."

"Your words have been heard, Emmett. Now leave me. I must face whatever this is alone."

Emmett moved toward the door and hesitated, looking back at her. "Remember who you are, *belle*," he muttered before he was gone

Taryn threw herself back into the armchair as he left, taking his words to heart. *I am Sedition,* she mused, draping herself in the chair in a pose of perfect assurance and mastery. *I have been granted authority by Erikkson. This is my home. Whoever this biomaton is, they cannot faze me in my own home.*

A knock came at the door. Taryn forced her voice into a quiet nonchalance she did not feel. "Come in."

The door opened. Taryn's heart pounded in her palm where it rested against the arm of the chair. Erikkson entered, a smile across his face that made Taryn's temples burn and stomach turn to lead. This was some kind of conspiracy against her!

"I have brought the newest member of our family to meet you."

A young man stepped into the room, his eyes downcast. He wore simple clothes in dark grey, his shirt was without sleeves to show off the strength in his shoulders. His right arm was made of robust clockwork. His black hair swept back from his forehead, slowly coming out of the careful way it had been styled. Taryn recognized him at once. She leapt to her feet, unable to contain the violent anger his face ignited in her chest. "How dare you come here!"

"Sedition, please. The boy has been through much in the last few weeks," Erikkson said in pacifying tones. His brow furrowed in pity.

The young man raised his eyes, and horror washed over Taryn in hot waves. Gone was the confidence he'd possessed. In its place was a sort of empty, stupid obedience borne from pain. Her throat ached. How could this have happened?

"Ace?" she questioned hoarsely. When he simply stared at the floor blankly, she repeated his name. "Ace? Do you remember me?"

He looked at her at last, his ice-blue eyes dulled by fear, devoid of feeling. "No, miss. I do not know you."

"You cannot do this to me, you bloody coward!" she screamed, losing control momentarily of the monster that lived inside her chest. "How dare you say you do not know me!" Her hands twisted into white-knuckled fists. She knew she was acting irrationally—could see in his eyes that his mind had been wiped—but the anger overpowered everything, heating her hands with the urge to finally take the revenge she could not take on him before.

Ace, though he could hardly be recognized by that name, flinched, backing away a step before Erikkson could catch him by the shoulders and hold him in place. "Sedition," Erikkson warned sternly. "Do not frighten our guest. He may remember, in time. For now, we must be patient with him."

Taryn paused, focusing on her breathing until the violence within herself receded. She flicked her eyes over Ace's submissive, hunched form. There were new scars on his left hand, new lines on his face. He was clean, but she guessed that had more to do with the auction than the conditions he had been kept in at the Black Castle. He shifted, and she caught a glimpse of a small black number carved into his left forearm: 745. She could not help but notice the corded muscle in that arm, too, sailor's muscle similar to Emmett's. She had to get him alone. Perhaps the real Ace was in there somewhere. "How did this happen?" she asked.

"Though I cannot be certain, I believe he was detained by Lord Bellham after I took you from the Black Castle. They must have wiped his mind after they changed him." Erikkson shook his head. "A clever tactic, if what Seraphim has told me of his skills is true. No doubt he could have broken free without the memory wipe and the dampers."

Taryn had forgotten Erikkson even knew who Ace was. But of *course* he knew. He *had* bragged of keeping a close eye on her all through the time they had been apart.

"And you have removed those dampers now, I hope?" she asked.

"Of course, little one. The circuits added to his mind are as near to normal as I can make them. His memory may be slow to return. I do not know how thorough they were."

"Let us hope they were not as thorough as you," she snapped, but the words were borne more of her own violent tendencies than any anger she still harbored for him. "Are you hungry, Ace?" she questioned, turning her attention once more on the new biomaton.

His uncanny, empty blue eyes met hers. "Is Ace my name?" he questioned in a soft voice, so familiar and yet so changed. Taryn's stomach clenched.

"Of course it is your name."

"Yes," he answered, turning his eyes to his bare feet once more. "Yes, I am hungry."

"Will you please get our guest something hot to eat?" Taryn asked, placing the full power and authority Erikkson had vested in her behind her voice. Even he could not argue when she used such a tone.

"Will you be all right?" Erikkson asked, placing a hand on Ace's shoulder. The boy nodded, and Erikkson seemed satisfied. He took his leave, shooting a final, significant look at Taryn. She ignored him. She slumped again into her armchair, kicking her legs over the arm to emphasize her invulnerability. At last, it was her turn to be the confident showman, the one holding all the cards.

"I do not like cowardice in my soldiers," she said, looking away from him, making a show of studying her nails.

"I am not a coward," he replied coldly.

"And yet when I raised my voice, you cowered like a dog that has been kicked too many times." Taryn allowed a smirk to cross her face, but she did not look at him. "I think it is *I* who shall decide whether you are a coward."

He glanced toward the mantle, where her pistol still lay. Catching her eye, he ducked his head again. Taryn's chest tightened. The man she'd known before had been unafraid of eye contact, possessing the kind of gaze that tore straight through her. Now, he could not even look in her direction. "Yes, miss."

"Tell me, Ace, do you have any special abilities?"

"I am strong. My grafts make me strong." The words sounded rehearsed, like something he had recited to himself in an effort to justify his grafts. Taryn thought it might even be something Lord Bellham or the handlers had told him at the Black Castle.

"Strength is nothing special," she muttered, allowing her authority and confidence to ooze from her words. "Many of my army can claim strength."

His ice blue eyes flickered from her to the mantle and back. "May I ask you a question?" She nodded her assent, just once. He continued. "Master Erikkson purchased me from Master Bellham, yet you command even him and he listens. How can a biomaton have that kind of authority?" He looked at her with a kind of eagerness that reminded her of a child, eyes wide and searching for answers.

A small smile crossed her lips. "That is the power of equality. That is the power I offer to every biomaton."

"Who are you?"

"I am Sedition, leader of the biomaton uprising."

A flash of something akin to recognition blinked behind his eyes, there for the briefest of moments and then gone. At last, she was getting somewhere. "Can you help me?"

She frowned, cocking her head to one side. "What is it you need?"

"I am looking for a biomaton with red hair like yours. Her number is 743."

Electricity raced down her spine at the mention of her old identification number, and she glanced down at her arm to reassure herself the black numbers had vanished from her skin. She noted Ace was touching his own forearm, and as his metal fingers moved, she caught another glimpse of his own tattooed numbers. She took a deep breath, pretending to consider, though in reality she was trying to decide whether or not to admit who she was. He clearly did not remember well enough to recognize her—or she was so changed from the timid girl he had known that he *could not* recognize her. "Ah, yes," she said at last. "I remember now. She came to me a fortnight ago. She requested to join my army but"—she clicked her tongue against her teeth—"she could barely stand, let alone fight."

"Is she here? May I see her?"

"The poor girl was injured and half-starved! I ordered my men to put her out of her misery." Taryn kept a haughty smile on her lips. If the real Ace *was* in there somewhere, this would draw him out.

"You what?" he asked, something dark and horror-filled

coloring the edges of his voice. She glanced at him to discover he had moved several inches closer to the mantle.

"What I did was a mercy. The girl was damaged beyond repair. Her clockwork arm had been crushed."

No flicker of recognition flashed behind his eyes this time. Instead, an icy cold fury was building there, no longer masked by the docile look worn by controlled biomatons. His dampers were wearing off. And so was his fear. "She is dead?"

"As dead as your right arm," she answered coldly.

He snapped. Leaping the final distance, he snatched the revolver off the mantle, leveling it at her with the ease of one who had been doing it his whole life. Taryn's heart leapt into her throat, thundering in her ears, but she leaned further back in her chair, glancing at him beneath her eyelashes. Though her throat constricted, she managed a dry chuckle, disguising her fear as bravado.

"What are you planning to do with that, Ace dear?"

"I am going to settle the score," he growled, his own voice as hoarse and constricted as hers felt. She could *hear* Ace in there somewhere, beneath the biomaton boy who had taken his place. "You took the only person I knew could tell me who I am. So—" he stuttered, his voice wavering. "So, I am going to take something from you."

"What will you take? My life?" She cocked her head, the showmanship painted over her fear so thickly she could barely recall the terror. At last, she'd fully slipped into the persona of Sedition, who feared nothing, least of all her own death. "As noble and romantic as that sounds, Ace, I remain your only chance at freedom. So go ahead." She rose, presenting him with a full, clear target, spreading her arms wide. "Shoot."

He cocked the hammer back. She expected his hands to tremble, but even in the midst of his belief that she had killed his only connection to his past, they remained steady. "She is really dead?" he asked.

"She is really bloody dead," Taryn answered coldly. "And would you like to know what she said as she died? She said, 'I hate him.'"

Bang!

Taryn froze, watching the black barrel of the gun smoke, waiting for the pain to blossom in her chest or gut.

It never did.

Instead, a searing pain shot through her left ear and across the side of her head behind it. Taryn raised hesitant fingers, trembling a little as she explored the round half-moon sliced in the top of her ear. Hot blood trickled down her jaw and neck.

Ace crept closer, his voice husky. "You really want to know my special ability, Sedition? My marksmanship. Whatever I aim for, I hit. That time, I was aiming for your ear. Next time, I shall not be." He cocked the revolver again. This close, the burned gunpowder was acrid enough to make her eyes water, and she could see where the firing mechanism had left black smudges on his hands. She was suddenly reminded of another time he'd held her at gunpoint, a lifetime ago in the halls of Grafton's School of Mechanicks. "Have you ever been shot at point blank range? It is messier than that hole in your ear." He stopped, just steps away from her. She could hear his breathing, a slight rasp on the intake she didn't think had been there before.

Taryn's eyes flickered down to the muzzle of the gun, then back up to Ace's eyes, a hysterical smile twisting the corner of her mouth. "I am listening."

"I want—I *need* to know who I am. You have destroyed the only person who could tell me. But because I prefer anything to slavery, I *will* join your army. But you must agree to something."

Erikkson and Emmett burst into the room, responding to the sound of the gunshot. Erikkson began to speak, but Taryn held up a hand to stop him. Ace, his back to the newcomers, moved nearer, touching the revolver's still-warm muzzle to her chest. Her breath caught in her throat.

"Stay back," she called, her voice strangled. "I am all right."

"Are you ready to listen?" Ace questioned. He pressed the gun into the hollow at the base of her throat, and Taryn choked. She nodded, just once. "You will not order me around. You will allow me to leave this place if I wish. You shall not *kill* any more biomatons, no matter how useless they seem. And you will immediately issue me my own pistol."

"I am not sure you have proven yourself trustworthy enough for—" She gasped, her breathing cut short as he pressed hard on the gun. "Very well. Very well. I agree."

He nodded, releasing the hammer of the pistol and lowering it to his side. Taryn stumbled backward, struggling to maintain the appearance of control; Sedition slipped through her fingers. "Show Master Ace to his quarters, please," she said, issuing the order to Seraphim, the third person who'd arrived in response to the gunshot. "Ensure he receives a room of his own."

He nodded and led Ace from the parlor. The young man showed no signs of recognizing the winged biomaton. Ace kept one hand firmly clasped around the pistol, as if it were a lifeline.

Taryn stumbled to the nearest armchair and fell into it, the last semblances of confidence falling away as her hands shook. Blood ran down her neck, staining the white blouse of her training uniform. Her vision spun as the adrenaline drained away, Sedition retreating into her mind and leaving weak Taryn in her wake.

Emmett dashed over to her, offering her a handkerchief for the bleeding. He tried to take her into his arms, but she shoved him away. His face lost all its color. Erikkson shut the door silently, his movements careful and stiff. Taryn's shoulders tensed. She knew what was coming.

"What were you thinking?" Erikkson yelled, turning on her. Taryn flinched. "You could have been killed! And then where would we be, Sedition? I cannot believe you would risk your life like that."

Taryn dropped her eyes, keeping the handkerchief pressed to her ear and temple with her clockwork hand. She knew what she'd just done had been incredibly stupid, and yet she felt no remorse. "I was helping him, Master Erikkson," she muttered.

"Helping him?" For the first time in her memory, he was really, truly yelling at her. Her entire body felt sick. She couldn't stand the knowledge that she had disappointed him. "How could allowing him to hurt and threaten you help him?"

Taryn's eyes fell to her feet. Erikkson would not understand the answer.

Emmett touched her shoulder, his expression twisting from concern to understanding. "It brought the old Ace out," he replied softly.

"Leave us, LeBeau," Erikkson snapped. "This is between Sedition and me."

Emmett squeezed her arm, nodding to her silently before leaving the room. Taryn lifted the handkerchief from her ear, only to discover the cloth was soaked with blood. The hole in the top of her ear had almost ceased bleeding, but the furrow across her scalp left by the bullet still bled profusely. She grimaced. A fraction's difference in the trajectory of the bullet —the merest tremble of his hand—and she would be dead now.

"I want you to explain to me why you thought that was a good idea." Her creator's voice was hard.

"It was just an idea, sir," she replied, turning the handkerchief in her hands. Her metal fingers were stained red. "I thought perhaps his memory would return if I provoked him. I thought he would remember long before he ever began shooting." A tear slipped from the corner of her eye, puzzling Taryn. What had she to weep for? This situation did not warrant tears.

Still, it was there, hot on her cheek, and she could neither explain it nor take it back.

"And yet there you sit, a bullet hole in your head, and he runs about the manor with the weapon he assaulted you with, free as a bird!"

"He will not hurt anyone," she mumbled.

"He already has! Blast it, Sedition, why do you never think things through? Why must you jump into situations without taking *all* the variables into account?"

Taryn cowered, the young, terrified child she could not remember rising to the surface. "I am sorry, Master—" she choked on her words, but she could not enunciate his name. She was just a reprimanded child in the presence of her commanding father.

He sighed and drew his own handkerchief from his breast pocket, handing it to her. He placed tender fingers beneath her chin, lifting her face to meet his eyes. "No one is your master, little one. And no one ever will be."

"I know what I did was reckless," she said, pressing the new handkerchief to her wound, wincing as the injury protested the pressure. "But I thought—"

"You thought it would help him, I know." He knelt beside her chair, shaking his head. "You make it very difficult to remain angry with you, little one. I love you too much."

She looked away, shame washing over her. "I have done little more than hate him for so long. He took me away from all I knew and left us to die at the hands of men he *knew* were cruel. But...he did come back, in the end, and he came to help. It was just too late." She paused, shaking her head. "And I still hated him." Slowly, she raised her eyes to meet her creator's. "Is that what love prevents? Does it keep the hate from taking over?"

"Not always. As long as there is love, there will also be hatred, and as long as there is joy, there will also be mourning.

But love helps us to see the good in others as well as the bad. Love teaches us to look beyond ourselves."

"Will I ever love again?" The words tumbled from her lips before she could stop them. She instantly wished she could take them back. She feared the answer.

"I hope so, little one," he replied gently. "I hope so."

CHAPTER SEVENTEEN

THEY BANDAGED her ear and scalp as best they could before Taryn headed to bed that night, but the wounds were difficult to bind well, and she found herself tossing and turning, unable to sleep for the burning in the left side of her head. At last, she rose, sick of attempting to sleep to no avail. She wandered the halls in the pale pre-dawn light. She stared in wonder out the windows at the grounds, her mind roaming freely over everything she had experienced over the last two months, from her final weeks at Grafton's School of Mechanicks to her training as Sedition. She had suffered much, but she had gained much as well. She no longer felt the spark of terror and shame each time she caught a glimpse of her metal arm. She could even say she took some pride in what—and who—she was. Her memories had not returned, and at this point she doubted they ever would. Still, she no longer felt as though there was a massive gap in her life. There was much she did not remember, but she was learning to fill in the blanks on her own, day by day.

"You are up early," Royal mumbled, walking up behind her, his eyes half-closed and hair mussed.

She glanced at him. "I could not sleep."

He seemed to really see her then, and his eyes widened, lingering on the bandages wrapped around her head. "What happened?"

A cold expression hid her emotions from his gaze. "I thought everyone in the manor heard the shot last night."

His mouth dropped open. "The shot? But I thought— Gor, Taryn, that was you? You could have been killed!"

Her mouth twisted into an expression that wasn't quite a smile. "But I was not killed. I am all right."

"We ought to get fresh bandages on that," he urged. "You bled through these." He reached hesitantly toward the bandages before pulling his hand back. "Come with me, Tiger. I will help you."

She hesitated a moment, then nodded and went with him, allowing him to lead her to Erikkson's study. "Please, take a seat," Royal said as he turned the gas lights up, the hiss of the flame a comforting sound. Taryn settled herself on a couch against one wall as Royal made his way over to the wall covered in drawers. "Let me see," he muttered, digging through them in no particular order. "I know Tony keeps medical supplies in here somewhere."

"Third to the right, eight drawers up," Taryn offered, remembering from the night before.

"Thank you," he replied, finding the correct drawer, and pulling out bandages, gauze, and a strong, clear alcohol for cleaning wounds. He brought them all over, sitting beside her. "Now, let me take a look at that wound."

Taryn held still as Royal removed her bandages, doing her best not to show how much the injury ached. Royal hissed through his teeth as he revealed the wounds.

"Oh, Tar. Does it hurt much?"

"Yes," she admitted honestly. "He took a piece out of my ear. Of course it hurts."

"He? Who did this to you?"

"Does it matter?" she snapped. "It is done."

"Taryn." He grabbed her shoulder, his voice taking on a gravity she had not heard in a long time. "Who hurt you?"

Taryn paused, staring down at her hands. "Ace."

"The man who took you from Grafton's? He was here?"

"He *is* here," she corrected. "He has been turned into a biomaton."

"What?"

"As far as we know, he was captured by Lord Bellham after he came back for me. He has lost his memories. He is so changed, Roy. I thought I could draw him out, but I am afraid it backfired." She chuckled a little, a bare scoff at the back of her throat. "Rather literally, I suppose."

Royal smoothed her hair away from the wound, trying to be as gentle as he could around the edges, where her skin was fiery-red and swollen. Blood and hair were matted into the wound, making it difficult to see just how bad it was. "I do not care how tragic his story is. He ought to be drawn and quartered for what he did to you."

A smile quirked the corner of Taryn's mouth. He sounded like Storm. "I appreciate your concern, Royal, but we do not perform capital punishment here. There is enough of that inflicted on my kind by the world without us also inflicting it upon one another. Ace was frightened and angry. Besides, I provoked him. You might even say I put him up to it."

Royal frowned, preparing a strip of cotton gauze by soaking it in alcohol. "This is going to sting, Tiger. It is difficult to even see your wound with all this dried blood, and I must clean it up so we can really know what we are dealing with. But I warn you: it is going to hurt."

Taryn clenched her fists on her knees. "I understand. Do what you must."

He nodded and pressed the cloth to her injury as gently as he could. Taryn squeezed her eyes shut, face white, a low moan rising in her throat. Royal winced in sympathy as he worked. Though he knew he had to clean her wound for her own sake, it still seemed wrong, so wrong, to be hurting her. She was his best friend. The mere thought of inflicting pain upon her chilled him to his core.

At last, he had cleaned the wound as best he could. He set aside the gauze, now dark with dried blood, and studied the wound carefully. The nick on the arch of her ear would heal well, he thought, in spite of the sheer amount of damage caused. The bleeding appeared to have stopped and seemed to already have begun to clot. The deep furrow across her scalp, on the other hand, was something entirely different. He'd considered stitches as he worked to clean it, but upon closer inspection realized there was nothing to stitch. It would have to be bandaged and allowed to heal on its own, and he could tell it would leave a nasty scar. He spoke not a word, only began to work on new bandages, making sure they were protective yet discreet as best he could.

"How is your father?" Taryn questioned softly, staring ahead at the wall as Royal worked.

"He was devastated when he received your letter. He wrote to me the same day, asking why you were leaving, where you were going, and when we would see you again. Of course, all I knew was what you had told me, so I did not have anything new to say." Royal shook his head. "I saw him in London just before you arrived here. He is ill, though he tries to hide it. I am afraid he may not live to see the new year."

"Oh, Royal, I had no idea. I am sorry."

He shrugged. "It is what it is, but oh, I wish I could tell him about you, about what we are doing here."

"You know he would not approve."

"No, but at least he would know that you did not disappear, and that I was doing something worthwhile."

Taryn grimaced. "Truly, if it had just been you and your

mother, I would have told you what I was. But as grateful as I am to your father, he terrified me. I know he would not take a biomaton in off the streets and treat her like family. And then..." She sighed, pressing her palms together. "And then I liked being a part of your family so much, I could not bear the thought that you would reject me if you knew. So, I kept it to myself." She ducked her head. "At times, I thought it would have been easier if you had never found me. At least then you would not have been heartbroken by my terrible secret."

"I always knew you were hiding more than just scars beneath that glove," Royal answered, touching her shoulder. "Perhaps not clockwork, but *something*. I am glad you no longer have to hide what you are."

Taryn looked at him, blinking her emerald eyes in surprise. "In a way, I still do. Here at Elmhurst, I am fully myself, but the world still sees me as either a missing schoolgirl or as property. That is the point of this entire rebellion, is it not?"

Royal stared at her for a few silent moments. "I suppose you are right." He grinned his familiar, lopsided grin, the one that would have made any human girl's stomach flip, but merely left Taryn feeling warm and accepted. "Think how appalled Father would be if he knew you were wearing trousers!"

Taryn laughed. "But your mother would applaud me."

Royal's smile grew, at the same time taking on a sort of quiet sadness. "True. She would have loved Sedition. My mother was her own person, regardless of convention."

She touched his hand. "Let us do this for her, then. She would be proud of us both."

Royal nodded. "Aye. For her."

"And that is another win," Taryn gloated, laying her cards on the table. "Another penalty to you, Roy."

Royal groaned and reached up, untying his cravat. "You are going to steal everything I am wearing if you keep this up."

A smug grin crossed Taryn's face. The twins, who were looking on in anticipation, already missing pieces of sparring armor and a shoe each before dropping out, laughed.

"I think that is her goal," Ari teased.

Royal's ears reddened with a blush, but he shoved the cards across the table toward Taryn. "Again," he ordered.

"Are you sure, Royal?" she asked, gesturing to the growing pile of his personal effects, each one marking a card game lost and a penalty he would have to pay later to get the object back. "That is an awful lot of penalties."

"Again," he repeated stubbornly, stretching his shoulders. Taryn's smirk grew, and she began to shuffle, deftly flicking the cards between her hands. The movement was not only impressive—it demonstrated the skill and dexterity of her prosthetic. Royal had never managed to get her to tell him where she'd learned to shuffle and play so well, but he was secretly convinced she'd run a game of three-card monte on the streets when she was twelve, earning ha'pennies in exchange for the chance to guess where the queen was hiding. He'd never been any good at the game. He would never have guessed it was rigged.

Taryn dealt five cards to them both and set the deck aside. Royal lifted his stack of cards. Pair of Queens. Not bad. The rest of his hand was rubbish, a three of spades, a four of hearts, and a ten of clubs, but he liked the look of that pair.

"Bid is to you, Roy," Taryn said, her face betraying nothing of the cards she held carefully in front of her. They were bidding with a handful of pocket change Royal had dug up, but the money wasn't what mattered. They were playing for forfeits, the kind of humiliating parlor games played at parties.

Taryn had never actually played a game with stakes like this with him before (likely because she had to keep her secret hidden, he knew now) and Royal was too exhilarated to stop, even though the next thing she could take was his waistcoat, and that was getting dangerously close to improper.

"I will bet two shillings," he said cautiously, dropping the coins in the center of the table.

"I see that," she murmured, dropping her own pair of coins on the pile. "How many cards would you like?"

He considered, then chose to keep the ten and the queens. "Two."

She nodded, taking the cards from him, and exchanging them with two new ones. She considered her own cards, then lay them face down on the table. "I shall take one."

The twins made interested *ohh* noises. Taryn drawing a single card meant she had something strong in her hand.

Royal picked up the cards she'd given him. Another four. An eight. He sighed, disappointed he hadn't gotten another match, but still. He had the pair of queens. He was doing well. He raised his eyes to see Seraphim had entered the room and was standing off to the side, quietly watching. The winged biomaton always disconcerted Royal, though he did his best to hide it. The sight of his silver fangs left a knot in the pit of Royal's stomach, and the way he looked at Taryn seemed shifty. Like he was hiding something.

"Your move, Royal," Taryn said over her cards.

He studied his cards again, making a show of looking them over, as though he had something worth considering. "Two shillings," he said, and pushed them to the center of the table.

One of Taryn's perfect, dark brows lifted. "I will raise you two more."

Royal shook his head, considering his hand again. He wasn't sure now if she was bluffing, and that worried him. He couldn't go on losing like this. He chewed his bottom lip.

"Go on," Taryn urged. "We do not have all day."

"I will match," he sighed, tossing the extra two shillings on the table. The corner of Taryn's mouth quirked up, and his heart dropped. He'd lost. Again. He knew it before they laid their cards on the table.

"What do you have, Roy?" she asked with that impish quality to her voice she always had when she won.

He laid his cards out, displaying his pair of queens, which had looked so regal before and now looked drab and disappointing.

She set her own cards flat on the table, and he saw he'd been right. "Close, Roy. I have three knaves."

He sighed and folded the cards, sliding them across the table toward her as she added the shillings to her respective pile. "I suppose you'll be wanting my waistcoat now?"

"If you please."

She began to shuffle the cards again, and he struggled with the top button of his navy-blue waistcoat. "I do believe you mean to undress me completely, Miss Roft," he said, trying to make it sound teasing. He hoped he'd see her cheeks color, her ears turn red, some indication she was embarrassed by the impropriety of his joke, but she just smiled as the twins guffawed.

"Anytime you like, we can stop, and you can begin to earn these things back," she replied primly. "I am sure the twins have already thought up some choice penalties to inflict upon you."

Oh, Royal was sure of that too, from the way the two big men grinned, their dark faces shining with mischief. He unfastened the second button of his waistcoat.

"Enough," Seraphim said, approaching. He had his clockwork wings folded tightly behind him, so they were barely visible. His arms, too, were crossed. "Give his things back, Sedition," he ordered.

Taryn looked up, blinking innocently at her biomaton sibling. "I think you misunderstand the point of the game, Seraphim."

"Give the boy his things back," Seraphim growled, lips curling into enough of a snarl to reveal a flash of silver fangs. He leaned forward, wings rising menacingly.

"No, Seraphim, really, this is how the game is played," Royal interrupted, his heart pounding. He'd seen the two of them spar—bold, brutal, and fast as lightning, exchanging blows like panthers locked in combat. He didn't want to get caught in the middle of that, especially here in the library.

"I know how the game is played," Seraphim hissed. He never took his intense green eyes from Taryn's. "I have not been *that* sheltered. What you do *not* seem to realize is that Sedition is cheating."

"What?" Royal found himself saying at the same time as Taryn.

"Show him your arm, Sedition," Seraphim insisted.

"Honestly, Seraphim, I do not know where you get such ideas," Taryn said, laughing a little, but Royal knew that face, knew that voice too well to be fooled by it anymore.

"If you are not cheating, show him your arm," he said, feeling the words grate between his teeth.

She shook her head and held out her left arm, the sharp angles of the armored plates always seeming a little treacherous to Royal, though he could not say why. "There, you see?"

Seraphim caught hold of her wrist, pinning her prosthetic, palm up, to the table.

"Seraphim—!" She gasped, but the bigger man didn't seem to be listening. He pressed his fingers against her forearm, opening the spring-loaded hatch—the one Royal knew was usually intended to hide her dagger. Half a dozen cards flew out, fluttering across the table. A pair of knaves. A king. Two aces.

Royal's mouth dropped open. Seraphim released Taryn's arm, straightening, his arms crossed over his chest again. "There," he said. "What have you to say for yourself?"

The twins looked on with identical expressions of surprise. *Now* Taryn's cheeks colored. "I—"

"You were cheating?" Royal exclaimed before she could finish. "I let you deal all this time, and you were *cheating?*"

Her emerald eyes flashed, and for a moment he saw that warrior inside her staring back at him, and then she ducked her head, copper hair falling over her eyes briefly. "I am sorry."

"Why?"

She shook her head. "It is the only way I know how to play."

"*What?*"

She splayed her hands on the table, flesh hand beside clockwork one, and shook her head again. Royal waited, holding his breath, hoping she would have a good explanation for him, though he could think of none good enough to justify what she'd just done.

And then Rorin began to laugh. He had a good laugh, strong, throaty, and infectious. It took only a few moments for his more stoic brother to start laughing as well. Even Seraphim's usually cold mask cracked, revealing a smile, and Royal sat, staring, as Taryn covered her face with her hand, refusing to meet his eyes.

"What?" he demanded. "What have I missed?"

"Nothing," Taryn answered, barely swallowing a giggle.

"No, what have I missed?" he pressed, looking back and forth between the others.

"For the first time in yer life, lordling, ye have not been allowed to win!" Ari said, letting loose a hearty guffaw that set Taryn laughing.

And then, though he was not certain it was entirely appropriate, Royal was laughing too. "No one has ever cheated me so thoroughly," he said when he could catch his breath.

Taryn shook her head. "Oh, Royal," she sighed, passing him the personal effects she'd collected in her rigged game. "I suspect you have been cheated far more thoroughly than that and never suspected it."

She was right. Good Lord, she was right. How many times had he lost pennies and sweets and beloved clockwork curiosities to the boys in his boarding school dorms? He'd always thought himself unlucky, but Taryn now opened a new line of thought. Perhaps he was simply naïve.

"You may be right." He replaced his pocket watch in his waistcoat pocket, comforted by its weight. "But regardless, next time you are letting someone else deal."

CHAPTER EIGHTEEN

Storm stood in front of the mirror in her cabin, studying the new white coat she'd been given to mark her station. Gold epaulettes decorated the shoulders and chains draped from them to the shiny double row of gold buttons down her front. She smoothed both hands over the stiff material, something sharp stuck in her throat.

Ace should be here, the little voice in her head that sounded too much like her mother's whispered.

Storm shook the voice away, raking fingers through her tangled hair. Beads and cogs jangled against one another, all the little trophies she'd kept from her many missions as a privateer making their own music, clinking like the heartbeat of her story. And now she wasn't just a privateer; she was a *commissioned officer* in the Queen's navy. *Admiral Storm Highmore.* The title was sweeter than honey on her tongue. She'd done what everyone had said was impossible, because of her past, because of her failures, because of her gender. She'd taken up arms, ruled her crew with an iron fist, and earned her title with all of England looking on in awe.

And she'd done it all while having to babysit her cowardly little brother.

She turned away from the mirror, fiddling with an Oriental coin tied into her hair, her fingers tracing the perfect bullet hole through its center. True, it would have been useful to have Ace along for the battle that had earned her this promotion. He'd been gone for less than half a day when it happened: Pirates had attacked the port just outside of London, in some sort of newfangled airship that could strike and disappear in moments; its sails, balloon, and white-painted hull had blended in with the sooty clouds that were almost always present in the city. With half the local navy's ships crippled, they'd called on the *Dauntless* for help. Storm's ruthlessness had ensured the pirates paid for the havoc they'd wreaked—with their lives.

But the promotion ceremony had taken weeks, which had left her and the *Dauntless* stranded in port, and while she'd expected Ace to eventually come crawling back to her, tail between his legs, he hadn't. That rankled her. She'd thought, before the whole red-headed biomaton debacle, that they'd had an understanding. She told him what to do, and he did it, because if he did, they rose in the ranks together. Yes, she'd demoted him after his stupid decision had gotten those ships destroyed, but she'd always intended to give him his position back, once he'd paid for his mistake. She needed him on her side.

But that little red-headed problem had changed all that. Three of her best crew members were now gone. She didn't regret losing Emmett; he'd been more trouble than he was worth, and her decision to send him into the Black Castle with Taryn had only increased her crew's fear of her. But Ace's decision to go after them had been an unwelcome surprise. When had he stopped fearing her? When had he decided treason was better than this life?

You can go find him. Get him back.

Sure, but where to look?

He is your brother. You're supposed to protect him.

Storm growled and threw the door to her cabin open, stomping up the steps loudly enough to silence the voices in her head. *I did this for the Crown, for the empire, for us!*

Above decks, her crew was working hard to keep the *Dauntless* in tip-top shape, just as she required. They saluted as she passed, halting in their work, eyes sharp and alert and full of that respectful fear she'd so carefully cultivated.

She stepped up onto the poop deck, holding onto one of the heavy lines anchoring the balloon to the deck. "Prepare to set sail! We make for the Black Castle in one hour."

She'd make use of the arrangement she had with Bellham and see if he knew where Ace had vanished to, with or without the biomaton. And if she had to crush some heads along the way, even better. Storm allowed the touch of a grim smile to grace her lips.

Time to get her hands bloody. Again.

"Ma'am, you cannot just—"

She caught the front young man's shirt in her gauntleted fist, the rip of fabric audible as he fell silent, staring at her with large, horrified eyes. "I wear the marks of rank, do I not?" Storm kept her voice even, calm, even though she wanted nothing more than to toss this young guard off the battlements and watch his body crunch against the ancient cobblestones of the Black Castle's courtyard. She wouldn't, though, at least, not yet. Not before she got what she needed from Bellham.

"Yes, but Lord Bellham is— I mean, he has—he is a very busy man—" The guard's eyes bulged, barely able to form coherent words as he stammered through excuses.

"I understand," she purred, eyes half-lidded, allowing a ghost of a smile to grace her lips.

He breathed a sigh of relief.

"But I must see him now." She pushed him backward, just a step, until his foot hit the edge of the stone wall and he had to lean backward over the edge of the battlement. Wind caught the guard's clothes and tore at her grasp on his shirt. "So, you can let me pass, or you can find yourself falling a very long way."

Paling, he quickly shook his head. "He is usually in his office at this time."

She put on a sickly-sweet smile. "That was not so hard, was it?" She dropped his shirt, shoved past him, and headed for the door she'd walked through weeks ago with that little red-headed biomaton who had ruined everything. Heels clicking against the stone floor, she kept one hand on the pistol at her hip and one eye out for any other pushover guards who might want to stop her.

Disappointingly, she reached the thick wooden door of Lord Bellham's office without incident. She pushed it open with a shoulder, catching the scent of acrid smoke and cherry wood and, beneath it all, the iron-salt tang of blood. "We need to talk," she said, before the gaunt Lord of the Black Castle could rise from where he sat behind his desk.

The door thumped closed behind her, and Storm twisted the lock with a *crunch* of metal on metal.

"Captain Storm, I did not expect to see you so soon." He did a good job of hiding his surprise at her arrival.

"It's Commodore now."

He stood, smoothing invisible wrinkles from the front of his waistcoat. "Do you have another biomaton for me?"

"I am looking for my brother."

A blink of colorless eyes. "I am afraid I do not follow."

She stepped forward in a flash, smashing her gauntlet into

the desk. He remained stock-still in the midst of her anger. "He left the *Dauntless* weeks ago to come after that Erikkson biomaton I left with you."

His eyebrows quirked up. "And why should I have any idea where he is now?"

"Perhaps you do not. I want to speak with the biomaton girl."

"Speak with, Captain, or interrogate?"

This time the smile that came to her lips was easy. Real. "A little of both."

"I am afraid that will be impossible."

"I promise not to do lasting damage."

"That is not my concern. Unfortunately, Lord Erikkson came and got her weeks ago. She is no longer here."

Storm scowled, processing this new knowledge. There had to be *something* about that girl, then, even if they hadn't been able to find evidence of it. Plans began to branch in her mind. "And you are certain you have not seen my brother?"

Bellham inclined his head. "We can check the records, if you like. We keep careful track of all visitors to the Black Castle." He drew a thick ledger from the desk. The slick hum of the drawer opening and closing set Storm's mood on edge. The ledger thumped onto the desk and Bellham flicked through it with long, skeletal fingers. "What did you say his name was?"

It stuck in her throat for a moment. "Ace."

He nodded and studied the book, the only sounds in the room the crackle of the fireplace and the hiss of pages turning. "I am not seeing an Ace, nor any Highmores besides yourself."

"May I look?" She had to ask through gritted teeth, anger and fear clotting in her chest. If Ace hadn't come here, where was he? Why hadn't he returned after he came here and found the girl already gone?

"Of course." He slid the ledger to her.

She rifled through the pages, barely feeling the thick, soft paper beneath her fingertips. Bellham kept meticulous records, and he was right. There was no entry for Ace, all the way back to the day she'd last been here. She even checked for his most commonly used aliases, Nicolas Hurst and Milton Granger, but they weren't there either. It was like he'd simply disappeared.

"You said he was here for the girl?" Bellham asked, interrupting her increasingly frantic page-turning.

"Aye."

"Perhaps he ran into Erikkson the day he came. He could have met with them outside, before anyone here had time to record his visit, and gone with them."

Treason, again. Storm's lip curled in disgust. She wanted to protest, to say Ace would never do such a thing, but after the way he'd changed around the biomaton girl, she didn't know anymore.

"Were you not trying to get enough evidence to accuse Erikkson of treason?" Bellham carefully took the book back from her. "Perhaps Ace thought he could get more information from the inside."

Of course. He'd gone in as a spy, been unable to inform her of his movements for risk of being caught. "Perhaps. Or perhaps the girl recognized him, and they kidnapped him. Took him back to Erikkson's labs."

Bellham nodded solemnly. "It is possible. We still do not know where he gets the subjects to create his abominations."

A chill settled into her stomach, a feeling she hadn't felt since she'd taken over the command of the *Dauntless.* There was only one thing that brought her any comfort: "To kidnap and torture one of the Queen's privateers qualifies as treason."

Bellham blinked, something deep in his eyes flashing with reflected firelight. A hesitation, a moment of cold calculation, there and then gone as a chilling smile crept across his thin lips. "You could easily get an arrest warrant for the girl with that accusation. The law is never in their favor. Kill two birds with one stone that way: find your brother, and get revenge on the girl who took him from you."

Storm felt the fear drain away, replaced with rich, glorious purpose. She grinned like a cat with a barrel of clipped-wing canaries. "*That* is a fine plan."

CHAPTER NINETEEN

"Ye can do better than that!" Ari crowed, standing over her with a triumphant smirk on his face. He was flushed from the exercise, his eyes bright and dark skin shiny with sweat.

Taryn shoved herself back to her feet, panting. Her wound throbbed with the pounding of her heart. "There are two of you and only one of me," she growled, taking up a fighting stance, her fists raised, her weight low in her hips. She kept her head turned, her periphery trained on Rorin behind her.

"Ye ought to be able to fight the two of us," Rorin answered in his thick Scottish accent. "Seraphim can take down five soldiers at once."

Taryn rolled her eyes. "Seraphim has massive blades attached to his back. You will not even allow me to use mine."

Ari beckoned with one hand. "Try again."

Taryn leapt into action, moving more out of instinct than conscious choice, ducking, jabbing, dodging, and weaving circles around her larger, less nimble opponents. Still, the twins worked together, attacking from both sides, hardly giving her time to prepare before coming in with fists swinging. Despite her best efforts, her wound, even four days after Ace had inflicted it, was slowing her down. The deep, insistent pain kept her from focusing fully on any one task. She gritted her teeth, working through it, trying to stay focused, but it was too late. Rorin's fist struck her in the side of the head, on her injury. Taryn crumpled to the floor, screaming.

Rorin swore. "I forgot ye were injured, Sedition. I am sorry!" He seemed flustered, unsure of what to do.

Taryn pressed one hand over her injury, struggling to breathe through the pain. Her vision swam, her entire body trembling.

"Are ye all right?"

Taryn shook her head. "I will be. Give me a minute."

The twins waited, silent, sheepish looks on their identical faces, until Taryn managed to control the pain and rose.

"Perhaps we ought to be done for the day—" Ari began, but she shook her head.

"No. We go again. I must learn to keep going in spite of the pain."

The twins exchanged leery glances. "I am not sure we should go on," Rorin mumbled.

"I am the leader. We keep going." Taryn took up another fighting stance. "Ready?"

"Can ye handle it?" Ari asked.

Taryn nodded. "Can you?"

The twins glanced at one another, then fell into formation, taking up fighting stances of their own. This time, Taryn was ready, her guard up, her senses piqued. She fought them both with an ease she had not possessed before. It was as if the blow to her head had unlocked something deep within herself, bringing to the surface the fighter she had been searching for all this time. She spun, ducked, and jabbed, allowing her opponent's momentum and her prosthetics to do most of the fighting for her.

She struck down Rorin first, as he seemed over-cautious of her injury. With a quick heel to the back of his knee, followed by the heel of her palm to his sternum, she knocked him to the floor. He stayed down, coughing, allowing Taryn to turn her full attention on Ari. The big biomaton had the physical advantage of being whole, so he had no weaknesses where clockwork met flesh she could exploit. But at the same time, his soft flesh was a weakness itself, especially when pitted against her solid metal fist, spikes protruding from her knuckles.

"Do you want to give in?" she questioned, flashing a razor-edged smile.

"Never."

They circled one another for a moment, each assessing the other, eyes darting, searching for chinks in their armor. Taryn attacked first, striking like a cobra, lightning-fast and deadly accurate. Ari barely had time to get his arms in front of his face before Taryn's fists were pelting him with blows. Her emerald eyes had taken on a wild look. He tried to twist away, to throw her off, but Taryn kept coming, never stopping with blows to his ribs, stomach, and arms where they protected his face. Finally, he reached out, catching her shoulder and pausing the assault for a moment.

"Enough, Sedition!"

She seemed to snap out of some kind of trance. Her fists slowed. She blinked. Recognition came into her eyes. "Gor, I am sorry. Did I hurt you?"

He shook his head. "But the way ye lose control is concerning. It is something Erikkson told us to watch out for."

"What do you mean?" Taryn swept her arm across her forehead to wipe away the perspiration.

Rorin pushed himself back to his feet. "Ari, we were told not to talk about it."

"About what?" She felt like she was repeating herself.

Neither twin would meet her gaze. "About Petrichor,"

Rorin said softly. "Master Erikkson asked us not to tell ye, but he said to watch for similarities."

"Similarities? Why is no one willing to discuss Petrichor?" she questioned. "She is mentioned, but when I ask about her, no one will tell me what happened. The only way I am going to find out is if someone tells me. My memories are not coming back."

Ari raked a hand across his tight black curls. "Petrichor lost herself in her persona before she left. Master Erikkson never intended us to kill for killing's sake. Petrichor began to enjoy the thrill of killing too much."

"It all went wrong after the Black Castle took her," Rorin mumbled.

"What?" This was new. Taryn looked at them both eagerly, waiting for them to say more.

"No one knows what happened there," Ari answered. "Not even Master Erikkson. But it changed her permanently. She left soon after that."

"It was not long after ye were sent away, or so I have been told," Rorin finished. "Master Erikkson was heartbroken, losing ye both."

Taryn absently toyed with a buckle on her hip. "And now he refuses to talk about it, but he asks you to watch me for similar signs?"

"Aye, he is worried about ye," Ari offered, in a rare, surprising moment of gentleness. "He does not want to lose ye again." He rubbed a hand over his chest and winced. "That is some punch ye have, though."

"I am sorry," she repeated. "I do not know what came over me."

"I think that is enough for one day," Rorin said. "We do not want to make yer injury any worse."

Taryn nodded, tucking her copper hair behind her ear,

displaying that missing half-moon, scabbed, and healing slowly. She shook hands with both biomatons, thanking them for sparring with her. "Speaking of my injuries, have either of you kept track of Ace these past few days? Do you know how he is settling in?"

Again, the twins exchanged looks. "He has begun training with our regiment in the mornings," Rorin said.

"He never puts down that bloody pistol," Ari replied. "I do not know why ye let him get away with it."

"I know what it is like to lose all sense of who you are. It is far better that we give him his space and treat him as one of us, rather than punishing him for what he did when he was frightened."

Ari's expression wrinkled into a sneer. "Still, I have no problem giving him a beating if given the chance."

Taryn smiled, using her fingers to work her hair out of its loose braid. "A few weeks ago, you would have applauded him for attempting to kill me."

"Sure, but that was before we knew ye," Ari said.

"Now, we would die for ye," Rorin confirmed.

"I certainly hope it shall not come to that," Taryn replied with a chuckle.

"I apologize for my interruption," a new voice interjected. Taryn turned to glimpse Seraphim approaching, his long hair tied back in a thick braid across the top of his scalp. "Master Erikkson has another assignment for us," he said, his eyes flickering to her ear before returning to her face.

Taryn nodded. "I shall be right there."

TARYN'S STOMACH DROPPED. "LORD THOMPSON?" SHE repeated hollowly, her mouth dry.

"That is what I said." Erikkson frowned at her. "Why? Is there a problem?"

"Could we not go after someone else? Mr. Cody claims to 'dabble' in biomechanicks..."

"Who?"

Taryn shook her head. "It does not matter. Someone else."

"Sedition, this man *flayed* one of his biomatons for attempting to escape. He brands them so they cannot be mistaken for another person's property. He is *precisely* the kind of man we want to stop."

Taryn leaned forward on the desk, slumping, her hands over her face. Her teeth grinding together, she said, "His son attended boarding school with Royal." Every fiber of her being demanded they stop this monster from hurting anyone else, and yet she dreaded it, concerned about Royal's reaction.

"So?"

"He will not like us attacking them!"

"Royal is not in charge of this army, Sedition."

"No, you are," she grumbled.

"*You* are. You command them, including Royal. Use your authority."

Heat flooded her cheeks, not from embarrassment, but very frustration. Though she hadn't really taken the time to admit it, the last mission she'd run with Seraphim had felt *good.* It felt like they were finally doing something. She wanted that again. She sat up, straightening her spine. "Who shall fly us there?"

"Royal, of course."

She slammed her fist against the desk. "Royal should *not* be involved with this mission. His emotions may get in the way. We cannot risk that!"

"Nonsense. He would not betray us. He will go with you, just as he did before."

She knew from experience how closely knit Royal's group

of peers could be, the way they covered for each other even if rules or laws had been broken. "I do not think it is worth the risk. I agree that Thompson needs to be punished. But someone else can fly us there."

Erikkson stared at her sharply. "Why do you not trust him?"

The words that leapt to her tongue—*because he is wealthy and sheltered and does not understand this, not really, not even if he seems to be more comfortable with it*—she quickly swallowed down. "I—I *do* trust him," she lied. "I am just afraid his connection to this case will be a problem."

"Then take someone else with you as well. I heard you mention that Emmett had expressed an interest in coming along?"

She nodded.

"Take him with you. He can keep an eye on Royal."

"Why do *you* insist he comes along?" she questioned.

"Because it is good for him to experience this, just as it was good for you to experience his world."

She huffed a frustrated grumble and pushed herself to her feet. "Fine. But if this goes wrong, I am blaming you."

TARYN CREPT THROUGH THE MANOR HOUSE WITH Seraphim close behind. As she padded down the hall, she remembered attending a party here once. It had to have been in the first year of her time with Royal's family, mostly forgotten now; she would have been thirteen. She had not fully recalled it until she entered through the upper floor window, memories flooding back as if she had broken open some locked door. *Funny,* she mused, creeping around a corner, *with so much of my memory already missing, one would expect me to remember the other parts of my life better than I do.* She wondered if this was a side effect of the dampers in her head, or perhaps just a symptom of being human.

Royal and Emmett were somewhere overhead in the air yacht, circling the manor silently. Royal had remained terrifyingly quiet during the hour and a half flight over, his face an uncharacteristic mask. Taryn had attempted to start up a conversation twice before giving up entirely. She wasn't certain what he was planning, but she didn't trust him alone and had left Emmett aboard the airship to keep an eye on him.

"We are just going to take the biomatons and go," Taryn murmured to Seraphim as they moved through the house. She had her mask pulled tightly over her face, in case young Master Thompson caught them. Heaven forbid he recognize her. Word would certainly make its way to Lord Stokker if they were recognized, and she could not have that.

Seraphim seemed hesitant, but at last he nodded. "As you wish."

Taryn found a familiar flight of stairs, but passed them by, moving more by instinct than conscious thought, certain that somewhere nearby there would be a set of back stairs leading directly to the servants' quarters.

They never reached it.

A loud bell began to toll, clanging through the halls of the house. Instantly, they spun on their heels, charging back the way they had come. Taryn's pulse thundered in her ears. Had they been discovered? The bell was some kind of alarm, certainly, but why had it gone off? Over the pounding of her heart, Taryn could hear shouts and hurried footsteps, the house waking. Seraphim slipped out a window, and Taryn followed. The door to the hall beyond the little private sitting room swung wide as they rushed to escape.

"Stop!" Taryn heard the words with one foot out the window, her hands gripping the frame. She turned to see

Royal's friend, Henry Thompson, staring at her, standing at the other end of the corridor.

"Hurry, Sedition!" Seraphim urged from above.

Taryn moved, praying her disguise was enough. She breathed a premature sigh of relief as Seraphim pulled her onto the roof.

"What alerted them?" she hissed.

Seraphim pointed over her shoulder, at the same time signaling to the yacht with his wings. Taryn turned, gasping as her eyes lit on the grass behind the manor, ablaze with yellow-orange flames. Half a dozen biomatons worked to get the flames under control, and, as Taryn watched, a young girl's skirt caught fire. One of the other biomatons knocked the girl to the ground, smothering the flames. Taryn swallowed hard, images of another fire, another skirt engulfed in flames flashing behind her eyes. The manor's roof seemed to tilt beneath her feet, and she had to throw her hands out for balance.

"Sedition!" Seraphim's voice snapped her back to the present. He held a narrow rope ladder, waiting for her to climb it before ascending himself. "We cannot stay any longer! Someone may see us."

"We were already seen," she snapped, but followed his lead, leaping up the rope ladder. She could not shake the horrid trembling in her core from the sight of the biomaton's skirt catching fire.

She heaved herself onto the deck of the ship, followed closely by Seraphim. Royal steered the ship away from the manor and the now-dying fire. Below them, people yelled. Someone was sobbing. But at least it seemed the air yacht had gotten away without being tracked. Taryn pressed her hands against the rail to stop them shaking.

"*Que s'est-il passé?*" Emmett shouted over the wind and the bells from below.

"The alarms woke the entire household. We could not stay

and risk being caught," Taryn shouted back. Inexplicably, her eyes went to Royal where he stood at the wheel, his back to her. Suspicion began to boil in her gut. "Seraphim, will you take the wheel please?" she asked in a slow, even tone. "I should like to have a few private words with Master Stokker."

Seraphim nodded, taking over for Royal. Taryn studied her best friend, catching the glint of mischief in his brown eyes. "You had something to do with this," she said without preamble. It wasn't a question.

"Why would you assume that?"

"Do not lie to me, Royal!" she yelled, the adrenaline in her chest all at once catalyzing to anger. "We could have been caught! We could have been *killed*! How could you do something so selfish?"

"Taryn, I had nothing to do with this!"

Her palm itched to slap him, but she forced her hands into fists by her sides, the wind whipping her words away as she spoke. "We were going to rescue the biomatons who were *suffering*. You had no right to interfere."

His cheeks had gone red enough to be visible even in the dim silver light of the moon. "Is that what you think of me? That I would betray everything you worked for to protect a cruel man whose son I knew years ago?"

"You are all alike," she growled. "You think you are untouchable, because you are wealthy, and your names are well-known. Because you are *whole*." She spat the last word at him like a curse, putting behind it all the vitriol she'd experienced for her own "incompleteness."

His brown eyes welled with hurt and anger in equal measure. "I cannot help where I come from. That should not influence your opinion of me."

"Taryn," Emmett interjected. She hadn't even noticed him come close. "We saw the fire start. A horse kicked a lantern over. Royal had no part in that."

Royal's eyebrows shot up at Emmett's defense, but he quickly recovered his composure. "You see? And even if I had thought of it, I would never have acted upon it! You are my *friend*. I want to see you free."

But her anger wasn't assuaged by the explanation, wasn't eased by Emmett's defense. "It is only a matter of time before you betray us. You have always been naïve, Royal. You do not understand what it means to be a biomaton."

"I am learning!" His eyes now swam with tears, brows drawn down into a painful-looking frown. "I do not know what else to say, Taryn. If you distrust me so much, perhaps it is time I take my leave."

"What?"

"I am *leaving*, Tiger."

She blinked, the old nickname stinging as if he'd slapped her. "You cannot—"

"I do not know what it is you want from me! You say you cannot trust me, and yet you do not want me to go?"

"I—"

"I have had enough of you treating me like I do not know what this means. I am going home."

He turned away, leaving her standing on the deck, shaking in the wind. Her mind spun, unable to fully process what had just happened. Emmett tried to touch her shoulder but she slapped him away, light-headed and stumbling over to the rail. She held onto it with both hands, squeezing until the wood cracked under the power of her clockwork hand, but nothing changed. She still *felt* betrayed, even if he hadn't done anything wrong. Deep down, she'd been waiting for him to betray them for so long it had almost felt like a relief when she'd thought he finally had. He was right. She didn't trust him. And maybe it was unfair to him, but she'd lived so long unable to fully trust anyone, it felt impossible to allow herself to let anyone in. The other biomatons risked the same fate as she did if they betrayed her, and Erikkson risked even more for building treasonous creations, but what did Royal have to lose? Maybe she was guilty of exactly what she accused him of. Maybe she could not see him, only what he was.

CHAPTER TWENTY

Royal paced around his room, fuming and unable to sleep, refusing to pack, refusing to believe his relationship with Taryn could end so abruptly. Could she really think so little of him? They were different people. He'd known that since the day he brought her home. But she was his best friend, and more than that, she sparked a fire inside him like no one else he had ever known. He'd expected her to call him back, to beg him to stay, but all the way home, she'd been silent and closed off. He needed more from her, needed an acknowledgement that he meant more to her than his title.

She had been slowly slipping through his fingers since she'd left him alone at Grafton's. He'd felt it first with Emmett, and then with the rest of the army; all those new faces slowly driving a wedge between them, pulling them apart. He did not care that she was a biomaton. She was still Taryn, still the beautiful girl he'd grown up with, and she was the only person in the world he felt this way about. She was the only girl he *could* feel this way about.

Grumbling to himself, Royal slammed his trunk closed, still empty. How could he go back to the life he had lived before?

This was where he wanted to be. Helping Taryn, learning from Tony. But how could he stay when she didn't trust him?

"I recognize that expression," a smooth voice came from the doorway behind him. "You and Taryn had a fight. A big one, by the looks of it."

Royal gritted his teeth, turning toward Erikkson. "She does not trust me."

A furrow appeared between Erikkson's brows. "What happened?"

Royal shook his head, turning away. "You would not understand."

"I was young and full of vinegar once. You may be surprised by what I understand."

Royal's eyes narrowed. "I told her I was leaving. You cannot stop me." He didn't really want to go, even though he'd said it, but it felt wrong to not stick by his word.

And maybe, what he really wanted was for someone to ask him to stay.

Erikkson's expression did not change. He remained the perfect calm to Royal's emotional hurricane. "I am afraid I am not quite following your non sequiturs, Royal. Begin at the beginning for me."

Royal heaved a heavy sigh. "There was an incident tonight, and Taryn blamed me. She thought I had betrayed them. I would never do that! But she does not trust me. Maybe never trusted me? She says that I am like everyone else, but is that not exactly why we are fighting this war? Ever since you told her that she is important to the world, I feel I have not been able to get through to her. I do not *want* her to be important to the world. She was important to *me* before any of this." He scowled, rubbing his cheek with a hand. "Do not tell her I said that. She does not know."

"I suspect Taryn is aware she is important to you, even if you have never said it aloud." Erikkson's eyes flicked to the window. "It is nearly dawn. Will you walk with me? I would like to talk with you about all of this."

Royal hesitated, studying the haphazard contents of his room, but at last he nodded reluctantly. Together, they strode out onto the grounds behind the manor. There were a few biomatons already training in the chill predawn air, their feet leaving long trails in the fresh dew. Erikkson skillfully avoided the soldiers, guiding Royal into the rose garden. Their feet crunched over the pebbled pathway as they weaved their way through the rich green hedges, a few sprouting buds in preparation to bloom.

His mentor's eyes studied the landscape. "I want you to consider Taryn's position very seriously for a moment. Place yourself in her shoes. Or in the shoes of any other biomaton, for that matter. Imagine for a moment that you were taken from your home or orphaned at a young age, forced to undergo a series of painful surgeries, and find yourself losing all sense of self, all sense of personhood. You are bought and sold, beaten and punished as your masters see fit, and you have no say in the matter." Royal opened his mouth to speak, but Erikkson stopped him. "The dampers inserted in biomatons' brains do not keep them from fully realizing the injustice of their situation, nor do they keep them happy. All they do is prevent the biomatons from speaking out, from acting on their discontent. It turns them into puppets." He paused. "If you do not believe me, ask Taryn. She was shut down while she was at the Black Castle."

Royal swallowed hard, the revelation making his chest ache. He was familiar enough with dampered biomatons; he'd grown up around their glazed stares and their neutral expressions. But imagining Taryn that way—it went against everything he liked best about her. Everything that made Taryn *Taryn*. He shook off the images. "What you are saying is that everything I was taught about biomatons in school is wrong..."

"Were you taught by biomatons, or by those who profit from biomatons?"

Royal nodded, understanding coming into his eyes. "They are exploited for the profit and benefit of the people who own them."

"And can you see why Taryn and the others must fight that?"

His expression became mournful. "I would hate to see Taryn shut down like some of the other biomatons I have seen." He hesitated, chewing the edge of his thumb. "But what does that have to do with her distrust of me? How am I to blame?"

Erikkson plucked a petal from a pink rose as they passed, toying with it between ink-stained fingers. "Consider this: she spent all those years hiding what she was from you. All that time builds fear and countless scenarios in which she imagined you or your family find out and do not accept her for what she is. Those things do not disappear overnight."

"She said it was only a matter of time before I betrayed her."

"Would you?"

"Never!"

"And I am sensing you do not really want to leave Elmhurst."

Royal dropped his eyes. "No, sir."

"Good. I would not want to lose my apprentice so soon." Erikkson pointed across the lawn to where Taryn was running, red-faced, her copper hair streaming over her shoulders as she raced around the track. "Give her some time to cool off. Then go and tell her how you feel. All of it, even the parts you are embarrassed by. Help her understand that you are here to help, not to hinder. That you are aware of your shortcomings and that you are learning. That you want to stay. If you are humble and honest with her, she will come around."

Royal's expression soured. "Tell her all of it?"

"All of it. She may not be able to feel romantic love, but she understands how it affects those of us who can."

Something fluttered in Royal's chest at those words. He ducked his head. "Yes, sir." Admitting how he felt did not come easily to him. It never had. But he would humble himself and do it. For her sake. He wanted to be better for her sake.

"Good. I suggest you give yourself some time to consider what I have told you. Rest, if you can. It shall do no one any good for our army to be sleep-deprived."

TARYN HEAVED A DEEP BREATH AS SHE PAUSED IN FRONT OF the heavy wood door to Ace's quarters. After the events of the night before, she had worked out in the chill predawn air, and then slept a handful of fitful hours. Though still tired, she had decided she may as well use the remains of the day to learn something useful. She pressed her hand over the pistol at her hip, taking comfort in the way it fit into her palm. She rapped on the door with her metal knuckles.

"Who is there?" Ace called. Through the door, he almost sounded unchanged.

"It is Sedition," she replied, surprised to find her throat dry.

"Come in."

Again, Taryn took a deep, steadying breath. She pressed the door open. "Oh, I am sorry!" She averted her eyes, shocked to find him half-dressed, naked from the waist up. His alterations were painfully obvious against his olive skin.

"Is something wrong?" he questioned with child-like innocence.

"No, no, I just—" she stuttered a little, sensible of how inappropriate the situation was. "Will you dress please?" He nodded and turned to the wardrobe. Taryn's eyes slid back to him. Her breath caught in her throat. Neatly glittering on the back of his head was a metal plate, the size of playing card. But that wasn't what made her blood run cold; it was the way the skin stretched between the clockwork replacing his ribs. His skin was puckered and red, stretched so tight in some places that she feared it would tear apart as he turned. He moved stiffly as he pulled a white button-down shirt over his shoulders.

"Does it hurt?" she questioned gently.

"What?" He turned to face her, the shirt hanging open as he worked the buttons with clumsy clockwork fingers. The muscles across the right side of his chest were torn and puckered where the clockwork bones were exposed, and it appeared that most of his sternum and all of his ribs on the right had been replaced with clockwork. How could his prosthetic make him stronger with damage like that? What could possibly be the purpose of such a cruel prosthesis?

"Your graft. Does it hurt?"

"Sometimes," he admitted, turning his eyes away from her. He lifted his pistol from the bedside table, tucking it into the leather holster someone had given him. Taryn refused to show any trepidation in the face of the weapon that had injured her just five days earlier, but her ear burned with phantom pain. "I have been remembering." He looked at her, his ice blue eyes dull and filmy, as though his lost memories somehow affected the color.

"That is good." She felt the need to be gentle with him, as if he could shatter if she was not careful.

"Just a little," he continued softly. "Images, really." He frowned. "I remember you. Your face, I mean. Did we meet before?"

A smile grew on her lips. All memory of the betrayal she'd felt when she had been around him before had vanished, leaving behind a strange sort of hope that at least he could get his memories back, and at last remember her. "Ace, it is me,

Taryn." When no sign of recognition registered in his eyes, she sighed. "743."

His face lit up. "But you—you said she—you—you were dead. She is dead."

"743 *is* dead. 743 is a meaningless number given to me by Lord Bellham to dehumanize me." Her eyes went to the numbers etched on his own arm. "I am more than a number. Much more."

"Then you can tell me who I am."

"Not as much as you think," she answered, taking her time to plot her words carefully. "You were a privateer for the Queen. You sailed on a ship called the *Dauntless.* Your sister, Storm, is the captain. She—" *She hates biomatons,* Taryn wanted to say, but somehow, she chose to soften the truth for him. "She does not like me."

"Why?"

"I—I do not know," Taryn stuttered, the lie tasting like poison on her lips. He would find out sooner or later, so why hide it from him now? Still, she hoped they would never encounter Storm again, and it seemed cruel to inform him his only remaining family member would detest him for what he could not control. It was not Ace's fault he was no longer human.

He sighed. "Oh."

"I am sorry I cannot tell you more," she offered gently. "Perhaps you will remember, in time."

He nodded and sat heavily on the edge of the bed. She could see the weight of his missing memories upon his shoulders, a weight she was intimately familiar with herself. He seemed smaller, somehow, than the man he'd been before, as if the loss of his memories left him hollow and shrunken. His eyes paused on the revolver at her hip. "You did not carry a pistol before."

She touched the cold metal of the pistol's grip. "I want you to teach me to shoot."

"Teach you?"

"You could easily have killed me, and instead you shot through my ear." She brushed her hair back, revealing the healing injury. "I have never seen anyone shoot the way you do. I want to learn."

He got up and moved nearer, his eyes locked on her injury. "May I...?"

She nodded, suppressing a shiver as his fingertips brushed the curve of her ear.

"I am sorry I hurt you. I was angry and afraid, but that is no excuse." He turned his eyes away. "I thought it would be like the Black Castle again, and I could not bear it."

His sincere apology felt like a knife under her ribs. What had they done to him to change him so? She could not bear to imagine what he must have endured. She tried to smile gently at him. "I will be fine, Ace. I understand. I know their cruelty." She paused, tipping her head so her copper hair fell over her ear once more. "Will you teach me?"

"Of course," he answered. "Anything for you."

Taryn winced, aware that his obedience was a result of the immense pain he had experienced, and of the changes the Black Castle had made to his mind. She hoped, in time, he would learn that he was free here. She hoped, in time, that she could draw out that man she'd seen in him aboard the *Dauntless*, the man who was gentle and noble. The man who'd left everything he knew to come back for her and Emmett. "There is a firing range in the forest beyond the gardens. We can go there." She turned and headed for the door, all too aware of his eyes on her.

"Taryn?"

She paused. "Yes?"

"Why were you so angry with me?"

"What?" She turned back to look at him.

"When I first arrived. Why were you so angry with me?"

She took a deep breath to steady herself. "You allowed your sister to sell us to Lord Bellham. You came back for us, but it was too late. I was hurt and I needed someone to blame. And you seemed to be the only person I could because you took me from my life in the first place. So, I pinned all the blame on you, until you came here and I—all that anger—exploded."

"I—I am sorry."

"I know."

"You are still holding it wrong," Ace said, shaking his head as Taryn once again missed the target completely. A scowl carved itself into her forehead.

"I am holding it just as you instructed. It bucks too much when I fire. I cannot even hit the bloody target!" She shoved the revolver back into the holster on her hip, cursing. "I ought to just stick with knives."

"Do not give up," Ace exclaimed, with so much spirit and vehemence in his voice it startled her. "You are so close."

She shook her head stubbornly.

"You cannot always fight your opponents at close quarters," Ace urged. "Try again."

Taryn sighed and pulled her revolver from its holster, hefting it in her right hand before pointing it at the target again. She cocked the pistol, drew a deep breath, and fired. It bucked in her hand; the bullet screamed over the target.

"You are still holding it wrong," Ace said, coming nearer to stand just behind her. "May I show you?"

She frowned at him but nodded, unsure what he intended to do.

Gently, he lifted her left hand with his, wrapping her

fingers around the butt of the pistol with his own. "Place your left hand here."

It was strange to Taryn, watching him manipulate her fingers like that without being able to feel his hand on hers. "It stabilizes the gun. And your right goes here." He adjusted the fingers of her right hand with his prosthetic, securing her grip with his palm. Her own hands appeared small compared to his. They stood close together, his head just behind her shoulder, arms overlapping, flesh on metal and metal on flesh.

"Now, feel how I aim, how I fire," he murmured. He leaned even closer, his head over her shoulder, his chest against her back. He was so close she could smell the scent of him, like salt and the sea and linen. Her mind searched for the last time they had been this close and came up empty. Even on the *Dauntless,* even when she was his prisoner, he'd kept his distance. All she could think of was the brief waltz he'd led her in at the Black Castle, when he was pretending to be a wealthy buyer interested in purchasing her. His breathing slowed, his exhale warm on her cheek. His forefinger squeezed slowly, pressing down on her own finger and, below it, the trigger. His other hand tightened around the butt of the pistol, keeping it steady. He released the breath he'd been holding, at the same time depressing the trigger.

Bang!

The pistol bucked in their hands, but not nearly as much as it had in Taryn's solo grip. Her eyes went to the target; a neat black hole marked the center of the bullseye. Ace pulled away from her. "You see?"

Taryn nodded, eager to try it herself. She took a deep breath, positioning her hands as Ace had shown her. She sensed the weight of his hands against her own, despite the fact that he now stood several feet away. She focused, sighting in on the target until it was all she saw.

She fired.

"Not bad," Ace said in approval.

It wasn't a bullseye—not by a long shot—but she had at last left a mark *within* the concentric circles of the target. She grinned, elated to have hit the mark.

"It is a start," Ace told her, a smile playing at the corner of his mouth. She thought perhaps it was the first time he had truly smiled since the *Dauntless*. He had a nice smile, warm and inviting. It softened the sharpness of his face and drove the cloudiness from his ice blue eyes. "Again."

CHAPTER TWENTY-ONE

Hours later, her arm aching from holding the gun steady and her thumb sore from cocking the hammer of her pistol, Taryn retired to her room to do a little reading before supper. As she swung her door shut, a voice spoke behind her. "I hope you had a pleasant training session."

Taryn spun, adrenaline surging through her veins, dropping her hidden dagger into her palm. Royal stood beside the door, where he had been hidden from her view until she closed it. "Do not do things like that!" she gasped. "I could have killed you."

He gave her an awkward, uncomfortable looking smile. "I suppose I am lucky you did not pull that pistol on me."

She glanced down at the gun on her hip as she sheathed her knife. Why hadn't she drawn it? It was far better for protection than the knife would be. But the truth was, she still needed practice. She was as likely to miss as she was to hit her target. "I thought you were leaving."

"Do you really want me to leave?"

She could not look at him, instead studying the grains of the wooden floorboards beneath her feet. "No."

"Then I ask you to hear me out."

His unusually grave tone left her no room for argument. She sat on the edge of her bed, beginning to unlace the leather forearm brace she'd worn for training earlier. "Go on."

He paced, the old treads creaking beneath his weight. One fist clenched and unclenched at his side, rhythmically counting words or heartbeats or something else cycling through his head. "I was hurt by what you said," he finally managed to say.

"I am sorry—"

"No, I am not finished." He turned on his heel and looked at her then, meeting her gaze with an intensity that surprised her. "Just wait, all right? This is not easy for me."

She folded her hands on her lap and waited.

"I was hurt by what you said, because you do not trust me. You said you *expected* me to betray you. As if, after all we have seen together, after all we have been through, that is all I am capable of." He raked his hands through his hair, then held them both out to her, palms up. "But what you do not seem to understand, Taryn, is that I *see* you. I have *always* seen you. I did not understand at first, and for that I am sorry. But I hope you know that I remain here because I want to learn. Because I am capable of being *better* than the men who came before me. If I have ever given you cause to doubt me, please, air it. Let me remedy what I have done to harm you, so that we can at last trust each other."

Something caught in Taryn's throat, choking all the air from her lungs. Royal looked at her with such a pleading expression, his blond hair brushing his shoulders as he waited for her response. She put her hands in his open ones, the rare touch of his calloused fingers surprising her with their warmth. "I am sorry. You have never done a thing to earn my mistrust. My fear is my own, and it is hard to fight. It is hard to uproot the very thing that has kept me alive all these years." As the words spilled from her, realization came with them. The emotions she'd thrown at Royal had been her own, not his. Letting go of Royal, she covered her face with her palms, ashamed. "I expect traitors because it is all I have ever known. And that is not fair to you. I am sorry I did not see how you have grown since you left Grafton's. I am sorry I did not trust you."

The mattress creaked as he cautiously sat beside her, giving her the half-foot of space she'd always demanded when she was still working to keep her secret. "I do not want to leave," Royal murmured. "But if I stay, I want to truly be part of this fight. Not the schoolboy you tolerate. Not the mechanick's apprentice you come to when you need someone to tend your wounds. I want to fight alongside you."

Quietly, Taryn reached out and grabbed his hand, squeezing his large, calloused palm against her own. She nodded. "I, and my army, would welcome you with open arms." She sighed, sitting up straighter. "I will work on my biases, Royal. I cannot promise I will get better all at once, but I do promise to never again accuse you of something without evidence."

He smiled, genuinely this time, that old crooked smile brightening the room with its appearance. He leaned across the space between them and gave her a hug, his smiling face buried in her shoulder. "Thank you."

She chuckled awkwardly and pushed him off, getting up and making her way to the wardrobe to put some space between them. They'd had a moment, yes, but that didn't mean she was ready for the smothering physical touch Royal gave to all his friends. "You should probably be on your way. I have to change for dinner." She turned and eyed his rumpled waistcoat, his bare shirtsleeves. "And you should probably do the same, if you are joining us."

"Will you be wearing trousers to dinner?" he asked, leaning back on the heels of his hands, making no move to leave. There was a teasing edge to his voice, the kind of easy camaraderie she'd missed recently.

"Perhaps. And what of it?"

"Are you sure that is proper?"

She gestured to herself. "I am a biomaton. I am leading a revolution. What about this is proper, Roy? Besides, since when did you care whether I was ladylike or not?" She tried to make the words come out light-hearted, but there was a tired edge to them. She'd been told for so long what she could and could not do, because she was a lady, because she was a biomaton. Becoming Sedition had promised to break those chains, and yet, every time she donned a gown, she felt it all flooding back to choke her.

His expression flickered, seeming to sense her inner tension. His voice, too, took on a forced lightness. "Think about after the revolution. What about when you have won your equality? What will you do if you have thrown away all your dignity?"

"I will not live that long," she muttered, turning her back on him in the pretense of selecting a dress.

His hand found her shoulder a moment later, and she felt herself flinch at the touch. "What do you mean?"

She sighed, chewing her lip. It was something that had haunted her since the beginning, but this was the first time she had a chance to voice it. He'd hate her for it, she knew that. He'd hate that she even had these thoughts. But she couldn't keep it from him forever, and maybe her voicing it would finally convince him of her part, her inevitable, terrible purpose. "This fight is for the biomatons' freedom. Not mine. I have known it for a while now. Some—many—will give their lives in this fight. But in the end, there must be a"—she searched for the right word—"a martyr. Someone to set the end in motion, something no one can ignore. It has never been an option, me living through this war." Her eyes took on a faraway look. "I think

Master Erikkson knows it, too. Someone has to set the end in motion."

His mouth hung open, all color drained from his face. "But — You cannot throw your life away like that. What about your future?"

A wry smile touched her lips. "What future has a weapon outside of war? Besides, is it really throwing my life away if it frees the biomatons for good? I have a purpose. A great and terrible purpose. But if I survive past it, I will have nothing to live for. I cannot go back to hiding what I am."

"You do not have to hide." He looked into her emerald eyes, words he had never meant to say tumbling from his lips. "You are more than a weapon to me. Do not throw your life away like this. I cannot live without you. Taryn Roft, I am in love with you."

As soon as the words left his mouth, he knew there was no taking them back. He grabbed her hands, and, leaning forward, kissed her.

CHAPTER TWENTY-TWO

TARYN FROZE with Royal's lips against hers, too shocked to move. After a moment's surprise, she pushed him away, her hand flashing out to slap him hard across the cheek. Her face flushed a deep red. The look of bewildered shock that crossed his face was more than she could bear. She shoved past him, desperate to get away from the discomfort of the situation. He caught her wrist, holding her back. "Taryn—"

She turned and stared at him. Where she'd slapped him, his cheek was bright red. His eyes brimmed with tears. She shook her head. "It is impossible. You know it is impossible." Overwrought as she was, her voice slipped toward those old Cockney consonants. Her words blurred together. "I'm sorry."

She ran from the room, leaving Royal in stunned silence. She could still feel the weight of his lips against hers, but that was all it was. Weight. She'd never felt more heartless.

"ACE?"

The boy looked up from the pistol he'd disassembled and

was cleaning with care, if only because it gave his hands something familiar to do; if only because he felt less empty doing it. A young man stood in his doorway, watching him with golden clockwork eyes. The boy nodded. He liked being called Ace, though he could not yet remember if it really was his name or not. It felt right.

"May I come in?" the newcomer asked in a soft French accent.

Ace nodded warily, watching as the visitor stepped into the room. He had a feeling this Frenchman was dangerous, but whether he was specifically dangerous to him or just dangerous in general, he wasn't certain.

"*Que s'est-il passé, mon ami?*" The Frenchman asked with a surprising tenderness to his tone.

"*Ils ont tout pris,*" Ace answered, the words falling from his lips as easily as his native tongue. He froze, one hand rising to touch his mouth, face twisting in confusion. "*Je parle français?*"

"*Oui,*" the Frenchman answered. "And you taught me to speak English."

Ace stared, waiting for something, anything to come back to him, some memory of this young man who so clearly knew him. Nothing stirred in a mind too damaged to recover even scraps of the past he had left behind. "What is your name?"

"*Je m'appelle Emmett LeBeau. Tu ne te souviens pas de moi?*"

Ace shook his head. "Emmett. No, I am afraid I do not remember you."

The Frenchman with the clockwork eyes sighed. "I was afraid you would not."

"Did I know you before?" Ace asked. As he spoke, he began to reassemble the revolver, sliding the well-oiled pieces together one by one with the ease of someone who had done it a thousand times.

Emmett nodded, watching closely as Ace worked. "*Oui.* We shared a cabin aboard the *Dauntless.*"

The name stirred something in his mind. Not a memory, not even an image, but a feeling bloomed in his chest, a combination of sorrow and longing. "The airship?"

"*Oui,* so something is coming back."

Ace shook his head. "I wish I could remember." He finished assembling the pistol and holstered it on his hip, standing up. "Do you need something?"

"*Non.* I just wanted to see how you were settling in."

"I am all right," Ace answered, but his voice trailed to a near whisper on the last note. He didn't know how to say that shooting Taryn had left a gaping wound of guilt in his chest, rivaled only by the wound of his missing memories. He *was* sorry he'd shot her, and even more sorry he hadn't recognized her in the first place, but even the bare scraps of imagery he'd regained could not compare to who she was, who she had become. This girl—this woman—could hold her own in the face of danger. She gave orders and people obeyed. Even Ace, with what little he knew of his past and what they were doing here, obeyed her. He'd enjoyed the little time she'd spent with him today, learning to shoot. It had been the closest to whole he'd felt in a long time.

"Tell me about the *Dauntless,*" Ace requested, looking up at the Frenchman. He gestured, indicating the room, trying his best to be welcoming. Some of the other biomatons were wary of him after what he'd done to Taryn, but surely, if he'd known this young man before, he wouldn't be afraid?

Emmett stepped into his room and perched himself on the narrow stone window ledge, swinging his legs. "She was *très belle, mon cher,*" he breathed, his voice growing soft and impassioned. "She was old and sleek, and she prowled the skies like a shark. Her balloon was navy blue, and we used to climb up and sit atop it on calm days. It was like flying." Emmett's face took on a far-away look. "I always thought you should have been captain, and not Storm."

Again, Ace felt that stirring at the back of his mind. "My sister."

"You remember?" Emmett asked, leaning forward eagerly.

He shook his head, toying with his clockwork thumb. He was used to the graft by now, and it responded to his thoughts as well as his own arm might, but it still felt like something was missing, something important he'd lost. "Taryn told me."

"You have spoken with Taryn?"

Ace nodded. "I am teaching her to shoot." A smile touched his lips as he remembered how poorly she'd done at first, how he'd had to retrain her fingers. He wondered if it was just the hollow, empty space of his life up to a few weeks ago that made those hours with her glow so brightly in comparison. They were the first truly happy moments he could remember spending.

"Ah, that is good. You will be a much better teacher than me, *mon ami*."

"You were teaching her?"

Emmett laughed. "I was trying. I am afraid I am not very good at it. It is hard when you can only see the outlines of the target."

"Taryn also told me—" Ace hesitated, unsure how to phrase his question. It was probably a clumsy thing to ask, and he didn't want to damage his potentially blossoming friendship with this person who seemed to know him. "I mean, were you— aboard the *Dauntless*, did you—"

"Was I a biomaton?" Emmett asked, gesturing to his golden clockwork eyes.

Ace nodded.

"*Non, mon ami*, I was whole. This happened recently."

"What happened?"

Emmett hesitated, his jaw tightening. "Let us say I was also the victim of the Black Castle's kindness."

Another flash of imagery: Taryn screaming at him, her left arm crushed. *I hate you!* Ace blinked, startled by the vivid memory. "That... That was my fault, wasn't it?" Emmett's face twisted, and that was all the answer Ace needed. "I am sorry, Emmett," he murmured. "For whatever I did, or whatever I failed to do."

Emmett shrugged. "Storm had you under her thumb, *mon ami.* There was not much you could have done without undermining her authority, and she would have punished you for it."

Ace shook his head, sarcasm flooding his voice. "She sounds like the kind of person one would want as a sister."

"*Certainement, elle n'a pas les mains douce.*"

"That is putting it mildly, from what I can tell," Ace answered.

"You will likely remember, in time."

Ace gave him a cautious smile. "Perhaps, if the person I worked for was so awful, and my own deeds were so ignoble, perhaps I am better off without those memories. Perhaps I have been given a chance to remake myself."

"You were in a corner, *mon ami,* but you have never been ignoble," Emmett answered, shaking his head. "*Mais...* If you want a chance to reinvent yourself, I can think of no better place to do it than Elmhurst Manor."

WHEN ERIKKSON FOUND TARYN OVER AN HOUR LATER, SHE stood in the shooting range, in front of a target with a six-inch hole torn through the bullseye.

"When did you learn to shoot like that?" he questioned, approaching from behind.

Taryn fired off another round, the bullet zinging through

the center of the target without touching the ragged edges. "This afternoon," she snapped, knocking the revolver's cylinder open, allowing the empty brass shells to clatter into the grass amongst countless others.

"Impressive."

She slammed the chamber back into place without reloading and holstered the pistol. Her jaw tightened. "If you came to invite me to supper, I am not hungry."

"Who taught you to shoot like that?"

"Ace."

She said no more. Erikkson's eyes narrowed. "What is bothering you, little one?"

She hesitated. "It is nothing."

"It is not nothing." His brow knit together. "Are you still angry with Royal?"

Her eyes snapped to his face, a jolt of shock racing down her spine. "What did he tell you?"

Erikkson raised his hands in a pacifying manner, taken aback by her vehemence. "We discussed what happened last night, that is all." He frowned. "He has not taken my advice?"

Taryn tossed her head dismissively. "We spoke, if that was what you suggested."

"Then what is wrong?"

She stared at him in silence for several seconds, considering whether or not she should even mention what happened. In the end, she decided it would be better to get it off her chest. The confession trembled on her lips. "I do not know what to do."

"What happened?"

"I—he told me he loves me and then—" Taryn averted her eyes. "He kissed me." She peeked at Erikkson, afraid to see judgement in his eyes, but found only sympathy and worry. "I have read enough books to know what a first kiss should be like." Her gaze turned inward, her fingers moving to her mouth.

"It should be like fireworks. It is supposed to make you *feel* something—" her voice cracked. "I felt nothing at all."

Erikkson sighed. "I am sorry, little one. It has been clear to me for some time that young Master Stokker was quite smitten by you, but I never thought he would have the courage to tell you..." A half smile crossed his face. "In a way, I am proud of him for taking my advice, though I did not suggest the kiss. I only wish he had fallen for someone capable of reciprocating his feelings."

She nodded. "He deserves better than me. He deserves someone who will love him and make him happy."

Erikkson's face folded in on itself, his green eyes brimming with tears. "Oh, little one, what have I done to you?"

She stared at him, a numb horror passing through her. "Do not regret what you made me. I am necessary for the future of the biomatons," she said mechanically. "You know this as well as I do."

"And yet I have stolen so much from you."

"To secure the freedom of an entire race," she insisted. "The ends justify the means." *And I shall not survive long enough to feel the loss of what I could have had,* she mused, but did not say the words. He already knew her inevitable fate. It was useless to spell it out. "Now, if you will excuse me, I have more training to do."

CHAPTER TWENTY-THREE

Taryn entered the dining hall, breathless and red-faced from her morning run, to the sounds of chatter, laughter, and joy. Emmett sat up straighter when he saw her, beaming. "*Chérie!*"

"Hello, Emmett," she said, returning his smile. "May I join you?"

"Aye," Rorin shouted from across the table. He was seated next to his brother, both of them grinning like schoolboys. Even Seraphim looked more chipper than usual, seated at the head of the table. There were six of them there in all: the twins, Rylan, Seraphim, Emmett, and Royal. She hadn't expected to find them all together like this—enjoying a meal together—especially not Royal, and something lifted a little in her chest at the sight of them. Despite the awkwardness between them in the days since the kiss, he was making an effort. He was making friends.

Taryn took her seat. "What are you mischief makers up to?"

Royal gave her a trademark crooked grin. "Seraphim was just recounting some of his exploits aboard the *Dauntless.*"

Taryn raised an eyebrow as Rylan passed her the tray of fresh *pain au chocolat.* "I thought you were mostly powerless aboard that ship," she said, repeating his words back to him.

"Only when it came to control," Seraphim answered. "I am still a warrior, after all."

"Seraphim, tell the story about the Spanish pirates," Emmett urged.

Seraphim shook his head. "That is not a story for the breakfast table."

"Now we really want to hear it," Rorin exclaimed, mouth half-full of a sausage roll.

Ari smacked him. "Table manners. Ye are in the presence of a lady."

Taryn smiled, sipping her tea. "This lady does not mind."

Royal gave her *a look,* but she just smiled demurely and sipped her tea again, enjoying the banter, basking in the warmth of her friends, new and old.

"Very well," Seraphim answered, shaking his head. "But Sedition, you may want to excuse yourself while I tell this story."

Taryn snorted. "Are you implying I may not have the constitution for this, Seraphim?"

He inclined his head. "I did warn you."

"Please," she murmured with a wave of her hand. "Continue."

"A little more than a year ago, we were in the Celtic Sea on the trail of a band of Spanish pirates who had been attacking merchant ships. We had been away from port for perhaps two weeks—meaning we were running low on hydrogen, but Storm refused to give up and return to refill supplies. She was determined to stop the pirates."

"She had even been sanctioned to lead a team of privateer airships," Emmett interjected excitedly. His golden clockwork eyes were trained raptly on Seraphim.

Seraphim ducked his head. "She and Ace were leading the band of pirate hunters. He was her first mate then, and she trusted him to give orders for her. There were six airships in all, strong British privateer vessels, including Captain Rosemary Todd of the *HMA Fidelis*: Storm's best friend."

Taryn's stomach tightened as she listened. She didn't know Ace had once been first mate. Perhaps this story might explain why Storm's vitriol had extended to Ace, and why he'd been so afraid to cross her.

"After weeks of searching, we caught one Spanish pirate ship in the midst of attacking a small fishing vessel and gave chase, but with our hydrogen reserves depleted, we could barely keep up. Storm kept ordering the airmen to vent the envelope so we could up our speed, but if they had, we would never have had enough to reach port. The Spanish schooner outpaced us and rounded a rocky craig, disappearing from sight." Seraphim paused dramatically, taking a sip of his morning tea.

"And that was when everything went wrong," Emmett murmured.

The winged biomaton glanced sharply at Emmett. "I was about to get to that."

Emmett's cheeks colored. "*Désolé.*"

"Ace gave the order: Three of our ships were to take the lead, the other two following after. The *Fidelis* led the first assault. We assumed it was only a single seafaring ship in the inlet. They would get off three or four shots from their cannon before we reached them, but that would be the extent of the attack. An easy mark. We were wrong."

Taryn leaned forward in her seat, elbows on the table despite how unladylike it was. Seraphim's soft-spoken accent was perfect for storytelling; he had a natural, easy cadence and chose his words with care, painting a scene for the biomatons sitting around the table.

"We were still beyond the cliff when we heard the cannons fire on the first wave. Not just three or four, but several *dozen* cannons all firing at once. And there was nothing we could do but wait as we rounded the rocks, guns at the ready, dread in the pits of our stomachs."

There was a haunted look in his eyes. "We'd severely underestimated the Spanish pirates. It was not just one ship: it was four. Two of them were air Man o' War, twice the size of the *Dauntless,* with over fifty cannons on their gundeck alone. Their ambush had crippled the *Fidelis* and the *Amare,* which were already burning. The *Hind* had been at the head and caught the brunt of the fire. Their ship was in pieces before it hit the water."

Taryn's heart pounded in her palms. Three airships and their crews, lost to the sea. No wonder Ace had been so cautious around Storm.

"What did ye do?" Rorin asked incredulously.

"We fought, of course. We had the advantage, as our cannons were primed and ready. We took them down before they were able to reload, and the crippled ships sank. But we lost three good airships full of brave privateers that day. Storm never forgave Ace for giving that order."

"It should have been Storm who died," Taryn grumbled.

"It was *my* order. Perhaps it should have been me."

The group twisted as one to find Ace standing in the doorway. He'd lost the glossy, empty look in his eyes, but he still didn't seem *whole,* exactly. He was more himself, Taryn knew, but he wasn't fully Ace. Not yet.

"*Mon ami,*" Emmett said reproachfully, always the first to find his tongue. "There was no way for you to know. Storm was wrong to place the blame upon your shoulders. The rest of us did not blame you for that."

Ace shook his head. He had one hand on the doorframe, as if afraid to fully enter the room. As if he still did not consider himself worthy to dine with them. "I do not remember what happened, but clearly, I bore the blame for it. Perhaps there was a good reason for that."

Taryn gestured, trying to welcome him into the room. "It seems to me Storm liked to blame you for her own shortcomings. You do not need to bear that burden any longer."

Ace offered her the slightest of smiles, approaching the dining table. He sat beside Emmett, who offered him a wide, friendly grin and a plate of croissants. Ace accepted one gratefully, tearing it in half with his clockwork fingers. Taryn stared at him, wondering at his transformation. In just a week's time, he'd gone from a glossy-eyed slave to this boy who smiled when he saw her. She could still see the weight of his time at the Black Castle on his shoulders, but something had eased that burden since he arrived. Maybe Elmhurst *really was* an oasis.

"Besides, you said you wished to reinvent yourself," Emmett offered. "That means releasing your past and moving on."

Ace's smirk stayed plastered on his face. "So, what you are saying is that I should be thankful I cannot remember?"

Seraphim inclined his head. "There are worse things than a missing memory. Sedition can attest to that."

Ace's icy gaze snapped to her face, and Taryn found her cheeks heating up. "Oh, no, I—" Had all the air been sucked from the room?

"You lost your memories too?"

She nodded, knotting her fist in the tablecloth. Royal noticed her reaction and set a comforting hand on her left forearm. She gave him a strained smile in acknowledgement, though she could not actually *feel* the touch. "I am missing about six years, between the fire that took my arm and the time I lived on the streets in London."

"And you are all right with that?"

Taryn swallowed hard, turning her eyes down to her plate

as she considered her answer. "I often wonder about what happened to me in those years. About how they shaped who I am now, about what important circumstances or people"—she nodded at Seraphim—"I have forgotten. But most days, I do not allow myself to dwell on it. They say if you dwell on the past, you cannot move forward, right?"

Ace nodded. "That is good advice. And you know," he smiled, and this time it was warm and broad and genuine, the kind of smile that might have turned another girl's heart in a somersault. "It is comforting to know someone else has experienced the same thing."

Taryn smirked and rolled her eyes. "Whatever makes you feel better, Ace."

Royal grunted, throwing another right hook into the padded gloves Rorin was holding. Ari had his arms crossed, standing nearby. "Oh, come now, lordling. Watch yer wrists. Ye fight like a schoolmarm."

"I do not," Royal snapped, throwing another punch into Rorin's gloves.

"Ye ever been in a fight before, lordling?"

Royal shrugged. "I got into my share of fistfights in boarding school."

"Probably ended up with broken fingers, too," Ari snipped.

"I did not!"

Rorin chuckled, adjusting his stance so Royal could better strike the gloves. "I find it unlikely that ye were the victor, though."

"I won a few and lost a few." He shifted, throwing three punches in quick succession. "Besides, I am better with a sword. I do not see why I need to improve with my fists."

"Because ye could be unarmed," Ari replied coldly. "And

our Lady Sedition will be disappointed if ye let yerself get run through just 'cause we did not take the time to train ye properly."

Royal grumbled and threw several more strikes before stepping back, shaking out his fists. "Give it a rest. We have been at this for a long time."

"We stop when they stop," Ari answered, inclining his head to the sparring ring nearby, where Emmett and Seraphim had been fighting endlessly. The two were perfectly matched, the bigger biomaton's wings clashing against Emmett's rapier in a whirl of blades almost too fast to observe with the naked eye. Seraphim was fast, but so was his opponent, and the two danced around each other without scoring a single hit.

Royal groaned and attacked again, fists pounding against Rorin's gloves, but his mind was on the mysterious biomaton and the story he'd told over breakfast that morning. "You know what bothers me?" he said, raising his voice to be heard over the crash of blade against blade. "How did Ace find Taryn? None of us at the school or at home knew she was a biomaton, let alone one built by Erikkson. So how did the captain know to send him after her?"

The crash of blades stopped. Seraphim and Emmett broke apart, leaving the room suddenly too quiet after the endless noise of their training. Royal glanced toward them to find Seraphim staring directly at him. A shudder raced down his spine and he turned his attention back toward Rorin. "Does this mean I can be done?"

Ari opened his mouth to say something, then closed it again, eyes sliding across to the winged biomaton. "I think Seraphim wants a turn."

Royal turned to find Seraphim standing directly behind him. He jumped, surprise shaking his shoulders. "Hello, Seraphim," he said, trying and failing to act nonchalant. He chewed at the side of his thumb. "Did you need something?"

He held out a hand, silent, green eyes sliding to the twins.

Rorin hurriedly set the training gloves in Seraphim's palm.

"I think it is time you and I trained together." His wings shuffled together with the hiss of metal on metal.

Royal shook out his sore fists, glancing at the twins for help. They just gave him identical shrugs. Rorin made a face that might have been interpreted as *good luck.*

"Now?" Royal asked numbly.

"Is now a bad time for you?" A flash of silver fang made an appearance behind Seraphim's lips.

"N-no. Now is fine." His heart in his throat, Royal followed Seraphim across the stone floor and out of the training room. "Um, where are we going?"

"I thought the fresh air might be a fine change of pace." Seraphim reached a heavy wood door and pushed it open, standing hunched over in the entryway. "After you, young Master Stokker."

"Royal is fine," Royal muttered, ducking past him and out into the yard. Though he'd spent time exploring the grounds, he realized this particular door wasn't one he'd used before. He stepped from the candlelit hallway to find himself standing in a secluded square, hemmed in on all sides by thick, eight-foot hedges. A soft drizzle fell from the sky, quickly dampening Royal's hair and clothes. He grimaced, but did not complain.

"Look, if I—" But just as he started to turn, something hard caught the back of his knees and he went down hard in the mud.

Spluttering, Royal coughed out something that *might* have been a protest before he felt a knee in the center of his back. He fell quiet, waiting for the biomaton's next move.

"There are questions that we do not ask," Seraphim hissed, his mouth so close to Royal's ear that the younger boy could feel the heat of his breath.

"*What?*" Royal tried to push himself up and failed, the full weight of a man who was half made of metal bearing down on his back. Slowly, all too slowly, he pieced it together. The question he'd yelled at the twins while they trained. The way Seraphim had reacted. "What are you talking about?"

A bladed wing touched his cheek. Not hard enough to leave a mark, but close enough that he could see the tiny drops of mist sliding down the honed edge. "Some knowledge is dangerous in the wrong hands."

"I am Erikkson's apprentice!"

"And you are Miss Taryn's best friend," Seraphim growled. "I have given you lenience up to this point because you were not a part of this war. But now you are a soldier, just like the rest of us, and you must understand that there are some things we do not question."

Royal gritted his teeth. "Let me up."

"Not until you understand that if you ever speak of this again, it will be the last time you speak."

"I understand!" The hedges seemed to muffle his voice, like they were absorbing all of this conversation, cradling the secrets within themselves. "Let me up."

The weight left his body. Royal pushed himself to his feet, spitting mud from his mouth and wiping his face on an already filthy sleeve in a feeble attempt to clean it. "At least explain to me why," he said, turning around.

The winged biomaton had vanished, leaving the heavy wooden door slightly ajar. Royal cursed. He stood there for a moment, trying in vain to wipe the mud from his clothes. There was one thing in life that rankled him more strongly than anything else. It had gotten him in trouble plenty of times, and he knew if he let it, this time would be the same. But as soon as Seraphim had pinned him, as soon as the threats had been spoken, Royal's already curious mind had been piqued. He couldn't let a mystery go. Not when he knew exactly who had the answers he craved.

Royal shoved the door open and stomped down the hall, following the wet footprints Seraphim had left in his wake, stringing curses along as he went.

The prints led him down the hall and up a flight of stairs before stepping into a small room. The door was open and Royal pushed inside, determination eliminating any better judgement he might have had. The room was equipped with a dark wood wardrobe and a small bed, but a hammock was slung in one corner, like a sailor's berth. A pile of books sat beside the bed. Royal glanced around as he closed the door behind him, realizing these must be the winged biomaton's quarters. The bare stone walls and floor shifted something inside Royal—this room was almost tragically impersonal; it was like Seraphim had no personality outside his role in Erikkson's army. Royal couldn't help but think of Taryn and how she'd been intended to have the same training. How different would she be had he not found her all those years ago on the streets? Would she be the same Taryn he knew, or would she be like Seraphim: stiff, driven, silent, a weapon?

Speak of the devil. The winged biomaton himself was standing near the wardrobe, his wings spread in alarm at Royal's entrance.

"You know what happened," Royal said without preamble. He leaned his back against the door, blocking the one way out of the room. His message was clear: There is no escaping this conversation.

"I am finished discussing this."

"You know how the pirates found Taryn, and I am not leaving this room until you tell me."

"You *will* leave," Seraphim growled, his wings clicking forward like a bird of prey mantling over its meal. "Or I shall make you leave."

Royal raised his hands in a pacifying gesture. He didn't know the world of rebellions or battles well, but he *did* understand people. He made a bid he hoped would pay off. "I have seen the way you shift about the place. You are Erikkson's secret keeper. And you are dying to let this one out. Let me carry that burden with you."

"What I know can *never* reach Sedition's ears."

"I understand." Royal was surprised by how steady his voice sounded, considering his heart felt like it was about to break out of his ribcage. But at least Seraphim's wings were beginning to lower, ever so slightly. "I know we do not know each other well, but I promise you, I can keep a secret."

Seraphim's face took on a skeptical glare.

"I kept the secret that I was in love with her for nearly six years," Royal offered, trying to lighten the mood.

"If I share this with you, you must keep it *forever*. It could change the course of the war."

If he hadn't already been interested, those words would have clinched it. "I swear, whatever it is you have to say, it will never leave this room."

Seraphim sagged, a heavy sigh escaping him as his wings tucked themselves back behind his broad shoulders. "Very well. Master Erikkson told the captain about her."

The color drained from Royal's face. "*What?*"

"He sent an anonymous letter to the captain telling her where Sedition could be found."

"You mean—" Royal shook his head, trying and failing to process this new information. "He's the reason Taryn went through all that? Why would he do that? Why not invite her home when he asked me to be his apprentice?"

"He said she still did not understand the injustices she faced well enough to lead. She was too comfortable with you and your family. So, he pushed her into a situation where she would better understand our predicament. Where she would find the fire to take up her mantle."

Unable to stand still and process this new information,

Royal turned and paced, chewing at a thumb that was beginning to bleed. He'd wanted this. He'd asked for this. But he hadn't known the sheer enormity of the secret Seraphim carried. "And Taryn does not know any of this?"

"She *cannot* know," Seraphim insisted. "She could turn on us, and we need her."

This gave him pause. Royal stopped midstep, turning back to Seraphim. "You think she would turn her back on the cause if she knew?"

The winged biomaton narrowed his eyes. "I think you know her and Master Erikkson well enough to know that if she were to learn this information, the consequences would not be pretty. She is a warrior now, Royal. She cannot just shrug that off. And to tear her cause away from her will only result in more pain. If you love her, you will keep this secret."

The words caught Royal like a slap to the face. *If you love her.* This man never ceased to see straight through him. He clenched his fists, pressing his bleeding thumb tight to his palm. He hated it, but he knew Seraphim was right. Taryn's words came back to him: *I feel more like myself than I ever have.* And he'd seen what good taking up the mantle of Sedition had done for her: she was more open, she smiled more, she had friends. She didn't flinch at his touch anymore. He swallowed hard and nodded. "I will keep your secret. At least until this war is completed. But I cannot promise that I will not tell her when all this is over. She deserves to know."

Seraphim ducked his head. "When the time comes, I am certain Master Erikkson will tell her himself. But until then, I thank you for understanding and keeping his secret."

CHAPTER TWENTY-FOUR

THE FOLLOWING three weeks passed with little incident. Ace joined Taryn in training most mornings. They seemed to share a silent bond because of their missing memories, and they got along well, working silently side by side. Taryn worked on hand-to-hand combat with the twins, learned specialized fighting and quarterstaves from Seraphim, sabre fencing from Emmett, and knife throwing from Erikkson. She spent the evenings poring over maps and schematics with Royal, plans made and remade in their eagerness to put the awkward kiss behind them. She endured strength training, and as she progressed, fittings for her armor from Gennifer. Not a single moment was wasted, until Taryn lived and breathed her role as Sedition: running drills, roll call, and keeping troop morale high atop all her other duties.

One morning, just after Taryn finished her early run, Ace by her side, Rylan came racing across the lawn toward them. "Sedition!"

She slowed, breathing in deep, steady breaths as he approached. His face had lost all color, making the freckles across his nose and cheeks appear even darker.

"You best change out of those clothes," he exclaimed, panting. "There is a Navy ship here; the officers demanded to speak with Master Erikkson."

Naval officers? Here? Taryn's heart thundered in her ears, and it wasn't from the exercise. Perhaps they were friends of Erikkson's, but she doubted it. She exchanged nervous glances with Ace, then raced to the house, feet barely touching the ground. She could not shake the feeling that her creator needed her.

She reached her room in record time, shrugging out of her training uniform and pulling on a dark blue cotton dress, the most "obedient slave" item of clothing she owned. Her mind raced. Why would the Navy suddenly pay Erikkson a visit?

Ace.

Her throat closed as she remembered the boy they harbored had been a privateer before he was a biomaton. Had been property of the Crown and gone rogue for her sake. She shook herself. It had been months since he left the *Dauntless*, and there was no reason anyone should suspect him to be here. This was probably just a social visit. But she couldn't shake the dread pooling in her stomach. She tucked her hair into a quick bun, then hurried down the hall to Erikkson's study. At the door, she saved a single moment to compose herself, taking a deep inhale before pushing it open, assuming a doe-eyed expression. "Master Erikkson, you called for me?"

She took in the scene in an instant: three Naval officers stood between her and Erikkson's desk, wearing their customary blue and white uniforms, each of the many buttons on their chests polished to a gleaming gold. Everything, from their immaculate uniforms to their square jaws and close-cropped hair, was militarily precise. Erikkson sat behind his desk, one hand holding a letter, the broken wax seal upon it bearing the emblem of Queen Victoria herself. His face was pale. His eyes met Taryn's with a sort of sick horror she had never seen before.

He lifted himself from his chair with some difficulty, moving like a man twice his age. "Not now, Taryn. Return to your quarters."

Taryn nodded, despite the fear and concern flooding her mind. Erikkson knew what he was doing. "Yes, sir."

She moved to retreat, but one of the officers called out to her. "Do not go yet, biomaton. Your master was just talking about you."

Her breath caught in her throat, but she turned back to the room, applying a pretty, porcelain smile to her features. Beneath her façade, her palms itched for a fight. "Good things, I should hope, sir."

"Taryn. Leave us. Now." Erikkson's voice hardened.

She bobbed a curtsy and turned again to leave. The nearest officer—a small young man with lapels that indicated midshipman ranking—caught her wrist. "Not so fast."

Taryn mentally restrained herself, though she was already calculating how she could defeat all three of them. It would take thirty seconds, she thought. Forty-five at most. In the same instant, she read the other officers' lapels: a commander and the captain. She wondered what could be so important they would send in their top-ranking officers. And the mystery of the letter bearing the queen's own seal refused to be ignored. Her mind flickered to the biomatons training in the west wing, only a few walls between them and these officers. Maybe this raid was far less personal than she'd thought. Her heart throbbed in her head, demanding she get out of this situation, one way or another. "Please, sir," she protested, but she did not know how to finish.

The midshipman shoved her into the room, moving between her and the door. Immediately, Taryn looked to

Erikkson, searching for some indication of how she should play this scene. He frowned at their treatment of her. "Do not touch her."

"M'lord Erikkson, were you aware you harbored a traitor?" the captain demanded slowly and deliberately, every word like a lead weight on Taryn's shoulders.

Her head spun. *Traitor? Do they know about our rebellion?*

"My Taryn most certainly is not." Erikkson held his head high. Briefly, he gave her a look that ordered her to do the same. Her mind raced, trying to figure out who could possibly have leaked the information about what they were doing here. She knew Erikkson sent spies out to keep tabs on activity in the bigger cities—could one of them have been caught? Or could they have been recognized on a mission to liberate biomatons?

"You may not think so, but we have it on good authority that says otherwise."

The commander produced a pair of handcuffs from somewhere. Taryn tensed, ready to fight her way out if it came to it. She forced her mind out of its downward spiral of speculation. There would be time enough to consider how this had happened later, and she needed all her wits about her.

"Her dampers prevent any kind of seditious act," Erikkson protested. She immediately understood his meaning. He wanted her to wait. For what, she did not know, but she quieted the violence inside herself, waiting for his signal.

"Despite your insistence on that fact, she *is* under arrest."

Under arrest?

"On what charges?" Erikkson exclaimed.

"High treason and conspiracy to overthrow Her Majesty, the Queen of England."

Taryn's mouth fell open. The commander approached her, forcing Taryn's hands behind her back and shackling her wrists. She stood numbly, allowing it to happen, her eyes half-glazed. How had she been accused of such a thing? Who knew about what they were planning? Who could possibly have reported her? Someone close enough to know what they were doing. Someone who wanted her to fail. The room wouldn't stop spinning.

"Please, do not take her from me." A frailty and fearfulness came into Erikkson's voice, at odds with everything she knew of him. "She is my best—my favorite of all my possessions."

It was all an act. She had to remind herself of that. He was putting on the guise of an elderly, eccentric lord for the benefit of the soldiers. Still, it was a bloody good act.

The commander dragged his eyes slowly over Taryn's body, sending shivers down her spine. An ugly grin crossed his face. "I am sure she is. Unfortunately, my lord, you cannot protest this. As you saw, the warrant comes directly from the Queen."

The midshipman slipped his hands down Taryn's bodice, from her ribs to her waist. She jerked backward, shocked, a wordless cry escaping her before she could muffle it.

"You dare violate her?" Erikkson demanded.

The young man drew his hands away instantly, his cheeks coloring in embarrassment. "N-no sir, I am required to check her for weapons—"

"If you *must* conduct such an asinine search, *I* shall do it for you," Erikkson declared.

The officers exchanged leery glances, then shrugged. Despite the charges, Taryn could read in their eyes and manners that they did not truly expect her to be armed. They saw what she wanted them to see: an obedient biomaton, falsely accused. She smiled inwardly as Erikkson frisked her. She could keep up the obedient charade to lure them into a false sense of security. She bore no weapons but the hidden ones, and of those Erikkson said nothing. He straightened, turning back to the men.

"I beg of you, do not take her and deprive an old man of his comforts. I can vouch for her. She is no traitor."

"Oh, and what of those other biomatons you built, m'lord? Strange, dangerous biomatons. I suppose we are to believe she is not like them?"

"I built them when I was young and restless, eager to show off my skills. Now I am old and would like no more than to live here with my creations in peace."

The commander scoffed. "We apologize for your loss, m'lord, but nevertheless we must take her. If you take your petition to her Majesty's court, they may find it suitable to provide you recompense for your losses. I am sure they can find a suitable replacement, capable of whatever this one does for you."

"I beg of you!"

Taryn shook her head. "I will go with them, Master Erikkson." He turned horror-stricken eyes upon her. She nodded to him, her chin held high. "My innocence will win out. There is no need to fear."

"There, it is settled," the captain exclaimed impatiently. "We must be off."

"Please, allow me a moment alone with her to say goodbye," Erikkson pleaded.

The officers looked at one another as if to say, *See what comes of spending too much time alone with biomatons?* but at last, they nodded.

"Very well," the captain growled. "You have five minutes."

The men filed from the room. As soon as they had closed the door, Erikkson spun on Taryn. "What are you thinking? They shall hang you!"

A clever smile crossed her lips. "Not if I break free."

"You have a plan?"

"The beginnings of one. I need you to make sure a small squad of our best are at my trial. Emmett, Seraphim, the twins, and Ace. Oh, and Royal, if you think he is combat ready. Send along an extra pistol and a sabre for me, if you can manage it." The words tumbled out breathlessly as she raced against the clock to lay out the foundations of her plan.

"What are you going to do?"

She grinned. "There shall be an audience at the trial, will there not? I think it is time we announced this rebellion to the public. The world should know that we are no longer going to be quiet."

At last, Erikkson caught on. "Clever girl," he exclaimed. He hesitated a moment, then embraced her. She stood awkwardly, unable to return the gesture with her wrists shackled behind her back. "Take care of yourself until we come for you, little one. It is a dangerous world out there."

Taryn nodded, her eyes crinkling at the corners. "Do not worry, sir. I have been trained by the best."

The door opened, and she applied her obedient, doe-eyed persona once more. "I am sorry to disappoint you, Master Erikkson. They shall discover these accusations are untrue."

He nodded. "I know, child."

"Time to go," the captain ordered from the door.

Erikkson took Taryn's face in his hands and ever so gently tilted it up, kissing her forehead. "I shall see you soon," he murmured.

The midshipman took Taryn by the arm, leading her from the room with a firm, steady hand. All at once, Taryn's heart leapt into her throat. They were taking her from her sanctuary. She was being forced back out into the hideous world which had rejected her, and this time, there would be no black silk glove to hide behind, no kind face to help her along. They passed out of the front doors of the manor and Taryn froze, staring at the massive Man o' War airship anchored in the drive. It was twice the size of the *Dauntless* and new, with shimmering paint and a brass lion figurehead gleaming in the afternoon sun. The navy-blue balloon above it was as large as Taryn imagined whales to be, keeping the craft afloat.

The officers did not stop, plowing right ahead to the basket on the ground beneath the ship. It was the same as a hot air balloon gondola, and the four crowded inside before the commander blew a shrill signal on his whistle. With a jerk, they ascended.

Once aboard the massive vessel, Taryn had no time to marvel. The midshipman took her shoulder and steered her down into the bowels of the ship, to the brig where three barred cells hung empty and waiting for prisoners. *At least there is a window*, she mused pessimistically.

The midshipman removed her shackles and replaced them with a bizarre cylindrical device that opened on a pair of hinges. The inside was packed with clockwork, but Taryn barely got a good look at the thing before it clamped around her forearms. Her arms crossed in front of her stomach inside the device, which covered her arms up to the elbow. There came a hiss and a click as it locked down and tightened to fit like a glove. Experimentally, she wiggled the fingers of her right hand. The cuff tightened ever so slightly. She made a tiny, surprised sound in her throat.

"If you move about too much, the cuff will tighten," the midshipman explained, almost conversationally, as he pushed her into the nearest cell and locked the door. "I have seen men come out of it with broken bones. Just a warning."

A scoff rose in her throat, but she stifled it, determined to play the doe-eyed slave as long as she could. Instead, she nodded. "Do you know why I have been accused of treason?"

"No, miss." He hesitated, his face twisting. For a moment, Taryn realized how very young he looked—no more than fourteen or fifteen. He turned away. "Someone will fetch you when we reach the Tower of London." He left without looking back at her.

Taryn's mouth went dry. *The Tower of London?* London was hours away, and only the worst traitors and murderers were held there. Her situation became more serious by the minute. She settled herself on the narrow bench against the wall of her cell, leaning against the pale oak-paneled wall. She forced her breathing to slow. Panic would not help her. She had to focus, to plan for whatever came next. Erikkson would ensure her soldiers would be at her trial. She just had to be patient.

CHAPTER TWENTY-FIVE

"You just let them take her?" Royal slammed a fist into the dark wood of Erikkson's desk. His brown eyes burned with fury.

"She wanted to go. What would you have suggested I do? Stand in the way of a direct order from the Crown?" Erikkson studied the other faces in the room, each and every one of the biomatons Taryn had requested. It had taken an hour for him to process that she was gone, longer to find the right words to tell them what had happened.

"Yes! We should *all* have committed treason before we allowed Taryn to be arrested," Royal cried. His official acceptance into the army had seen him grow from awkward outsider to eager participant. He was still fumbling and childlike at times in his understanding of their fight, but he was trying so hard to make a difference. And as for his attitude toward Taryn, his fierce protectiveness had only grown. "You yourself insisted she is the biomatons only hope, so why would you allow them to take her?"

"I had *no choice*," Erikkson exclaimed, at last raising his voice. "We ought to be focusing on how to rescue her before they hang her for treason, rather than arguing over whether or not I did the right thing."

Royal's face curled into an irritated scowl, but he fell quiet. Seraphim stepped forward. "Who knew what we are doing here well enough to accuse Sedition of treason? And why did they not arrest us all?"

Erikkson rubbed his face with one hand. "I do not think her arrest is about what we are doing here. I believe whoever accused Sedition had a vendetta against her alone. Perhaps Lord Bellham—he would have known she was with me—or..."

"Or Storm," Emmett murmured, his golden clockwork irises locking onto Erikkson's face. "That is possible, *non*?"

Erikkson shrugged. "Anything is possible, I suppose."

The room shifted, discomfort floating over the men like an invisible specter. A few threw glances at Ace, who stared doggedly at his feet, chewing on the inside of his cheek.

"It does not matter why they took her," Ari growled from his place near the door. "We need to get her back first. *Before* anything happens to her."

"I was a privateer for the Queen," Ace spoke up in a painfully meek voice. He stood against the left wall, his hands nervously fiddling at his waist. "Perhaps if I turned myself in..."

"*Non*, Ace." Emmett patted his shoulder. "They are not after you, *mon ami*."

"I believe Sedition's plan of attack is our only option," Seraphim said.

"Though it seems more suicide than actual plan," Rorin retorted.

Erikkson held up his hands. "You shall have to go in disguise. We must ensure your grafts will not be noticed until the time is right." He sighed. "Petrichor ought to be here."

"Petrichor is more volatile than the rest of us combined," Seraphim shot back. "She would be more harm than help." His wings rustled in agitation.

"You three were built to work together. She is the missing link to this battle."

"She is a broken link." Seraphim's green eyes suddenly flashed with cold hatred. It was the first time any in the room—Erikkson excepted—had seen him get angry. "We shall be better off without her. *She* left us; we did not send her away."

Erikkson sighed and raised an eyebrow at the biomaton towering over him, wings half raised in a threatening manner. "Nevertheless, Petrichor shall return to us before the end. And you will all work together once more. But now, I think, you ought to prepare for your mission to rescue Sedition. Tonight, we leave for London in my airship, so we have no chance of missing the trial. We shall stay in my townhouse on Hanover Square."

The others took their cues and moved off, headed to pack their bags, clean and sharpen their weapons, and get last minute disguises from Gennifer. Seraphim waited, chastened, his eyes on the floor, until all the others left the room.

"I apologize for my outburst, Master Erikkson."

Erikkson looked at him tenderly. "Seraphim, my child, there is no need to apologize. She hurt you just as much as she hurt me when she left. I am only surprised to discover you cared so much." The older man smiled. "Truly, still waters run deep." He turned away and began to collect a stack of papers from the drafting table near the window.

Seraphim's mouth twisted into an expression that was not quite a snarl. "I learned from the best how to keep secrets and play my hand close to my chest."

Erikkson stilled in his movements but did not turn back toward Seraphim. "What are you trying to say to me, Seraphim?"

"I am saying your methods have once again put Sedition in danger. I warned you this would happen. She learned her impulsiveness from you."

Erikkson spun on his heel, green eyes bright with a fire Seraphim had seen only twice before. "No, she learned that from her two older biomaton siblings, who were supposed to train her to be a warrior and instead twisted her into a *killer*."

Cold raced down Seraphim's spine at the reminder of what Taryn had done, the final straw before Erikkson sent her away. His lips curled back in snarl. "You made us *all* killers! We were children. We knew only the world as you painted it." Seraphim's wings rose, spreading to fill the space between himself and the door, between Erikkson and his way out. The message was very clear: You are not leaving this room until I am satisfied. "And Sedition *still* does not understand the way you have her twisted around your finger. I would not be surprised if you had reported her for treason as well, to set the rebellion in motion."

Pain flashed across his master's features, and Seraphim immediately regretted his words. "Even I am not that stupid, Seraphim."

"Then why did you let them take her?"

"I had *no choice*." Tears glittered in his master's eyes.

Seraphim's usually cold heart twisted at the sight of his master—his father figure—so close to tears. He ducked his head. "We will rescue her. She is smart and strong; she will be just fine until we can arrive and begin the war."

Erikkson nodded and cleared his throat. "I know. She is quite the warrior. She can handle herself."

Seraphim tucked his wings tightly against his back, inclining his head. "I will go help the others prepare. We should leave as soon as possible."

He turned away, headed for the door. He'd nearly crossed the threshold when he heard Erikkson call out. "Thank you for being so loyal, Seraphim. This rebellion would be nothing without you."

The winged biomaton could not help the smile that graced his lips as he headed for the west wing.

✦

TARYN LURCHED, STARTLED OUT OF HER DOZE BY THE *CHINK chink chink* of metal against metal. All at once, the warm drowsiness offered by the steady swaying of the airship and the thrum of the engines dissipated, replaced by an ugly, gut-wrenching sense of dread. She raised her eyes to discover a metal gauntlet being slowly dragged between the bars of her cell. *Chink chink chink.* And above it, a wicked face she'd prayed never to see again.

Storm.

She wore a new coat: white, with gold trim and epaulets, the marks indicating she'd been promoted to commodore. The jacket hugged her curves, accentuating her powerful feminine figure, and its tails fanned behind her like a skirt. Taryn thought she'd ask for one like it if she ever saw Gennifer again.

"I missed you, biomaton," Storm said with a sinister grin. "How long has it been since I sold you to Lord Bellham?"

"Not long enough," Taryn growled in response. She no longer feared Storm; she had faced far worse than the captain since they last met. The only thing Taryn feared was being unable to defend herself.

Storm seemed taken aback by Taryn's easy reply, but she quickly recovered. "I see you got a new arm, freak."

The word no longer hurt. Taryn met Storm's ice blue eyes, so alike to her younger brother's and yet so very different. "I seem to recall the last one was crushed."

"It needed to be. The thing was hideous," Storm sneered. "That one is not much better. Perhaps I ought to smash it too."

Taryn did not rise to the bait. "Did you accuse me of treason?"

"You are working with Erikkson."

"No, he owns me. I work *for* Erikkson. There is a difference. What evidence do you have?"

"I do not need evidence to accuse a biomaton," Storm said, an icy calm coming into her voice. "Treason always ends in a hanging for biomatons. Since you are not human, it is better to be rid of you. That way there are no loose ends."

Taryn's stomach lurched into her throat. *Always?* It could not be true. And yet, she knew Storm was not lying. She hoped Erikkson knew how crucial her rescue was.

The captain leaned closer to the bars, tapping her gauntlet against them again. Taryn grimaced at the sound. *Clank clank clank.* "How does it feel to know you are going to die, biomaton?"

Taryn glared. "How did you find me again?"

"That was easy. Lord Bellham keeps a thorough account of each biomaton bought and sold by the Black Castle. He and I have a special arrangement."

Taryn stared numbly at Storm, slowly realizing she was facing down the one person in the world she could rightly call her nemesis. Storm seemed to hold all the cards. "Why do you hate me so much?" Taryn questioned, her voice hoarse.

The captain rolled her eyes. "What list would you like? One of your kind killed my parents—"

"That was not *me*. I did nothing to you."

Storm lurched forward, gripping the bars with her metal gauntlet. "You *stole* my brother."

Taryn kept her features neutral, but her stomach plummeted. *That is what this is about.* "You accused me of treason because you think I know where Ace is? Is he not aboard the *Dauntless*?"

"Do not act so innocent with me! I know you know where he is. And you *will* tell me, if I have to tear it from you piece by piece." The ugly smile Storm offered made it clear she hoped

Taryn would be uncooperative so she could question her. A shudder ran down the biomaton's spine. Despite herself, Storm's cruelty chilled her to the core. Whatever happened, she could not risk being left alone to the captain's mercy; she had none.

"I do not know anything about it," Taryn said with all the conviction she could muster.

"I will ask you nicely one last time: Where is Ace?"

Taryn shook her head. "I do not know!"

"Fine," Storm grinned. "I shall enjoy forcing it out of you. It has been too long since I performed a proper interrogation."

"Somehow, I doubt the Queen's finest will allow you to torture me."

"They will allow me to do whatever I like. This ship is under my command. Or did you think I wear these epaulets because I like the color?"

Taryn's chest tightened. Inside the complex clockwork handcuffs, her palm began to sweat. She twisted her wrist, trying to adjust her position, and the handcuff tightened around her arms. She stopped moving. She knew how sadistic Storm could be, and she could not risk infuriating her. At the same time, the captain would be livid to know Ace had been turned into a biomaton and was now living with Taryn's newfound family. No, she would *not* be the one to tell her that. She chewed the inside of her cheek.

"So, biomaton? Do you have anything to say?"

"I do not know where he is."

Storm slammed her gauntlet against the bars. "I do not believe you!"

Taryn shook her head. "It does not matter how many times you *ask,* it is not going to bring him back."

"Then you *do* know what happened to him."

"Think about the place you left us, Storm. If Ace got caught up in there—perhaps Lord Bellham took a liking to him

—he would be as good as dead to you. I do not know what happened to him, but I can guess."

Storm stared coldly at her for a few long seconds. "I shall leave you to decide if that is your final answer, biomaton. I will see you when we reach the Tower of London."

She turned to leave, and Taryn relaxed, breathing a sigh of relief. She was safe, at least for a few more hours. She would have to concoct something to tell Storm, or risk being tortured—and she could not afford that. She had to be in shape to fight, and Storm's interrogation techniques would doubtlessly ruin her form. No, Taryn would have to tell her *something*.

At the door, Storm paused and turned back, a look of puzzlement on her face. "Tell me, biomaton. You are meant to be obedient, are you not? How can you defy me if all your mental dampers are in place?"

Taryn cocked her head. "Quite a mystery, hmm? It is almost as if I am just as human as you."

Storm spat. "The world will be better with you swinging from the gallows."

She vanished through the open door.

Taryn shut her eyes, controlling the raging monster in her chest. There would be enough chances to fight Storm in the future. For now, she had to bide her time. She heaved a heavy sigh, praying Erikkson had readied her troops. It was becoming increasingly clear that she would not escape without them.

CHAPTER TWENTY-SIX

THE MOMENT the airship reached London, Taryn knew. No single factor tipped her off, but rather a combination of indicators told her they were at last above her city. She knew by the way the engines whined, slowing the ship; she knew by the way the scents upon the air changed from farm animals and greenery to coal smoke and the metallic, swampy smell of the Thames; she knew by the sounds she could hear beyond the engines and the sailors aboard the ship: sounds of clattering cobbles and street salesmen hawking their wares, of bobbies chasing street urchins and blowing their whistles as they raced away. She *knew*.

Thus, she was not surprised when the midshipman returned to the brig, the engines whirring to a standstill, his hand on the sword at his hip in a way that was authoritative without being threatening. "Step to the back of your cell, please."

Taryn backed up as far as she could, studying the young man as he unlocked the door. His dishwater blond hair fell over his forehead as he worked, the top grown a little longer than the sides to allow it to be slicked back. There was something odd about this young man, though Taryn could not put her finger on what. It was not just how young he seemed, nor was it his slight frame, but something less tangible, below the surface.

"Step out, miss. Nice and slow."

She followed his instructions, stepping from the cell obediently. She considered fighting him off, attempting to escape, but it was more a thought experiment than any real consideration. She had no way of knowing how many sailors were upon this ship, and regardless, she doubted she could free herself from her clockwork restraint. The cuff tightened even if she so much as shifted the position of her wrists.

The midshipman led her back through the maze of halls that made up the underbelly of the ship, until at last they emerged into the sunlight above decks. Taryn caught her breath, staring at the Tower Bridge where it loomed beyond the far rail, the massive, familiar architecture never seeming so beautiful and so baleful as it did in that moment. The ship hung level with the top of the Tower, and a gangplank had been extended, connecting the ship and the battlements with a narrow wooden walkway.

Taryn was not allowed time to stare. She marched steadily toward that gangplank, aware of a few curious eyes watching. Storm stood near the rail. She caught Taryn's shoulder as she passed, hissing in her ear. "I shall see you in a few hours, biomaton."

Taryn gave her a saccharine smile.

Once upon the battlements of the Tower, Taryn was forced down several flights of stairs by the young midshipman and into the inner courtyard of the structure. The Tower was a fortress, a keep of massive walls surrounding an inner courtyard, in the center of which stood the White Tower, a tall, imposing castle gleaming in the afternoon sun. Ravens bobbed about on the green lawns which grew between the stone walkways, and beefeater guards in their red uniforms patrolled the grounds.

Taryn tried not to think of all the lives that had ended within these walls.

She was led across the courtyard and to a small wood door in the wall, where a beefeater stood guard. He nodded to the midshipman as they approached.

"A biomaton in the Tower, eh, Cobb?" the guard asked. "Seems a bit much, if you ask me."

"She is here on the orders of Her Majesty," the midshipman answered.

"Ah. I suppose she must know what she is doing. Still, this little girl does not look threatening." He gave Taryn a wink, and she smiled sweetly at him in return.

I could kill you as soon as look at you, old man.

"Just help me keep an eye on her," Midshipman Cobb snapped. He moved in front of Taryn, and using a small brass key like those used to wind delicate clocks, unlocked her cuff. The mechanism clicked open; she could at last move her hands again. Her palms itched to attack, but once again she held herself back. Attempting to break away now would be suicide. The Tower was notoriously difficult to escape. She rubbed her numb fingers as the midshipman and the beefeater escorted her up a set of narrow stone steps, worn smooth by the hundreds of pairs of condemned footsteps that had passed before her. Taryn's heart lurched into her throat as the walls narrowed, hemming her in.

At the top of the steps, there was a single, thick wooden door. The beefeater unlocked it, and Taryn stepped into the small, octagonal cell as instructed. The room was unfurnished, save for a narrow wooden bench near one wall. Small, open windows let in a little light and noise from outside. The walls wore the carvings of thousands of condemned hands: poetry, names, dates, prayers, even curses, and elaborate designs were etched into the stone, the only remnants of people long forgotten.

Behind her, the wooden door slammed shut. She heard the rattle of keys in the lock. Taryn leapt to the door, gripping the bars in the small window embedded there. "Please," she gasped, more to keep them there than anything. The knowledge that she would be left alone with all these doomed inscriptions threatened to suffocate her. "When is my trial?"

"Three days' time."

Footsteps began to descend. Taryn reached her fingers through the bars. "Wait! Please!"

No response came.

She turned away and came face to face with an inscription of a man's name carefully carved into the stone. Below it was a date. The reality of her circumstances struck her like a blow to the face. This was where prisoners came to die. This was not where they kept common murderers and petty thieves. This was where they held traitors to the Crown. She was trapped. The rebellion would die before it had even begun.

She breathed a deep sigh, trying to slow her mounting heart rate. It would do her no good to panic. Taryn curled into a corner of the cell, her arms around her knees, sick to her stomach with terror. She rested her head on her forearms, wishing someone, *anyone*, would return, so she would not have to be alone. Even Storm would provide a kind of morbid company, and at least then Taryn would not have to face the dreadful thoughts running through her head.

TARYN DOZED OFF AND ON THROUGHOUT THE AFTERNOON and into the evening. Late that night, she awoke shivering; the night air coming through the windows was ice-cold. The stones beneath her robbed her body of what little warmth remained. Her prosthetic was freezing to the touch. Taryn rose and paced the cell, breathing on her hand to warm it. It seemed cruel and unusual punishment to not be provided a blanket in the chill of the early English spring, but at least she knew she would not freeze. It would be far worse to be trapped here in the dead of winter.

Taryn stepped to one of the windows and leaned into the narrow stone slit, trying to see beyond the walls of her prison. She glimpsed the glow of a few streetlamps far below, but all else was lost to shadow. Try as she might, she could see no stars. *Three days*, she mused, returning to her pacing. Three days of this cold, this solitude, this terror of what came next. If Storm only knew how close to the truth she had come with her accusation, Taryn would never see her friends again. The English were not above lynching a traitor, no matter what moral high ground they claimed above their lawless kinsfolk in the American West.

Footsteps came from outside, and Taryn froze, trying to read how many soldiers were approaching. The stone distorted the sounds too much, and it could have been two or twenty sets of feet headed her way. She set herself in the center of the room, facing the door, her stance automatically setting her weight low in her hips, prepared for a fight. The violent part of Taryn's mind stirred eagerly, but she held it back, aware that her survival depended on her ability to act like a helpless slave.

The door to her cell opened, and Storm entered with half a dozen brutal-looking men, a few of whom Taryn recognized from the *Dauntless*'s crew. The young midshipman who had brought her into the Tower stood just behind Storm, a look akin to pity in his soft hazel eyes. Taryn did not break Storm's gaze as the men surrounded her.

"Seven against one. Are you really so frightened of me?" Taryn asked, though beneath her cocky façade, her heart thundered against her ribcage.

"Are you ready to tell me where Ace is?" Storm growled.

"I. Do not. Know."

Two of the men surged forward, catching Taryn's wrists and shoulders, restraining her. Their grasps were like iron. The fingers of her right hand began to go numb. "I will ask again," Storm said slowly, as if speaking to a child. "Where is Ace?"

"You are a coward if you truly need six men to back you up while you torture a helpless biomaton."

Storm struck her hard across the face with her metal gauntlet. Taryn tasted blood, her vision going crimson as the violence inside her chest begged to retaliate. She held herself in check. The blow would have sent her to her knees two months ago, but Erikkson's training had taught her to take a beating without flinching. She spat blood on the floor before meeting Storm's eyes with cold determination.

"Where is he?"

"He is as good as dead to you. What does it matter where he is?" Taryn growled. Sedition begged to be unleashed, to take revenge on those who dared to subdue her. Taryn swallowed the violent thoughts.

"You *will* tell me."

Taryn offered her a crooked, bloody smile in response.

"Hold her," the commodore commanded.

The soldiers holding Taryn's shoulders and wrists tightened their already vise-like grips. Though her mouth had gone dry and her heart pounded in her ears, she forced herself to hold Storm's gaze as the admiral stepped forward, gauntleted fist raised threateningly.

The blow landed just below Taryn's ribs. Her knees buckled, her breath momentarily impossible to catch. The soldiers held her up by her wrists and shoulders as she coughed, her lungs desperate for a breath that would not come.

"We can keep going." Storm's voice, smooth as silk, wormed its way into Taryn's mind. "Just tell me where he is."

"No," she answered. This was what it meant to be Sedition

—to put her life on the line for those who could not do so for themselves.

Storm struck her again, this time catching her off-guard with a second backhand across the face. Taryn shook her head against the stars dancing across her vision.

"Where. Is. Ace?" Storm asked again, punctuating each word with a blow. Taryn sagged, coughing, relying on the soldiers to hold her weight. She clenched her fists, struggling to breathe. The copper salt tang of blood flooded her mouth.

A whirr came from behind her, and instantly, the two guards dropped her, stumbling backward, cursing. Taryn pressed her palms against the floor, gasping for breath. Murmurs of horror spun around the room, beginning and ending with the soldiers who had held her up. Taryn lifted herself into a kneeling position, aware of all the horrified eyes trained on her.

"What is that?" Storm snapped in shock.

Taryn twisted her shoulders, and at last realized what they were staring at. Her blades had snapped open, leaving mirror image cuts across the forearms of the men who'd held her. She forced herself to her feet. She wanted to use the blades. It was a suicidal thought, one she nursed for a single moment before abandoning. She was completely surrounded, and she couldn't start the rebellion if she died here. "Just an extra bit of prosthetics," she replied meekly, clicking the blades shut once more. Her common sense told her the only way to get out of this situation was to give in, and though she hated it, she knew what she had to do. She forced herself to look damaged, beaten down. "I cannot tell you where Ace is, but I do know where he is going to be."

Storm narrowed her eyes. "Go on."

"My trial." She stared at her feet, lacing her fingers together in a posture she hoped looked nervous and penitent. "He will be at my trial."

"If you have done anything to harm him—"

"He will be there of his own volition," Taryn interrupted. "He is neither held against his will nor eager to leave."

Storm's gauntlet clanked into a fist. "If I discover you are lying, biomaton—"

"You will what?" Taryn's tongue let the words go, and she could not stop them. "If I remember correctly, I am going to be hanged in a few days. What more can you do to me?"

A fire burned in Storm's eyes. "Boys, you have my permission to teach the biomaton a lesson."

The soldiers moved nearer, and Taryn's stomach dropped. She should have *known* Storm would hurt her whether or not she gave up the information. She tried to back away, but they surrounded her on all sides. There was nowhere she could turn. She tried to keep up the weak girl act: "Wait! Please! I gave you what you wanted!"

The words fell upon deaf ears. One of the sailors caught her by the shoulders, spun her around, and struck her hard in the gut. Taryn collapsed to her knees, struggling to catch her breath. *Fight back!* a voice in her head screamed at her, but she rebuked it. It was not yet time to fight back. She had to play the weak biomaton for just a little longer. Another sailor grabbed her clockwork hand, forcing her wrist behind her back, and accidentally nudged the switch that triggered her blades. They snapped open once more with a whirr, further shredding the back of her dress. Taryn tried to turn, but a fist caught her in the temple. Stars danced across her vision.

Someone grabbed the base of one of the fan-like blades protruding from her back, wrenching it the wrong direction. Taryn screamed, collapsing to the floor. She curled into the fetal position, trembling from head to toe, her arms raised to protect her head. A dreadful, animal whimper rose in her throat. Footsteps neared and she tensed, waiting for the blows to come. A tear slipped down her nose, unbidden and unwanted. *Defend yourself!* Sedition screamed at her, and she could not silence the voice in her head any longer. *Fight back! Defend yourself!* Another blow. Steel-toed boot to ribs. Another whimper escaped her.

Defend yourself, or this is where our story ends!

CHAPTER TWENTY-SEVEN

"No."

Someone stood over her, arms spread, refusing to allow the sailors any nearer.

"Get away," Storm snapped.

"No," the voice insisted, stronger this time. "You will not hurt her anymore. She is to stand trial in two days. The law shall decide what to do with her then."

"Can the law avenge my brother?" Storm questioned. Taryn dared to raise her eyes to discover the midshipman standing over her, his slight frame somehow keeping Storm and her lackeys away.

"According to her, your brother is still alive."

"Biomatons are all liars," Storm growled.

"Would you take your revenge now and be as bad or worse than she?"

Storm stared at him for a moment. "If she matters so much to you, you may stay with her."

Hands shoved the midshipman away, hauled Taryn to her feet, before throwing them both roughly to the back of the cell. Taryn sagged, crumpling to her knees, one hand pressed to the sore spot on her ribs. The midshipman kept his footing as the sailors left, standing between them and Taryn. The door slammed shut, the ominous clang of the lock clicking into place pounding through her aching head.

The midshipman stepped up to the door, glaring at Storm. "The Queen would be appalled at what happened here today."

"She would be appalled that you are siding with a biomaton accused of treason," Storm retorted.

"When I swore fealty to the Queen, part of my oath was to serve and protect. I will uphold that oath with my dying breath."

"Then you will be tried with her. Enjoy your time with the biomaton, Midshipman Cobb. Keep a weather eye on her, or she may try to kill you."

The sailors guffawed with laughter, the sounds fading as they left the two alone. Cobb punched the wall hard, exclaiming wordlessly in frustration. He had a remarkably high voice. Taryn shoved herself into a sitting position against the cold wall, eyeing him warily. She pressed the switch to close her blades.

"Why?" she questioned hoarsely.

He turned his young hazel eyes on her. She wished she could put a finger on what was odd about him.

"Why would you protect me?"

"I could not let them kill you."

"Why? I am as good as dead already."

"Not yet, miss. You have yet to be tried."

"I might as well have been," she answered coldly, her eyes drifting to the narrow strip of sky through the window. "The results are already determined." A chill breeze swept over her, and her head throbbed with the blows she had received. Still, she puzzled over this young man.

"You must not give up yet, miss."

She glared at him. "Oh, so you believe I am *not* a traitor?"

"I believe you are innocent until proven guilty."

"Not biomatons," she spat. "That law only applies to humans."

He fell silent, cheeks reddening, his eyes once again going to the locked door of the cell. Taryn studied him closely.

"How old are you?"

"Fifteen."

She narrowed her eyes. "It takes three years of service to gain the rank of midshipman."

"I started young, as a cabin boy," Cobb swallowed hard, shifting his stance. He would not meet her eyes.

Understanding hit Taryn all at once, and intense admiration for the figure standing in front of her flooded her chest. "What is your name?"

"Jack," Cobb scowled. "You ask a lot of questions for a biomaton."

"Your full name," Taryn insisted, ignoring the jab.

"Just Jack!"

"Not Jacqueline?"

Cobb's face paled. His—her—whole body slumped. When she spoke, her voice was hoarse. "How did you guess?"

Taryn smiled. "Call it a woman's intuition." She paused, studying the girl. She was slight, and her navy uniform hid most of her more feminine curves. Taryn guessed she was closer to eighteen than fifteen, but the markers were clear. She hid it well, but she *was* a she, enlisted in the Queen's Navy, flying on an airship. Taryn couldn't help but admire her. It had been a dream, once, a flight of fancy when she still lived on the streets and could barely scrape enough money together for bread. She'd considered chopping her hair, disguising herself, enlisting as a cabin boy, but the added secret of her clockwork arm had made it an impossibility, even if she had found a proper disguise.

Jack glared at her. "I should have let them kill you. If you tell *anyone*—"

"I will be hanged in a few days. Not much time for me to spill your secret. There are worse people to confide in." Taryn shrugged. "Now that I know, it is rather obvious. Have none of your shipmates guessed?"

Jack shook her head. "Only one of the others knows, and he got me the job in the first place. The others see what they want to see." She narrowed her eyes as the words spilled out, shooting a suspicious glare at Taryn. "If you breathe a word of this—"

"Who shall believe me?" Taryn asked, holding her hands up in a pacifying gesture. "I am not only a biomaton, I am accused of treason. Can you think of anyone less trustworthy?"

Jack merely stared at Taryn. For a long moment, the two examined one another. Then, Jack turned away, settling herself at the far end of the cell. Taryn leaned back against the cold stone, resigning herself to a chilly night of silence from her cell mate. *That is all right,* she thought. What did she care about this young woman who had saved her life? And yet, Taryn knew what it was like to disguise her true identity in order to survive. She knew what it meant to wear a mask, in constant fear of someone peeking through it. So as the hours drew on and the cold became colder, Taryn kept one eye on Midshipman Cobb, trying to figure her out.

LORD ERIKKSON'S HOUSE ON HANOVER SQUARE WAS NEVER designed to hold so many anxious young men. Which is not to say it was too small—five stories tall and squashed between two taller houses, it was the epitome of the upper-class city getaway. Though Erikkson rarely spent time within the house's walls, several of the biomatons had been there before, on scouting missions or errands for Erikkson. Four biomatons lived in the house full-time, reporting back to Erikkson any news from London, but the interior still felt dark, cramped, and dusty. Remnants of the eclectic tastes of his many ancestors remained to clutter the rooms, from the flowery, pastel shades and extravagant gilding of the French Rococo style in a few of the upstairs bedrooms to the more muted, Regency neutrals and heavy draperies of the study and library. Dust hung thick in the air of the rooms no longer in use, and the narrow windows stood in want of a good wash.

Ari and Rorin sat in the parlor, playing a game which mostly involved throwing knives at a massive painting of a fox hunt hanging over the fireplace. They awarded one another points depending on where the knives struck: one for any of the eight men represented in the picture, five for the horses or hounds, and forty-five for a hit on the small, fire-orange tail of the fox in the far distance.

Seraphim stood in the doorway for a few seconds before entering and clearing his throat disapprovingly. Twin pairs of dark brown eyes looked up from their game.

"I know you are anxious, but that is no reason to deface the art," Seraphim growled.

Ari twirled a throwing knife over his knuckles. "If we do not get Sedition back, will ye be our new leader, Seraphim?"

"Do not say things like that. We *will* get her back."

"Aye, but *if* we do not—" Ari shrugged. "We think ye ought to be the leader. Ye have been with Erikkson the longest."

"We were built for different purposes," Seraphim replied. His wings clicked in agitation.

"She to lead and ye to terrify?" Ari scoffed. Rorin glanced at his brother.

"Ari, ye mustn't say things like that."

"He is allowed to speak his mind," Seraphim answered. "It does not mean anything to me." He flashed his silver fangs.

"We are all restless. I only came to inform you both that it is your turn to keep watch next."

"Why can Royal not continue to do it? He blends in best. No one will notice another bloody rich bairn hanging around the prisons."

Seraphim huffed and turned away, sick of their disregard for leadership or protocol. Seraphim had better things he could be doing than arguing with the twins.

Somewhere downstairs, a door slammed.

"Tony," Royal yelled, an edge of panic coloring his voice.

The three biomatons exchanged glances. As one, they raced downstairs.

Everyone in the house had heard Royal's cry, and they hurried toward him from wherever they were, converging in the front hall where Royal stood, red-faced and panting, the door still hanging open in his rush.

"What has made you so upset?" Erikkson demanded.

"Taryn—" Royal spoke through gasps; it was clear he'd run all the way back from the prisons. "Taryn's—sentence—has been—attaindered. She is not—getting—a trial."

Everyone began talking at once, exclamations of shock and horror racing around the crowded entry hall. Erikkson held up his hands. "How do you know this?"

In response, Royal thrust the crumpled paper he held at Erikkson.

With trembling hands, Erikkson took the sheet, smoothing it open. His face paled. "By decree of her Majesty, Queen Victoria—"

CHAPTER TWENTY-EIGHT

By the way the sunlight streamed through the windows and the sounds of the harbor outside, Taryn guessed the time to be around eight in the morning when a beefeater brought them breakfast. She sat quietly against the wall as he passed the food through the door to Jack, then rose and went to take the bowl of porridge from her. The beefeater paused outside after relocking the door. "Eat well, girl," he said, though not unkindly. "I heard your sentence will be carried out tomorrow."

"Sentence?" Taryn frowned. "You mean my trial?"

The beefeater shook his head. "No, miss. Your sentence. Her Majesty bypassed your trial by act of attainder."

Taryn's mouth fell open. Her throat dry, she croaked a horrified noise. "You should not make such jokes to a condemned woman, even if she is a biomaton. Attainder is for landed gentry, not nobodies like me."

"It is no joke, miss. I am sorry."

As he turned away, Taryn sank to her knees, unable to breathe. Her hands shook so hard she could barely grip the bowl of porridge she held. Great, shuddering gasps verging on sobs wracked her shoulders.

"It—it is not fair," she choked. "I ought to at least be granted the dignity of a trial." She'd expected death to come for her, yes, but not like this. Not so soon. Not without even being able to speak for the biomatons. She'd expected to die in battle, a Valkyrie claiming her right to paradise, not the quick snap of a hangman's noose.

Jack stared at her, a look of puzzlement on her face. "I thought biomatons had no capacity for dignity."

Taryn stared at the girl, her green eyes filling with venom. "The only difference between you and I is a bit of clockwork. I am human, too, and I would like to be treated like it."

"You are no longer human. That was taken from you by your master." The words had no emotion behind them, flat and static, like something she was reciting from a page for class.

"If you truly believe that, what was the point of saving my skin? There is no nobility in saving an abomination." Taryn spat each word like an accusation, all of her terror coalescing into a need to convince one *solitary person* of her humanity. If she could convince one person outside her circle, she would know the cause wasn't entirely futile. She would know they had some hope.

Jack scowled. "I saved you."

"Yes, but why? Did you perhaps see something besides my clockwork that compelled you?"

The girl's scowl deepened. "My father taught me that nothing should die needlessly. And—there was something in your eyes—"

"Something human?" Taryn demanded.

Jack nodded, though it appeared to pain her to say it. "You are...*different* from the other biomatons I have met. More... real."

"I have no mental dampeners to hinder my mind," Taryn replied. Her cheeks colored, and she stared down into her bowl, still gripped tightly in her palms. "I should not have told you that."

"You are illegally built?" Jack questioned, aghast.

Taryn nodded. "Please, if you have any decency, do not tell anyone. My master will be arrested for such an offense, and he is a good man." She shook her head. She'd just taken on the role of obedient slave with surprising ease. "It shall be enough that I am hanged and gone."

Jack frowned, but at last nodded her consent. "I suppose I must honor the last wish of a dying woman. And you promised to keep my secret, so I shall do the same for you."

Taryn nodded her thanks and began to eat. The porridge was gluey and tasteless, but it helped to fill the gaping ache in her stomach. She considered the ugly truth she faced, visions of the hangman's noose dancing behind her eyes. She prayed Erikkson would discover what had happened and ensure her soldiers would be at her execution.

Execution. The word sent shuddering bolts of electricity down her spine. It was a ghastly beast of a word, four syllables of pure, hopeless dread. *No, not execution,* she told herself. Tomorrow would not—could not—be the end of Sedition's story. Rather, it would be her triumph, her manifesto, the moment the world would be forced to recognize the biomaton's equality and value. Taryn clung to the tiny kernel of hope like a life preserver in a vast ocean, a sea of uncertainty that threatened to drown her if her grasp slipped even for an instant. Taryn closed her eyes and vowed to survive, for each and every one of the dear friends she'd made.

EARLY THE NEXT MORNING, THE BEEFEATERS CAME FOR Taryn, shackling her hands behind her back before leading her from the cell. One of the men tried to dismiss

Midshipman Cobb, but she refused, insisting on attending Taryn, wherever she was headed. Though the two beefeaters exchanged glances, they shrugged and allowed Cobb to remain. Taryn held her head high, her messy copper hair streaming down her back. The morning sun seemed to gild her locks.

In the courtyard, one of Scotland Yard's infamous Black Maria carriages stood, awaiting its dire cargo. The men who attended it were not as courteous as the beefeaters, jeering at Taryn and her midshipman companion as they approached. Taryn held herself with grace and dignity, even in the face of such abuses against her. She had endured far worse than name calling.

Strong soldier's hands lifted Taryn into the back of the Black Maria. She gasped, face going pale as fingers found the bruise on her ribs. She stumbled into the dark interior of the cart.

Without a word, Cobb swung into the carriage behind her.

"You are welcome to ride up front," one of the soldiers shouted.

"I shall remain with the biomaton," Cobb replied. "Someone ought to ensure you do not lose her on the way."

Both soldiers' faces turned purple at the thinly veiled insult, but they made no reply. The doors of the carriage slammed and locked with a click.

Taryn stared out the narrow-barred window. She could see little besides the dreary walls of the Tower outside. The carriage swayed as the soldiers climbed to their positions. Taryn turned her eyes to Cobb.

"How far is it?" she asked. She was no stranger to the public hangings held occasionally outside Newgate Prison; she had always avoided them at all costs. There was something shockingly morbid about gathering to watch as someone was put to death, and she had never participated. She hadn't the heart to watch someone die, no matter what their crimes might be.

"Perhaps fifteen minutes, if traffic is not bad," Cobb replied. Her young hazel eyes studied Taryn.

A smirk crossed her face. "I would tell you to take a photograph to remember me by, but I am afraid there is not time."

Cobb's face twisted. "I am sorry you did not get a proper trial."

Taryn shrugged, surprised by how serene she felt now the day was upon her. "The verdict would have been the same."

Jack leaned forward a little, staring down at her hands. "Miss..."

"Call me Taryn, please."

"Taryn," the girl choked on her words. "I—I lost my brother. He was part of the British army. He was serving in India when the Bhutans revolted."

"I am sorry," Taryn replied, unsure why this girl was confiding in her *now*. "That war was costly."

"No, that is not how I lost him. He came home. He was given a simple clockwork prosthetic to replace the hand he lost in the fighting. And then he—he was not allowed to stay with us. Because he was a biomaton." The girl picked at a hangnail. "He was taken from us and returned to the army. They said he was the property of the British empire now. And when I went to see him, he was—he was changed. He didn't know me."

Taryn said nothing, but nodded to show she was still listening. The story was a similar iteration of the story every one of her soldiers shared. It was as familiar as her own clockwork arm. And every time she heard a new story like this one, it made her ache deep in her bones.

"That is why I joined the navy. I wanted to get as far from all of that as I could. I knew the navy did not employ biomatons, and that was enough for me. I had to become someone new. I had to disappear. I could not go on knowing my brother had been shattered like that."

Taryn's lips twisted into a thin line. "I am sorry you had to face that."

Cobb nodded. "You—I saved you because you reminded me of my brother."

Taryn was silent for a long time, the weight of Cobb's admission sitting squarely on her shoulders. She sighed. "I do not want you to get in trouble for helping me."

Jack shrugged. "What can they do?"

"We are escaping. My master is sending a team to get me out of this mess, and we are escaping." She hesitated again. "We are fighting for the freedom of the biomatons. You may join us, if you like. You would not have to hide any longer. And we could free your brother."

Jack smiled. "You really *are* a traitor. Thank you for the invitation."

She nodded. "It stands until we escape...or I am killed."

Noises in the distance, becoming audible over the clatter of hooves and the wheels against cobbles, distracted them from their conversation. Taryn listened closely, trying to discern the meaning of the din. It grew exponentially as they rounded a corner, and Taryn suddenly understood. Her heart leapt into her throat. The noise came from the crowd gathered to watch her execution.

CHAPTER TWENTY-NINE

"We are gathered here today to witness the execution of Taryn of Erikkson, accused of treason and conspiracy against the crown."

Taryn stood on the platform that had been erected in the square, staring out at the massive crowd that had gathered in spite of the drizzling rain. Her eyes raked over the crowd of cold, unfamiliar faces as the bailiff at the front of the platform continued to read off the long legalese document detailing her supposed "crimes"—including, she noted, the kidnap and murder of one Ace Highmore, privateer to the crown. And then she spotted him in the audience, ice blue eyes flashing with concern. And there, Royal and Seraphim. Emmett. The twins. All of her warriors, there as she had requested, standing in the crowd near the platform. Seraphim caught her eye and gave her a nod, just enough to say, *We are ready*. He opened the front of his cloak to reveal the hilt of the rapier hidden beneath it.

"—shall be hanged by the neck until dead," the bailiff concluded, and Taryn bristled as the hangman pulled the noose over her head, tightening the knot just beneath her chin. He bent to tie another rope around her ankles, securing her skirt in place. *At least I shall have my modesty intact as I die,* she mused. She was surprised by her calm, by the lack of pounding heart or shaking hands, all the things she would have expected to feel with the hangman's noose around her neck. But she stood still and strong, her eyes on her friends, her soldiers, and she was unafraid.

"You came here today to see a biomaton hang," she called out, her voice ringing clear and cold across the square. People exchanged glances. The hangman seemed at a loss. The condemned addressing the crowd wasn't just unusual. It simply *was not done.* "Though I have had neither trial nor chance to defend myself. But what is the passage of justice to a biomaton? What am I but a machine to be recycled when I have lost my usefulness? You came here today to see a spectacle, and I will not deny you that. But I am *not* Taryn of Erikkson. I am Sedition, leader of the biomaton rebellion, and we refuse to be silenced by your whims and your cruelty any longer!" With a flick of her fingers, she triggered the razor hidden in her wrist, slicing through her bonds. She raised her fists, signaling to her soldiers. "We demand our freedom! We demand equality! We will not stop until we are freed!"

"Silence her! Stop this treasonous speech at once!" the bailiff cried. Taryn reached for her dagger, twisting toward the hangman, whose hand was already on that lever that would open the trap door beneath her feet and send her plunging to her death. Her fingers grasped her blade, but in her haste, she forgot about the rope around her ankles. She stumbled, hobbled by the bindings.

The hangman pulled the lever.

The trap door dropped out from beneath her. Taryn shut her eyes, waiting for the *snap* of her neck breaking— A jolt stopped her fall before the rope pulled taut. Strong arms wrapped around her legs, keeping her just inches from that fatal tension on the rope. She opened her eyes to find Ace below her, face red with exertion as he held her up. "I trust you still have those hidden knives?" he grunted.

Understanding, Taryn reached for her dagger again. It took some balance, but using Ace's shoulder to steady herself, she slashed through the rope above the knot. The sounds of a battle were already ringing all around them, shouts and the clang of swords, the *crack* of gunfire. Ace set Taryn on her feet, and she leaned down to slash the rope around her ankles. Straightening, she gave him a teasing salute. "I owe you one."

"Duck," he growled.

She did.

He fired his pistol over her back, felling the red-coated soldier just inches from plunging his sword beneath Taryn's ribs. She straightened, smoothing the front of her frock, and gave him another grin. "So now I owe you two."

There was something new about Ace here in the midst of the fight, something *fuller* than he had been in the weeks since arriving at Elmhurst. He seemed more himself than he had in a long time, and there was a light in his blue eyes that ignited something unfamiliar in her chest.

"Sedition!" Seraphim ducked beneath the platform, wings already bloodied, wearing an expression Taryn would have called exhilaration if she had not known better. He had to stoop beneath the platform because of his height. "Your army needs you," he said, tossing her a cutlass.

Taryn caught the sword, the weight in her palms firm and reassuring. She snapped her shoulder blades open. "I am with you. Let us show them we will no longer be silenced."

The three charged into the fray, wielding weapons, wielding prosthetics-turned-weapons, nothing so important in that moment as the fight and the rush of blood in their ears. At last, Taryn let the violent monster in her head out to play. *Time to show them what we are made of.*

The square had emptied of onlookers. The only people

remaining now were the red-coated soldiers and Taryn's band of misfits. Despite the soldiers' superior numbers, the biomatons' training was clearly better, and a number of red-uniformed bodies already littered the square. But more soldiers were coming, and the biomatons had no reinforcements, no fresh comrades to fall back upon.

Taryn caught her opponent's sword with her own as he swung down, slashing at his ribs with the dagger in her left hand. He jumped out of the way just in time, swinging at her again with his own sword. She blocked, ducked beneath his arm, slicing his forearm with her shoulder blades. He cried out and dropped the sword, leaving his guard open. She finished him off with a single, powerful blow.

Taryn bent and cut her skirt, tearing it off just below her knees to stop it from encumbering her. "Sedition, look out!" a familiar Scottish brogue yelled. A soldier charged her with a lance. She flipped into a roll, somersaulting beneath the blade, and came up inside his guard, plunging her dagger into his ribcage.

She was on her feet before her opponent hit the ground. Nearby, Ace struggled with a big soldier. Without hesitating, Taryn raced to his aid, attacking the big man from behind. Between the two biomatons, it didn't take long to fell the man. Ace nodded to her, his face and hands splattered with blood. "Thank you." He'd taken a blow to the jaw, and it was blossoming into a dark bruise.

The click of a flintlock pistol being cocked came from behind them. Taryn threw herself at Ace, knocking him to the ground. She hit his chest hard as the gun fired. They locked eyes for a moment, the fight slowing to a crawl as he gave her a wide, perfect smile. How long had it been since she'd seen him smile like that? *Had* he ever smiled like that?

She shoved herself off him, searching the square to find the person who'd fired the bullet. She spun, Ace at her back, each of them scanning the chaos for their attacker.

Taryn spotted her first, standing near the edge of the square, a manic grin on her face. Storm. She caught Taryn's eye and spun on her heel, racing down an alleyway. Her white commodore's coat billowed behind her.

"Coward," Taryn growled, digging in her heels to give chase.

Ace laid a hand on her arm. "Taryn, you are needed here. I will go after her."

"Ace, that is Storm! She is," Taryn gasped. "She—"

"I know," Ace answered. "Emmett told me." He squeezed her arm, then raced after Storm.

"Be careful!" Taryn called after him. "Come back to us."

He glanced back at her over his shoulder and gave her another one of those earth-shattering smiles. "Worry about yourself, Sedition."

THE FARTHER ACE RAN DOWN THE ALLEYWAY, THE narrower it became. The large brick buildings on either side towered above him until they blocked out nearly all the light. Ace slowed as he reached the end of the alley, a brick wall ahead. The woman had led him into a dead end. But where was she? He turned, searching the heavy shadows, and spotted her as she melted from the darkness of a doorway. "Clever, very clever," she purred. Ace's hand leapt to the pistol on his hip as she stepped into his path—blocking his one escape route back to the square and his friends. "You know, for a while there, I really believed you were gone."

Taryn, in her kindness, had kept the truth of Storm's nature from him, but Emmett had filled in everything he needed to know about the airship captain. A shiver of dread raced down

Ace's spine as he stared at the woman who was his own flesh and blood, and yet a stranger. He could see the resemblance between the two of them, like looking into a circus mirror that stretched and distorted his shape, but it was there: in the curve of her jaw, in the blue of her eyes, and in the dark hair curling around her face, adorned with little trophies and treasures like a magpie's nest.

"You can remove that disguise now, Ace. The biomatons are still being slaughtered in the square."

He raised the pistol, heart pounding. "Stay back. If you are who I think you are, you know what I can do with this." He hated the way his voice trembled, but he could not deny that the tales of Storm's cruelty had shaken him. And worse, he feared he might be complicit in her crimes, though he had no memory of it.

She held up her hands. The left one was encased in metal and for half a second, he thought she was a biomaton too—but no. It was a vicious-looking steel gauntlet, a deadly weapon when used properly. "I do," she answered in a voice cool and smooth as silk. "But I also know you are afraid. Your hands are shaking, brother dear."

Ace tightened his grip on the pistol, all too aware of the trembling. He thought of the last person he'd held at gunpoint; the way Taryn, too, had stared so coldly down the barrel of the gun. He mentally shook himself. He had to stay present, *now*, in this moment. He could not allow himself to go wandering off into the dark corners of his own mind. And most of all, he couldn't let himself get mired in the fog surrounding Taryn. "That does not mean I cannot shoot you."

She took a few steps toward him, toying with a coin tied into her hair. The currency had a hole through it. "What made you decide to change sides?" she asked. "We could have done so much damage to those little biomaton rebels together. But now..." She tsked, the noise setting off an automatic guilt response in his chest. "You are a traitor to the Crown, you know. You will be hanged with your red-headed automaton mistress."

"We will not be hanged," Ace choked the words out. He drew back the hammer of the pistol, comforted by the familiar click. Something stirred in the back of his mind, something nameless and lumbering, dangerous as a bear waking from sleep. A piercing headache throbbed between his eyes.

"You have been so different since you met her," Storm murmured. "Come back with me. Whatever happened to you, whatever that freak did to you, I can fix it."

"The only thing I want fixed is my missing memory," he gasped as she stepped nearer. And it was true, he realized, though he'd never put it into words before this moment. He didn't hate being a biomaton. He didn't *want* to be whole again. He'd found something through these trials, something he was certain he'd never had before. In spite of Storm's blood relation to him, he'd found a *family*. A cause. A purpose. Sweat dripped down his temple, and he stepped back, heel catching on an uneven paving stone. "Stay back."

"Oh, Ace." A pained, patronizing look crossed her face. She stuck her lower lip out in a mocking pout. "You really have become one of them." She slipped a dagger from her belt, the sharp blade glinting even in the dim light. "You know what that means, of course."

His head pounded. He couldn't breathe. His throat had gone dry. He knew the words before they left her lips.

"It means I have to kill you."

CHAPTER THIRTY

He hated the feel of his wings snapping through blood and bone and gristle. He hated the stink of sweat and the taste of copper in the air. He hated the way his vision brightened, the way everything took on a diamond-sharp sheen. He hated the way his pulse beat faster, and he hated the way he relished the fight. Worst of all, he hated that he was *made* for this, that he could do it better than anyone else, except for perhaps his biomaton siblings. And yet, every time he did it, it took him right back to the days he'd spent as a ring fighter, the time when his own abilities, his own skill set had been turned against him. Since then, war left a bad taste in his mouth, and even when it was justified, as he believed this fight was, the battle remained abhorrent to him.

He brought one wing around, blocking a stray bullet, the ricochet stinging his ears. To his right, Sedition fought hard, her forehead shining with sweat, cheeks splattered with blood, a wild light in her eyes. Seraphim knew that look too well. He'd seen it on Petrichor's face a thousand times, and now he saw it in Sedition. It broke his heart. She'd become what Erikkson wanted, and he'd had a part in forcing her into it. Seraphim ached with the knowledge that he could have saved her from all of this with a word and he'd stopped himself. He'd kept quiet because Erikkson had told him to.

"Seraphim, watch your flank," she exclaimed, catching him looking at her.

He swept one bloodied wing out in time to stop the lance aimed to pierce his ribs. Metal grated against metal as the soldier tried to drive the lance's point between his bladed feathers. Seraphim grimaced. The delicate clockwork mechanisms of his wing ground together with the strain. He swung his quarterstaff, trying to dislodge the lance, but it stayed put, stubbornly trapped between two bladed feathers. The screech of machinery grinding against itself assaulted his ears. With a growl, he lurched forward, slicing his other wing across the shaft of the lance. It broke with a *snap*, splintering in the soldier's hands. But something else snapped too: Seraphim's primary flight feather, the long blade clattering to the ground. As soon as the blade fell, Seraphim folded the damaged wing tightly. The internal workings of the prosthetic were exposed. One well-aimed hit could cripple it for good.

He lunged with the quarterstaff, striking the soldier in the temple. The man crumpled and Seraphim took a moment to catch his breath, stretching his full fifteen-foot wingspan. His left wing *definitely* wasn't responding properly. He muttered a curse and pulled it close again. He was down one wing. That could come back to bite him.

ACE WAS STRUGGLING TO FOCUS. IMAGES LINGERED IN THE corners of his vision, like hot fire brands dancing in his periphery. He couldn't blink them away, couldn't breathe for the weight on his chest. Memories rippled beneath his skin.

And Storm kept coming, gauntleted and wielding a dagger, always making sure she stayed between him and the alleyway leading back to the square. Back to his friends. Back to Taryn.

"You are not really here, are you?" Storm asked sharply.

Ace's back hit brick and he froze, holding his pistol at arm's length between them like it could stop her from getting any closer. His finger shook on the trigger. "I do not know what you mean."

Her eyes narrowed. A shaft of light caught her blade, dazzling his eyes for a moment. There were things in his head that didn't belong there, voices and names and pain he couldn't remember. *Why* couldn't he remember?

"Use that pistol or put it away," Storm growled. That tone was familiar, the way her voice grated against her back teeth when she was angry. He blinked away the pain clouding his vision. His memory *didn't matter* right now. He had to fight her. He had to win.

He fired.

The bullet whistled over Storm's shoulder, knocking her hair aside with its speed. A severed ribbon slipped to the ground, carrying with it a bird's skull. Ace's mouth went dry as the skull hit the paving stones and shattered, the tiny, fragile bones fragmenting. Storm's attention snapped down to the object and then back to him, fury building behind her blue eyes. "You know how much that meant to me."

He shook his head. "No." And yet, something deep inside him had been crushed with the skull. He'd known it was important, even if he couldn't remember why. "Stay back. The next shot will not be a warning."

A slow smile crossed her lips, the expression so inhuman it chilled him to his core. With a speed he hadn't known she possessed, she lunged forward, dagger slashing across his wrist. The cut wasn't bad, but it was enough to cause him to recoil on instinct, temporarily loosening his grip on the pistol. She caught his metal wrist with her gauntleted hand, steel screeching against steel, and yanked, pulling him away from the wall. The heel of her boot caught him behind the knee, and Ace stumbled, barely catching his balance. He whirled, training his pistol on her again, but he was too slow. Her elbow caught him across the ear. Pain whispered behind his ribs, the old friend he could never be rid of.

"Disappointing," Storm clucked. "I thought you would at least offer me a fight. But I suppose this is easier. I will finish you off, and then I will have time to return to the square and kill your little redheaded revolutionary. What is it she's calling herself these days? Sedition?" She spat the word in his face like a curse.

Ace's stomach lurched into his throat. He wouldn't let Storm hurt Taryn. Not again. He raised his pistol once more. "You will not touch her."

"And what are you going to do about it, brother dear?"

"I will stop you."

CHAPTER THIRTY-ONE

THE SQUARE LOOKED LIKE A WARZONE.

Blood spattered across the cobbles, and red-uniformed bodies lay strewn about, ugly testaments to how well the biomatons had been trained. Taryn and the others fought bravely, but their small numbers meant they had a distinct disadvantage. Still, they refused to give up. Each and every one preferred death to being forced back into slavery.

Seraphim fought three soldiers at once, a quarterstaff in hand and his undamaged wing fanning out behind him with a mind of its own. The clockwork blades whirred through the air, too fast to see, and the true reach of his wingspan became apparent. With a twist of his shoulders, the long primary feathers of his right wing slashed across one soldier's throat, as he struck at another with the quarterstaff. Even before the first soldier fell, Seraphim rounded on the other two, snarling, wing whirling toward them.

"Give no quarter!" Taryn shouted from across the square, locked in her own battle, using every secret weapon Erikkson had placed at her disposal. "Show them no mercy, as they have shown us no mercy!"

Emmett, fighting near her, glanced at Taryn momentarily before returning his attention to his duel. With ease, he parried, side-stepped, and plunged his sabre through the soldier's ribcage. The soldier fell, choking, and Emmett ran to assist Taryn.

"*Chérie,* every moment we stay is a moment we risk lives. We must go," he cried as they fought back-to-back. He could not help the grin toying at the corner of his mouth. Fighting alongside Taryn like this thrilled him in a way nothing else ever had; he could hear her panting, feel the heat of her skin against his, and though he knew it was futile, he had never felt more in love than he did at this moment.

"I trust you brought transport?" she called back over the noise of gunfire and the clash of metal against metal. She turned away from him, using her shoulder blades in a wide, spinning arc. Her bustled skirt had been further torn away during battle, revealing her legs from the knee down. Those legs, too, were a weapon. She incapacitated another soldier with a well-placed kick, followed by a knife to the throat.

"There is a cab waiting," Emmett replied. With a quick double-slash, he slew both soldiers left facing them, then gave Taryn a devil-may-care grin. "Cannot allow them a chance to stop us."

She smiled back, but he could see fatigue behind her emerald eyes. She likely had little food and less sleep in the past few days, and though she would never admit it, he could tell her strength was flagging.

"We cannot win this, *chérie.* We must retreat."

"I am not leaving until Ace returns," she growled. She ran toward Seraphim, throwing herself into the fray once more.

Emmett ran alongside her. "What if he does not come back?"

"He *will,*" she insisted. "Go help Royal. No one is being left behind today."

Emmett turned, obeying her command, but he no longer relished the battle. He knew they could not keep this fight up much longer. Already, the twins sported flesh wounds, and one of Seraphim's deadly flight feathers had snapped. If this continued much longer, it would become a suicide mission. Emmett gritted his teeth, throwing himself into the battle, refusing to dwell on the knowledge that Ace could very well be dead. Storm would show him no mercy.

ACE HIT THE COBBLESTONES HARD ENOUGH TO KNOCK THE breath from his lungs. His head slammed against the granite. Stars danced across his vision. The pain between his eyes had spread to the back of his head, like spikes being driven into his skull. He watched, dazed, as Storm pried the pistol from his fingers and kicked it away. It skittered over the paving stones, lost in some dark shadow. Something stirred in the back of his mind, begging for his attention, but he shoved it away. It would have to wait until he finished with Storm.

"I am disappointed in you, brother dear," Storm purred, her voice dangerously soft. She drove one steel-toed boot into his ribs. Ace bit back a scream, rolling away from her, clutching at the place on his ribs where skin and clockwork met. His hand came away sticky with blood. His chest heaved. He tried to shove himself upright. Storm planted a knee on his chest, constricting his breathing further. "You always were weak, but this is a new low."

Bile rose in his throat as she leaned over him. Her long hair brushed across his cheek. He lifted his head, trying to speak, but she drove the butt of her knife hard against his forehead. His head hit the raised stones again, and this time it wasn't darkness dancing behind his eyes. With a final explosion in the back of his brain, Ace cried out, a thousand images dancing through his mind. Understanding came into his eyes. He knew who he was. He knew what she was.

He *remembered*.

A new strength flooded him, racing through his veins like lightning. He lunged, twisting the knife from her hand, wrenching it from her grasp. The hilt felt good in his palm. His clockwork hand caught her around the throat. Her eyes widened, her shaking hands grasping at his metal wrist. "I was weak when I trusted you," he growled. A fire burned behind his eyes. He rose, never relinquishing his grip for a moment, forcing her to her feet.

"Ace—" she choked, all her languid confidence lost.

"No, Storm." He shoved her backward, backing her against a wall. He pressed the knife below her jaw. He was stronger than her, even with the pain in his ribs. Stronger than he'd ever been aboard the *Dauntless* when he fought so hard for her approval. "I remember. I remember *everything*. And I will not be stupid enough to follow you again." He swallowed hard. "How could you do that? They were our own parents!"

Her blue eyes, dark mirrors of his own, flashed with anger. "They were traitors and you know it! It was only fitting that the bloody creature who destroyed them was part of the very slave race they wanted to free." An ugly, bitter bark of a laugh escaped her constricted throat. "I wish they could see you now, brother dear. They would be so *proud*." She spat the last word, spittle spattering Ace's cheeks.

He slammed the butt of the dagger into her temple, hard enough to knock her unconscious. She slumped over, collapsing, and Ace let her fall, gasping in pain. He pressed his hands against his torn ribs, all the fight draining from him at once. He stumbled to the shadow, on the other side of the alleyway, where his pistol had fallen. He bent, picked it up, and looked over his shoulder to pay his sister a final glance. He had already decided not to kill her. He did not know if he truly could; and besides, he needed to get back to the square. To his new family.

"We will meet again," he grunted. "And only one of us will make it out alive." He grimaced, his face twisting in agony. "And you are wrong, Storm. Mother and Father would not have cared about my prosthetic, as long as I continued their fight." He turned away, using the wall for support, allowing Taryn's red hair to once more be the beacon to guide him home.

CHAPTER THIRTY-TWO

THE BIOMATONS COULD NOT KEEP up the fight much longer. Each one of them knew it. They fought close together now, allowing the soldiers to take the initiative, defending one another as they could. Most were injured to some degree, and all were battle weary. One of Seraphim's wings hung crippled and useless, slowing him down. Rorin's breathing came in heavy, wheezing gasps, his iron lung unable to keep up with the sheer exertion.

"*Chérie, we must go,*" Emmett cried, charging the soldiers she faced, beating them back with a savagery borne of exhaustion.

"Not without Ace," she exclaimed, spinning, a throwing knife leaving her fingertips and finding its mark. The soldier behind Emmett stumbled and fell, clutching the hilt that protruded from his chest.

"It has been too long," Royal called from her left. His face was streaked with sweat and blood. He fought shoulder-to-shoulder with Taryn. "He is not coming back. We cannot wait any longer."

"He is," Taryn insisted. Royal broke a soldier's arm with a

blow from the hilt of his sword. Across the square, Seraphim circled slowly, prowling like a caged tiger, staring down the four soldiers who had him surrounded. "Go assist Seraphim," she ordered.

Royal cursed beneath his breath but obeyed. The soldier Taryn now faced measured twice her size, but his girth made him clumsy and slow. She dodged and danced circles around the big man, but Emmett could tell her strength was exhausted.

"Why are you idiots still here?" Ace stumbled into the square, hand pressed to his ribs, his olive skin drained of all color. An ugly, crimson stain spread over his side, seeping between his fingers.

"Ace!" Taryn cried, turning. For half a moment, she forgot her opponent. He raised one of the heavy wooden beams broken from the gallows during battle.

"Taryn!" three boys called at once. She twisted, green eyes wide and questioning. Her gaze met Royal's. Time slowed to a crawl.

Royal dug in his heels, yelling soundlessly, helpless to do anything but watch.

The beam splintered across the back of Taryn's head. Her expression twisted. Her knees buckled.

Her best friend screamed her name again, time snapping back into focus as two gunshots rang out. Ace swore. Taryn's attacker fell. Royal rushed across the square, bundling her into his arms, breathlessly begging her to be all right. "No no no, Taryn. *Taryn!*"

Her eyes stared blankly up at the sky, her breath coming in hiccupping gasps—but she *was* breathing. He lifted her, cradling her head to his chest, almost without realizing this was the closest he had ever held her. She was heavier than he expected, until he remembered how much of her body was augmented with metal.

"We are leaving *now*," he screamed.

CHAPTER THIRTY-THREE

Dodging gunfire, the biomatons raced around the corner to where their cab waited, Erikkson's driver, Emilio, already sitting in the driver's seat. Royal ran at the front of the pack, cradling Taryn to his chest like a child. Her breathing hitched in her throat, uneven gasps catching in her chest, and her fist clutched at his shirtsleeve. Her clockwork hand spasmed uncontrollably.

As Ace clambered into the brougham so he could help lift Taryn inside, a young sailor ran up behind the biomatons. "Seraphim," Ace exclaimed. "Behind you!"

The biomaton spun, his left wing flashing out, a mere hair's breadth from cutting the young man's throat. The midshipman held up his hands. "Please, Miss Taryn said I could join you! I am on your side."

Seraphim sneered suspiciously, revealing his silver fangs. "What do you think, Rorin?" he asked the twin standing beside him.

"Kill him," Rorin wheezed. "He is one of them. He is trying to trick ye."

"No," Taryn choked the word out, clutching the doorframe of the cab. Every biomaton turned concerned eyes toward her, staring at their leader, who seemed to be fighting for her life. "Let her come."

Seraphim retracted his blades but flashed his fangs once more at Cobb. "If you betray her, I will personally ensure you do not take another breath."

Cobb swallowed hard but nodded to indicate her understanding. She hurried toward the cab with the rest of the biomatons. Ace collapsed inside, his hand pressed to his ribs. Taryn lay in Royal's arms, clearly losing her grip on consciousness. It had taken everything she had left to call out, and now her mind drifted toward the comforting dark.

"Hurry!" Royal screamed.

Bang!

A gunshot rent the air in two, the sound echoing off the buildings around them. All eyes went to the twins, who froze in their tracks, steps away from the cab.

But it wasn't the twins who had been hit.

Just behind them, Cobb sank to her knees. Storm stepped from the shadows of an alley, her flintlock pistol still smoking. Despite the blood trickling down her cheek, a smirk of triumph split her face. The twins and Emmett moved at once, swinging into the cab. Seraphim leapt onto the back of the carriage, pounding on the roof.

"Drive!"

The pirate captain reached Cobb and caught a fistful of the girl's hair, already taking aim at the back of the brougham as it began to move. Cobb coughed, blood bubbling between her lips, but she managed to cry out in a hoarse voice. "My brother! Sedition! Help my brother!"

Her voice was drowned out by another gunshot, narrowly missing the cab as it raced away. "I shall not rest until every last

one of you traitors hangs for this, starting with the midshipman!" Storm screamed, red-faced, at the retreating biomatons.
"Do you hear me? You will all hang!"

CHAPTER THIRTY-FOUR

ROYAL BURST through the front door of Erikkson's London townhouse. "Tony!" He held Taryn's unconscious body in his arms, horribly aware of her labored breathing. She had passed out shortly after they escaped the square and remained unresponsive the rest of the trip. The other biomatons stumbled into the house after him, closing the door in a rush, each nursing their own wounds. Emmett supported Ace, whose shirt was soaked with blood. "Erikkson!" Royal screamed again.

At last, the biomechanick came dashing down the stairs. His face paled when he saw Taryn in Royal's arms, his usually rosy cheeks losing all their color. "What happened?" he demanded breathlessly.

"She was struck from behind—" Royal's voice shook. "She passed out on the way here. I cannot wake her. I am afraid she will stop breathing—"

Erikkson held out his arms, taking her tenderly from Royal. He frowned. "This should have waited. She was not ready." He shook his head, glancing at the other biomatons. "I will tend to her. Assist the others with their injuries." He eyed Ace. "In particular, Mr. Highmore looks as though he could use some good medical care."

Royal nodded, but he found himself rooted to the spot as Erikkson carried Taryn upstairs. "Come on, Tiger," he whispered, his heart in his throat. "You must pull through. You *must*. Do not leave us all alone here."

"Royal, *s'il vous plait,* we are as concerned about Taryn as you are, but we must take care of our wounds," Emmett interrupted.

Royal turned, at last acknowledging how bad Ace looked. He teetered on the edge of passing out as well, his left arm over Emmett's shoulder, his whole body sagging in pain and fatigue. His right side was soaked in blood. It would help to have something to occupy his mind, until Erikkson had news regarding Taryn's condition. Royal nodded. "Can you make it to the lab?"

Ace heaved a heavy sigh. "Aye."

Seraphim came to support Ace's right side, and together they made their slow, painful way to the small medical lab Erikkson kept stocked at the back of the house. Royal turned the gas lamps as high as they would go as the others helped Ace sit up on the small metal examination table. Royal rummaged through a few drawers, finding bandages, gauze, and some sort of clear alcohol for sterilizing tools and cleaning wounds. Seraphim left to tend to his injuries in private. Emmett followed him, looking lost now that the fight was over.

"Will you remove your shirt, please?" Royal asked, laying his tools out in a careful line.

With some difficulty, Ace pulled the shirt over his head. Royal turned toward him, and his eyes widened at the sight of his brutal graft. "Gor. They really did some damage."

Just below Ace's fourth rib, the skin had torn away from the metal, blood still seeping from the wound. Royal tipped alcohol onto a cloth. "What happened?"

"Storm's bloody steel toes were intentionally designed to do damage. My graft just made it easier—" Ace grunted, his jaw clenching as Royal began to clean the wound.

"Sorry," Royal mumbled. He pressed the cloth more carefully over the injury, trying to clear away enough of the blood to see the real damage. "Whatever hack did your graft did not have proper training," he said, then seemed to backtrack. "I mean—"

"No, I know," Ace growled. "I look like Frankenstein's monster."

Royal stared at Ace for a moment, then grinned. "You said it, not I." He finished cleaning the wound and studied it for a moment before turning away, grabbing a box of small metal pins and a tool like a narrow awl. He returned, glancing at the injury once more. He shook his head. "I need to access your control panel. We should not do this without anesthetic."

Ace's lip curled. "Morphine?"

"No. Just turn your head. There is a lever that will shut down your pain receptors. It is temporary, but it should help."

Ace turned his head, allowing Royal to access his control panel. The small metal hatch in the back of his head was far less sophisticated than those Erikkson had installed in his creations, and Royal easily found the proper lever. With a flick of his finger, he flipped the switch. "There. Now this should not hurt. I can make no promises, though."

Ace flexed his fists, the muscles in his jaw standing taut beneath his olive skin. "Just do what you must. I have experienced worse."

Royal wondered about that, but he began to work without comment. He took one of the small copper pins from the box, a thin strip of metal with spikes on either side. Using the tool, he first affixed the spikes to Ace's exposed metal rib, then used the other side to pin the torn skin in place, the pin acting like a stitch, binding metal and flesh together. It would require many, many more to sufficiently seal Ace's wound.

"Your sister seems charming," Royal muttered while he worked. He could read Ace's discomfort, despite the neural dampeners, and spoke to keep Ace's mind occupied more than anything.

"My sister," Ace spat with a derisive laugh. "I cannot believe I am really related to *that*. I cannot understand why I ever followed her."

"Your memories have returned?"

"Aye, during our fight. I remember too much now."

"But that is good! Taryn will be glad to hear—" Royal stumbled over his words and fell silent, crestfallen as he recalled her situation.

"Taryn will be all right," Ace said gently, clapping him on the shoulder. "She is strong. She will not go down so easily."

Royal tried to smile, but his lopsided grin ached and he turned away, reaching for a roll of white bandages. "I hope so." With Ace's help, he wrapped the clean bandage around his chest. "Let me know if any of the pins break open, or you begin to bleed again." He tapped Ace's metal shoulder. "You ought to have Tony look at that. He may know how to help you with it."

"Thank you," Ace said, shrugging. "He saw it when he purchased me. He said there was nothing he could do."

"Ah."

Ace rose, a little unsteadily, and lifted his bloodstained shirt, as if to dress. Then he set the garment down again, shaking his head. "I will find a clean one."

"I am going to find out if Erikkson knows anything more about Taryn's condition," Royal said quietly.

"Let me come with you," Ace replied.

Together, they walked toward the bedroom Tony had reserved for Taryn. Now that the adrenaline had drained from his body, Royal had grown stiff and sore, and the two boys hobbled along like old men. They reached the room just as Erikkson was closing the door, his expression grim. Emmett came racing from the other end of the hall, nearly colliding with them. Royal caught a glimpse of his best friend through the door as it swung shut; she lay in bed, eyes closed, as peaceful as if she was sleeping.

"Will she be all right? Will she wake up?"

Erikkson sighed and shook his head. "The blow to her head did a lot of damage. She will have a difficult time healing."

"But will she be all right?" Emmett asked.

"It is too early to tell. But I believe if she can wake from the coma, she will be all right."

"Coma?" Ace asked. "Why should she be in a coma?"

Erikkson glanced between the three boys. They each cared for Taryn so much. He was not sure how they would react to the truth. He took a deep breath, held it for a moment, and exhaled. "She has a severe concussion, and anything I could do would require surgery. I haven't the tools to perform such an operation here. The impact jarred some of her mental controls as well, dislocating pieces of the prosthetics in her brain. If—and this is a big if—*if* she wakes, she will be able to love again."

To Be Continued...

ACKNOWLEDGMENTS

Here we are at the end of my second book, *Seraphim*. It's been a journey getting here. If you've followed my career at all, you know just how long it took to get *Seraphim* out into the world. But it's finally here, and I'm so thankful to have had the endless support and dedication from my team at Parliament and my friends and family to make it happen.

First and foremost, to my husband, best friend, and partner Paden Belleque: you endlessly encourage and believe in me, even through my breakdowns, even when I want to give up, and I thank you for that. I am so thankful I've been blessed with someone like you in my life. Let's tell stories together until we die. I love you.

To Nadia Nelson, who read some very early drafts and helped me talk through plot holes over Salt and Straw ice cream: you rock. This book would probably not exist without you, and it certainly wouldn't look the same. Thank you.

To my parents: Thank you for inspiring and feeding my love of stories from the earliest of ages. Thank you for reading to me, for showing me that books can be windows to other worlds, and for your unconditional love as I've found my path to telling my own stories. I love you.

To my other friends and family who have encouraged me every step of the way, whose names are too many to list here; if you ever read an early draft, talked me through a confusing piece of lore or plot hole, listened to me talk about my characters or my struggles, or in any other way had even the tiniest part to play in the creation of Taryn's world, thank you. This one's for you.

To my Lord and Savior, Jesus Christ: nothing would be possible without You. Nothing. Thank You for gifting me with the ability to tell stories.

And last but certainly not least, to Malorie and the rest of the incredible team at Parliament House Press. This book would only be half of what it is without you. Thank you for challenging me, and believing in Taryn's story.

ABOUT THE AUTHOR

E.M. Wright is an author and editor living in Salem, Oregon. When she isn't reading, she's probably playing with her four cats or taking trips to the bookstore with her husband. She's been writing stories since she was old enough to hold a pencil, but it's only recently that she's begun to pursue publishing. *Seraphim* is her second book. You can find her on X and Insta-gram, @EMWrightWrites, or contact her directly: authoremwright@gmail.com.

𝕏 x.com/EMWrightWrites